ARMY OF FIRE

The Elementals Book 1

Jennifer L. Kelly

This is a work of fiction. All of the characters, organizations, and events portrayed in this novel are either products of the author's imagination or are used fictitiously.

Library of Congress PCN: 2016917251

BoxerBull Books

Cleveland, OH

ISBN: 0-9977764-2-0

ISBN-13: 978-0-9977764-2-3

TO MY DEAR READER~
HEAD OR HEART?
-J.L.K.

OTHER BOOKS BY JENNIFER L. KELLY

THE LUCIA CHRONICLES

THE PROPHECY
THE DISSENTIENT
THE BEACON
THE GIRL WHO WASN'T LOVED (NOVELLA)

STAND ALONE FICTION

THE FRACTURED LIFE OF JENNY MCCLAIN

PROLOGUE

The Day the Sun Went Out

I wasn't alive when it happened. Well, what I mean is that I wasn't yet born the day the sun went out. I've heard about it though, probably more than I ever wanted to hear about anything. Like one of those rumors or urban legends that circulate for decades or whatever. And they grow more and more elaborate, each generation adding something to the story until it's almost—*almost*—unbelievable.

I guess they'd been talking about it on Earth for years, the sun going out. After all, the sun is just a star. Sure, it sustained all life on the planet, but by their very nature stars die. *Poof!* Gone forever, just like that. The scientists thought we had more time, like, they thought we'd be good for *billions* of years. But even I know that nature isn't as predictable as that. I mean the Universe has been around forever and in comparison humans are just a blip on the Universe timeline.

The scientists' reports said the sun was burning through all its gases and we had to make a decision as a species. We could stay on Earth and potentially be engulfed by the resulting supernova, along with the planets Mercury and Venus. Or—and that's a big *or*—there was the possibility that the resulting explosion would sort of change the elements of the Universe. As the sun burned through its gases trying to prolong its own inevitable death, it had the potential to change the habitats of other planets. And so a sort of lottery was set up and the people of Earth could enter to be randomly selected to start a colony on one of those outer, unnamed planets of our galaxy. Some people, of course, refused to enter: better to stick with the enemy you know, in this case death, than the one you don't. In this circumstance, that strategy worked out more favorably, because there were only 3,000 names drawn. 3,000 names out of every man, woman, and child left on the planet.

So, before the sun went out forever, the scientists sent out probes searching for habitable zones on other planets. And much to their own surprise, not to mention everyone else's, they found a planet just past our own solar system. A planet, surprisingly like Earth. Below its surface it had liquid water, and on the surface it had mountains and some vegetation, albeit slightly different than that back home. But still it had potential. And potential is all that we needed. So those 3,000 people—doctors, teachers, scientists, political leaders, and children—I even heard there was a movie star, a garbage disposal man, and the inventor of this weird chemical that can get out absolutely any stain from any item (that's all just rumors, of course) among the lottery winners—so they flew in their little space shuttles and set up a colony for the surviving people of Earth to continue their existence.

The story goes that the people who stayed behind were happy that humanity could continue, even without them. But I know people; I may only be seventeen, but I know that people would not just go gently into that good night. They'd go out kicking and screaming. I know, because that's what I'd do too.

And so Xon 9 came to be. Xon as in exonerate because the original colonists of Xon 9 should not feel guilt for having been selected to propagate the species of *Homo Sapiens*. The 9 is for the nine original planets in our own solar system, before they gave Pluto the boot so to speak. Not that any of that matters now. That was over eight hundred Earth years ago.

The year that the sun engulfed the Earth.

The year that the sun died.

CHAPTER 1

I'm nobody. I don't stand out in any way whatsoever. I have mousy brown hair that hangs limply to my shoulders and I have brown eyes that my dad describes as molten chocolate lava. Whatever that means. I keep to myself. I don't make trouble—usually. I fly under the radar or at least I try to, but sometimes it doesn't always work out that way.

I stare at the front of the classroom where Teacher 4 stands, droning on about the history of Xon 9. He's very excited which is one of the things I admire about Teacher 4, his enthusiasm for his subject matter. It's more than I can say for Teachers 8 and 13, Ancient English and Earth Arithmetic bore me to tears—literally. But Universal History is kind of cool, even when Teacher 4 goes off on one of his tangents like he is right now.

The dim red light of Xon 9's sun filters through the heavy,

dual-paned glass windows of the classroom. The pinkish-red light glints off the side of Teacher 4's face, making the silvery-green ridges on the right side of his face glisten and sparkle like the beautiful jewels for sale in the Black Bazaar. Teacher 4 is very tall and thin. He's not very old either, maybe only a few years older than his students. He keeps a large jug of water on his desk and periodically pauses to take a drink from it. His gills wiggle in delight as the water equilibrium in his system is restored for the time being.

I glance around the classroom. My class is small, maybe only about twenty students. Some are staring out the window at the red, brown, and white landscape. Others appear to be writing down notes as Teacher 4 talks. Li pokes me in the back with his pencil and I turn around and glare at him. His black hair flops carelessly into his brown eyes and he gives me a sinister smile. I scowl and try to scoot my desk further away, bumping into the back of the chair in front of me. The blonde ponytail whips around, almost catching me in the face, and the cool blue eyes of Diadona glare at me. "Watch it, Loser," she hisses. I feel myself instinctively shrink away before, satisfied, Diadona turns back around in her seat and feigns attention at whatever Teacher 4 is lecturing.

I take out my pencil and begin to absently sketch in my notebook instead of writing down the notes. I can always get them from my best friend Ahna later. Ahna always does exactly what she's supposed to, not that I don't, but, yeah, okay, who am I kidding? I don't. My mind drifts to my moon. I'll be turning eighteen in seven days. Seven days until my Pronouncement. I keep trying to tell myself it isn't a big deal. I mean, who cares, anyways? Everyone makes a Pronouncement. But I have this deep fear, the kind that sits in the pit of my stomach, that I'm going to make the wrong choice. Ahna says it's impossible to make the wrong choice, but I disagree. Once I make my Pronouncement there's no going back. Your Pronouncement is a label that stays with you forever. It's how people categorize you for the rest of your life, all two hundred remaining years of it. I look down at my notebook and realize I've sketched Teacher 4 without even realizing it, catching his shaggy brown hair and lithe posture perfectly. I squint at my notebook, yep his scales and gills are perfect too. I feel my cheeks flush and hurriedly close my notebook, knocking my pencil to the floor.

I bend to pick up my pencil, noticing Ahna who is repeatedly tilting her head toward the front of the classroom while looking at me, her brown eyes wide. As I sit back up everyone is turned and looking at me expectantly. *Uh-oh.* I've been asked a question and I have no idea what's going on. Teacher 4 stands with his hands on his hips waiting. I cough nervously. "Um, I-I'm sorry, Sir. Could you please repeat the question?" Giggles erupt around the classroom.

"Yes, Ka, the question was what ancient Earth civilization established the first functioning universal monetary system?" Teacher 4 gives me a tight smile. His face looks agitated, but it's betrayed by his eyes, which have a sympathetic expression in them.

"I, um…" *Rrrriiinnng!* I let out a relieved breath as the bell rings and the rest of the class gathers their belongings and make their way out the door. I pick up my books and press them into my chest making my way up the narrow row of desks. Suddenly, I'm reeling forward, my books flying out of my hands, my knees hitting the tile floor hard.

"Oops, sorry about that, Ka," Diadona smirks at me as she gingerly makes her way around my sprawled out form. For a second Teacher 4 looks like he's going to say something, reprimand her, but instead he squats down and begins picking up my books. Ahna scurries past and I know that she'll be waiting for me just outside the door. Ahna may be my best friend, but she's a good student. She doesn't get failing grades and she never gets in trouble. I know that she wouldn't want to get on Teacher 4's bad side.

Teacher 4 stands up and reaches out a hand. I thankfully grasp it as he helps me to my feet then hands me my books. He gives me a small smile. "You really need to daydream less in class, Ka."

I nod numbly. For a minute, only a minute, I think that I could tell him what's been occupying my mind, but for some reason I don't. I mean he'd be the perfect person to confide in. He's not my parent; there'd be no fear of disappointment, but just as I'm about to maybe mention it, he continues. "I'm sorry about Diadonna. But, Ka, you really shouldn't let her treat you that way." He perches on the edge of his desk and takes a long drink of water. His gills waver back and forth slightly.

I shift awkwardly from foot to foot wishing I could sink into the floor. It's one thing for your classmates to think you're a nobody, but it's a whole other thing for your teacher to think you're one too. "Anyways, Ka, it's the end of the school year, eh?" I nod dumbly again. "Alright then, let's make it a good one?"

"Yes, Sir," I mumble and this time he smiles a little bigger, a dimple appearing on the non-scaled side of his face. He pats me on the shoulder gently, or what I guess he assumes is encouragingly.

"Alright, off you go. Oh, and you may want to get the notes from Ahna." I feel my cheeks redden and hurriedly nod before practically running out of the classroom.

"Well?"Ahna presses as we make our way out of the building and into the warm air. On Xon 9 we don't have seasons. The weather just…is. All of the time. She walks beside me wringing her hands anxiously.

"Nothing," I finally answer. "He didn't say anything. Just that I should get the notes from you." I leave out the part about not letting Diadona treat me the way she does. I don't know why Diadona bothers, I don't do anything, don't stand out in any way. I just blend in; just like the weather of Xon 9, I just *am*.

Ahna reaches into her bag and pulls out a notebook and hands it to me. I take it and put it into my bag along with my own books that are still cradled in my arms. The sun feels warm against my cheeks; it sits high in the sky, casting a red aura all around it, pinkish clouds floating past its surface.

"Have you decided yet?" Ahna asks. I know she means well, she is my best friend after all, but I think she's more obsessed with my Pronouncement than I am.

"No, I haven't."

"But it's in seven days."

"Yeah, I know. It's just…I mean, how do you even decide?" I ask. I'm not really looking for her to give me an answer, but she does anyways, because that's what Ahna does. Whereas I'm no good at school; Ahna gets straight As. Whereas I am not athletic and always seem to get hit in the head with any type of ball during any type of sport; Ahna is captain of the basketball team and cheer squad. She is also class president and the leader of the Xon 9 Docious Youth. I am none of these things.

"I want to be an Earth Elemental," Ahna smiles dreamily and I can't say that surprises me. All the Earth Elementals I know are reliable, kind, and nurturing. All qualities that Ahna already possesses, I mean she's friends with me isn't she? I look at Ahna in the red sunlight, her creamy, tawny-colored skin and deep chocolate brown eyes, her long black hair in a thick braid down her back. Ahna is named after the Anasazi, one of the first peoples who inhabited a country called America that used to be back on Old Earth. Supposedly, her family is descended from that tribe. With a name like that, how could Ahna not be destined for greatness? Of course she already knows her Pronouncement even though her moon is after mine, we all have our Pronouncement on the same day, which just so happens to be my moon.

A hooded figure slouches down the sidewalk toward us and I'd recognize that form anywhere. He reaches us and turns to fall in step beside us. "Thanks a lot for that in class. I think you may actually have left some graphite in my skin." I bump shoulders with him and Li flips his hood off and smiles bemusedly at me.

"I couldn't resist. You make yourself such an easy target," he grins.

"We're supposed to be friends, remember?"

He flips his black hair out of his eyes. "It's not like everyone needs to know." I've known Ahna and Li my entire life. We live in the same concrete block housing development reserved for families of the scientific colony. "I have a reputation to maintain."

"What reputation?" huffs Ahna. "One for being a giant jerk-face?"

"Yeah, yeah Sis, whatever." Li grins. I don't have brothers and sisters of my own, so Li and Ahna are as close as I get. Li turns to me. "Any big plans tonight, Ka?" I'm secretly grateful for the change in conversation. The longer I can put off thinking about my approaching Pronouncement the better.

"Not really, no." I shrug.

"We have that gigantic Ancient English paper due soon. We should be working on that." Ahna points out.

"Well, aren't you a barrel of fun," Li quips sarcastically. Then I see the twinkle in his brown eyes, the eyes that match his twin sister's in color, but that's about it. He wiggles his eyebrows at me. "How about we go to the Black Bazaar?"

"Li, I think that's a horr—" Ahna starts. But I'm quick to cut her off. "I think that sounds like a great idea." The Black Bazaar is sort of off limits for me. It's not that my parents have said I couldn't go to the Black Bazaar, it's more like it's strongly discouraged.

"I can always count on you for a good time, Ka." He raises

an eyebrow at his sister.

"No way. I'm going home and getting started on that paper," she glowers, "And don't even think for one minute that either of you is going to be copying mine. You're on your own."

"Sis, it's the weekend. I mean what's one day?" Li begins, but the expression on Ahna's face stops him short. "Well, maybe I'll pick you up something, like a Pleasure Patch or something." He winks at me.

"No thanks, Liwald Sollomon. You can keep your patches to yourself." Ahna glances at me. "Are you sure, Ka?" I can tell from the look on her face that she disapproves, which for some reason makes me want to go with Li all the more.

"That's my girl," Li grins. He flips up his hood and takes my hand with a *whoop!* We run down the concrete walkway, the warm breeze whipping my cheeks, my bag thudding against my legs, leaving Ahna behind, scowling after us.

We run past the concrete buildings, some above ground, and some partially below ground. The temperature of Xon 9 never changes; it is a constant sixty-seven degrees, day or night, and there are no seasons like on Old Earth. We run past the greenhouses where our food is grown and past the warehouses where our food is stored. We run past the reddish-brown crags sticking out of the earth like gnarly fingers reaching for the sky, and we dart past the twisted trunks and grayish green leaves of the giant trees, forming a canopy over our heads and blocking out the red rays of the sun. His hand holding mine tightly, Li and I run until the buildings become fewer and farther in-between, until we reach a darkened alley with a small wooden-sign staked into the ground. The sign has a faded painted arrow that points down the alleyway, which from the other times I've been here I know leads to a concrete stairwell to the Underground, where the Black Bazaar is located. Li yanks me down the alleyway and heads for the concrete steps, leading me away from the safety of the surface and toward the enigma known as the Black Bazaar.

CHAPTER 2

The Underground is an odd place. It has the ability to make you feel both intrigued and frightened at the same time. The Black Bazaar is no exception. I tighten my grip around Li's hand as we enter the Bazaar under the tattered sign hanging between the two rows of buildings flanking either side of the entrance.

The Bazaar consists of various vendors, all housed in what appear to be beat up trailers. Only they aren't attached to any sort of vehicle because they never move. Some of the trailers are rusted out or dented, and some have their metal sliding doors closed tight: not open for business today. Other vendors lean out the windows of their trailers, calling out to customers: rare Old Earth jewels here, moon rock over there, and other goods salvaged from space wreckage.

A woman leans out a window, several of her teeth are missing and leave gaping black holes that have the effect of a jack-o-lantern. Her gray hair is a nest atop her head and her apron is smudged with dirt. She calls to me. I can see the metallic strands of metal that thread across her cheek in the dim light. "How about you, Honey? Yer need yer fortune told. I can see it in yer eyes." I pause and turn, curious. "Aye, that's a good lass." She beckons, but Li quickly yanks me away.

"Not now, thanks!" he calls behind him as we hurry through the crowds of people. The earthen floor is covered with trash and there are sets of tables and chairs scattered about. The Underground has many delicacies which we aren't supposed to have in the above ground: things like candy, sugary soda, and alcohol. Li drags me to a vendor that's slightly pushed back from the others. The door is slid down, but Li raps on it anyway. He glances at me, still holding my hand when the door slides open.

"Yup," answers a gruff voice. The voice belongs to a large man with a black beard and bald head. He too has streaks of metal reaching out across his cheeks and forehead, glinting silver against his dark skin. On his neck is a jagged black tattoo that seems to be clawing its way out of the collar of his leather jacket. "What can I do for you?"

Li steals another glance at me, then confidently turns to the man. "Pleasure, please."

"And for your friend?" the man asks nodding his head to indicate me. Normally, in these kinds of situations, Li just answers for me, but this time he turns to me instead and raises an eyebrow.

I clear my throat nervously. Despite my curiosity about the Underground, the cool whispers of fright make my hair stand on end. "Uh, um," I shift from foot to foot as my hand grows clammy in Li's. And that's when it comes to me. What it is I need, if even for only a few moments. "Adventure, please." The man nods as if satisfied by my response. He disappears and returns sliding two small packets across the dented chrome countertop. Li rummages around in his pockets and pulls out two silver coins that he drops into the man's outstretched palm.

"All sales are final," the man grunts.

"Keep the change," Li smirks as he takes the two packets and the man slides the metal door closed with a bang. "He was a friendly guy." Li grins at me as he tears open the packet labeled: *Pleasure.* Inside is a clear bandage. He pushes up the sleeve of his hoodie and slaps the bandage onto his bicep. "Your turn." He tears open the other packet as I roll up the sleeve of my sweater. It won't roll past my elbow so he carefully presses the bandage onto my forearm. I've been to the Bazaar a few times, but I've never gotten a patch before.

I wonder what will happen. Will I suddenly be overcome with the desire to jump from the roofs of tall buildings? Or will I finally throw caution to the wind and let Li kiss me? The cosmos know he's tried so many times, maybe just this once I'll let him. *Adventure.* His hand still rests complacently on my forearm and his eyes melt into mine like thick molasses. He gives me a syrupy grin. "That was fast." His patch must have kicked in, but I don't feel any different. Maybe the guy gave me a dud.

We walk past other vendors: tattoo artists and glass cases full of colorful candies, until we reach one with large wooden barrels. Li orders a bottle from the man behind the counter, a tall thin man with the same metallic threads running across his cheek. I notice that even his skin has a grayish hue to it and I wonder if it's a side effect of too much Metal.

We continue to wander around the Bazaar, Li holding me tightly with one hand and sipping from the brown bottle in his other. He buys me some candy and it's so sweet that I can only manage to eat one, my teeth feeling coated in a saccharine chalkiness. I shove the rest into my bag for later.

Eventually we sit down on a dirty, metal bench. Li scoots so close that I can feel the heat radiating off of him. His face is so close to mine I can smell the bitter scent of whatever he was drinking from the bottle earlier. He leans in toward me and I can feel an odd sensation come over me. Normally, whenever Li tries to kiss me I pull away and shove him playfully, telling him he's like a brother to me and how weird would it be to kiss my brother? But this time it feels *different*. I hear a voice in my ear, like a whisper blowing in the wind: *Adventure*. Li presses his lips to mine and I think maybe it's not a dud after all.

. . .

"Are you sure it's such a good idea?" Li asks as I lead him back to the front of the Bazaar, back toward the woman with the missing teeth.

"Is your Pleasure wearing off already?" I challenge, dragging him through the thick of people.

"No, of course not. It's just, I mean, Mom always says the one thing you don't mess with is the future. There's a reason it's called the future—you aren't supposed to know what happens." I look back at him, his eyes are still molten and lazy, drunk with the feeling of Pleasure. After Li kissed me something suddenly clicked. I felt brazen with the sense of Adventure and I had an idea. I'd go back to that fortune teller and maybe, just maybe, she'd be able to tell me what my Pronouncement will be. If I knew for sure what it was going to be, well, then there's no way I could make the wrong choice. A breeze tickles my ear, even though we are in the Underground and there is no breeze—another whisper: *Adventure.*

"Adventure," I say as I turn around and stop in front of the beat-up trailer.

"I knew I should have made you get something else," Li mumbles behind me.

The woman with the missing teeth and dirty apron appears at the counter. "Aye, yer back. I knew ye would be."

I feel a slight wave of apprehension, but I swallow it down. "How much is it?" I ask. "For a fortune, I mean?"

The woman peers at me curiously. "Fer ye, lass, tis no charge." I glance at Li who shrugs.

"Are you sure, ma'am?" I ask quietly feeling my sense of Adventure waning. The patch must be starting to wear off.

"Tis no charge for a young lass simply seeking Adventure."

How does she know? She must be able to see my patch. I finger the end of my sweater sleeve which is pulled down to my wrist and a shiver runs up my spine. The woman motions for me to come inside and I make my way to a door on the side of the trailer. Above the door is a tattered white awning. Li follows, but the woman quickly puts out a hand to stop him. "Ye stay behind. The fortune tis only fer the girl." Li steps back awkwardly and the woman grabs my arm, her boney fingers like icicles wrapped around my wrist, and pulls me inside.

. . .

I follow her down a short hallway and past a small living area to a curtained partition. The vendors must also live in their trailers. She pulls the curtain aside and behind it is a small wooden table with a stack of cards and two red velvet chairs. "Sit." The woman orders and I do. I am slowly beginning to regret my decision, the Adventure definitely having worn off by now. The woman lights a small candelabra and sets it on the table. She sits down and begins to shuffle the cards. My stomach roils about nervously as she lays out several of the cards in a sort of overlapping pattern on the table.

She mumbles to herself, her brow furrowed, causing the metallic threads to wrinkle. "Impossible," she mutters. And then she mutters it again. My heart beats in my chest so loudly that I'm sure she can hear it, but she shows no indication that she does. Suddenly she picks up all the cards, shoving them mindlessly back into the deck then sets them aside. "Yer hand," she demands and I lift my hand tentatively to the table. What are those cards and what did she see in them?

Her fingers are like ice as she turns my hand palm up. She stares at me for a moment, her steely gray eyes boring into mine, then she closes her eyes. But her grip doesn't loosen. She begins to sway awkwardly back and forth in her chair, mumbling words I can't quite make out beneath her breath. And then she stops. I can hear the muffled voices of the vendors in the Black Bazaar. "Yer fortune, lass," she finally says, but this time her voice comes out raspy and old sounding, not like how it sounded earlier when she was trying to entice me to have my fortune read. "Metal," she says and I feel the urge to yank my hand away because I don't want to be like this woman or like the man with the gray skin. I don't want to proclaim myself as Metal, but her grip only tightens. "Earth, Wood, Water." I think of Teacher 4 and the large jug of water he's always carrying around to satisfy his insatiable thirst for it. "Fire." At this the woman's eyes fly open and instead of gray, all I can see is a milky white. And I'm frightened, but her grip is like a handcuff around my wrist. "Ka, girl whose name means fire." Frightened no longer even begins to describe it. I'm beyond frightened now. How does she know my name? Her voice is not her own. "You are all and yet you are none. You are Metal. You are Wood. You are Earth. You are Water. And you are Fire. You are all possibilities and yet you are impossible. You are the Impossible Girl." Suddenly, the woman begins to convulse, knocking the cards from the table, and her grip loosens ever so slightly, just enough for me to run away, but I feel like my feet are glued to the floor. The woman's eyes roll back from her head, stony gray now looking back at me. The flames of the candelabra blow out ominously and I hear the voice on the wind once more: *Adventure.* The woman lets go of my wrist. "Go. Go and never come back," she barks at me. "Go!" And I find that I suddenly remember how to use my feet again, hurrying down the short hallway past the living area and out the side door where Li waits for me with a bored expression on his face.

The look on my own face must be both pale and stricken because he immediately asks, "Are you okay?" An expression of concern replacing that of boredom.

"Home." My voice comes out strangled, like it doesn't even belong to me and that one word is all I can manage to say.

He takes my hand, pausing to rip the bandage from my forearm before tossing it to the trash-strewn ground. "I think you've had enough Adventure for one day."

CHAPTER 3

That night I toss and turn unable to decipher the words from the fortune teller. *You are the Impossible Girl.* I mean, what does that even mean? I didn't tell Li what she had said and he didn't ask. Smart guy. If Ahna is going to become an Earth Elemental, then I wonder what Li will be? They may be twins but they're as different as night and day.

That's actually a weird saying because night on Xon 9 isn't like what I've learned about night on Old Earth. On Xon 9 we've always followed the Old Earth clock the best we can, but the sun never actually sets. Heavy curtains block the red light from my windows, but a small gap allows some pinkish light to cast a slim rectangle across the concrete floor. The sun is steadfast in the sky like a flame that will never blow out. It seems eternal and never-ending, but as we found out all those years ago, even the sun can die.

Fire. That's the Elemental Li will announce. It has to be. It fits his personality. He's impulsive, passionate, and seeks instant gratification. My stomach stirs at the thought of his lips pressed to mine. It was exciting, intoxicating almost, but it's hard to tell where the patch ended and my own feelings began.

My mind drifts to Teacher 4. He's not much older than us, maybe twenty-one or twenty-two. He just had his Pronouncement only a few years ago. Some people are freaked out by the Water Elementals' scales and gills, but I think they're beautiful. With his sea green eyes, I can't imagine Teacher 4 proclaiming any other Element. Waters always make the best teachers because they're both kind and gentle. Teacher 4 really is a great teacher, even if Universal History is extremely boring. I mean who cares about the past, right? I'm more concerned with my future and this stupid Pronouncement. Whose idea was it anyway to have seventeen and eighteen-year-olds decide how they want to be labeled for *the rest of their lives?*

Pronouncement was not an Old Earth tradition. I try to think of what Teacher 4 told us during our unit on rituals. After we left Earth and set up our colony on Xon 9 our bodies began to adapt to the new environment, but there were some unexpected side effects. The Elements of Xon 9 had a unique effect on our human physiology. Over time we learned that the mind has a strong influence over the body as well, so instead of having no control over which Element most affected us, we harnessed the ability to decide. Although, often it's clear what Elemental someone will become even before their Pronouncement. Like Ahna, Li, and I'm guessing even

Teacher 4. So why do none of them seem to fit me?

Maybe I really am just a nobody.

I hear my bedroom door open and the soft tread of my mom's footsteps across the floor. She sets something down on my nightstand and sits on the edge of the bed, gently brushing my brown hair off my forehead. "I brought you some warm soybean milk. I could hear you tossing and turning down the hall. What's on your mind, *Kata?*" Kata isn't my actual name, my name is really Ka which means fire, which is a bit ironic considering my personality is anything but Fire. Kata means pure one and has been my mom's nickname for me since I was a baby.

At first I don't want to answer. I don't want to tell her that I've disobeyed again and went to the Black Bazaar. It's not exactly that I'm not allowed to go, it's just that my parents have always told me nothing good comes from a visit to the Black Bazaar and now I can see how right they were. I turn my head away so that I'm not looking at her, can't see her imploring brown eyes. I decide on a half-truth. "Just my Pronouncement."

"Oh, Ka. You still haven't made a decision?" Her voice isn't chastising, but is soft and gentle. "It's only seven days away."

"I know," I mumble and for some reason tears sting my eyes. Sometimes I feel like I'm a big disappointment to my parents. I know they'd never ever in a million light years admit that. But what else can you be if you're a nobody? I've always gotten mediocre grades, never excelled at any sports like Li, wasn't a class leader like Ahna, and now I can't even find the courage to make the biggest decision of my life.

I turn my face back to my mother. Even in the almost dark room I can see the curlicue of green vines that run down the side of her face, curling to the back of her neck where they become interspersed with soft green leaves. Even though her brown eyes are identical to mine, sometimes I swear that I could look into them and see the sky, not the red sky of Xon 9, but a sky of a long time ago. Then I'd blink and it would be gone. My mother is an Earth and my father is a Wood. Whereas my mom is nurturing and soft-spoken, my father is logical and practical. I suppose it's a nice balance.

She pats my hand gently and whispers, "It will come to you. Don't worry. I wasn't sure I would be an Earth, I wanted to be. But I felt like Fire was running through my veins." I peer at her in the darkness. It's hard to imagine my mother as a Fire: carefree and impulsive. Fire and Wood are a dangerous combination too. If she had been a Fire she'd never have been able to marry my father. If she had, it most likely would have been volatile. She seems to read my mind and nods. "You're right, but I already knew your father and knew that he felt his Pronouncement would be Wood. So, despite the Fire I felt pulsating through me, I denied it. I concentrated on Earth: calm, serene, grounding Earth." She smiles at me and I can see her white teeth in the darkness. Her eyes are faraway. "And, obviously, it worked. So you see, Ka, really anything you think you want to be, you will be."

I think of the Black Bazaar and the vendors with metallic threads running along their cheeks and across their foreheads. The tattooed and bald patch-selling man. The fortune teller with her missing teeth. These people who live in the Underground amongst darkness and filth. "But who would want to be a Metal?" I find myself asking out loud. I push myself up to a sitting position.

Mom sighs as she hands me the glass of warm milk. "You went to the Black Bazaar again, didn't you?"

I look down into the glass, my cheeks growing warm with shame. She pats my leg beneath the crisp bed sheet. "Kids will be kids, but I really wish that you wouldn't go there. Remember—"

"Nothing good can come from there," I mumble.

"I don't think his mother will be too happy about Li going there either." I feel my cheeks redden even more and take a sip of the warm milk to distract myself. "And to answer your question, Metal is a tricky Elemental. Metals are very brave and faithful to their kind, however, Metal is known to run rampant if it isn't carefully managed through a lot of self-control. Metal is invasive and too much Metal can cause someone to become unkind and even destructive to themselves and to others." She pauses for a moment, gets up and moves toward the window, peering between the curtain panels at the red night outside. She continues, still looking out the window. "That's why it's safer for Metals to stay in the Underground. In that way the damage they inflict on others with their deceitful ways is minimized. But, *Kata*, even though you can choose your Elemental, it doesn't mean that everyone does." She turns and looks at me across the room. "Do you understand what I mean?"

I wonder who she is referring to—who it is that she is remembering as she says these words. You can choose, but it doesn't mean that everyone does. Are some people too weak, so that the Elemental chooses them instead? Or maybe some people are too apathetic to even care. Even though I really don't understand her words, I nod anyways. She smiles tenderly, coming to the side of the bed and kissing the top of my head. "Good." She leaves closing the door softly behind her.

I set the glass back down on my nightstand and sink back beneath the safety of the cool sheet, tucking it around me so I'm in a sort of snug cocoon. I lie and stare up at the ceiling, the same rectangle of light dances above me as well as below me. I think of my mother's words. Did my father choose Wood? Did Teacher 4 choose Water? Even though you can choose, not everyone does. I drift off to sleep with these thoughts swirling through my mind.

. . .

I dream that I'm in a vast ocean, weighed down with the overwhelming choice that looms before me. I am sinking slowly toward the bottom of the sea floor, salty water fills and stings my lungs. The choice has me trapped, worn like shackles around my ankles that I can't escape. Water continues to fill my nose and lungs. I can't breathe. I know that I am drowning. Everything is blurry and I feel my eyes slowly starting to close, resigned to the fact that I can't make a choice; I can't label myself forever. What if I make the wrong choice? My chin begins drifting down to my chest. There's nothing I can do now.

That's when I feel strong hands grab me firmly and begin pulling me back toward the surface. I feel the shackles slowly falling away, sinking to the seafloor below as I'm pulled further and further away. I gasp as I break the water's surface, sucking in deep breaths of cold air that immediately burns my lungs. Coughing and sputtering. The hands are gone and I wipe the water from my eyes looking around for whoever it was that saved me.

But I see no one. Just miles and miles of ocean. I look back down into the water below me, in the direction I was sinking only seconds before, and for a moment—so brief a moment that I'm not even sure whether or not I imagined it; *surely* I imagined it—beautiful green eyes gaze back at me from beneath the surface. I move my hand tentatively as if I could touch them, determine whether they're real or not. But as soon as I draw my hand nearer they disappear.

Gone.

CHAPTER 4

The day is dragging. That is until Universal History. As I slouch in my seat I find my stomach is filled with butterflies. The bell hasn't rung yet and Teacher 4 is nowhere to be seen. My heart is beating fast and I can feel it pulsating in my ears. Diadona is snapping her gum at the desk in front of me. Ahna is scribbling madly in her notebook; taking notes I guess even though class hasn't even begun yet. My hands are clammy and I run them down the sides of my jeans. Li is running the tip of his pencil lightly up and down the back of my neck and I swat him away annoyed.

Teacher 4 walks in and the chattering of the class dies out. Teacher 4 isn't mean or even strict, but he always commands a sort of quiet respect. *Just like the ocean*, I find myself thinking. Then, *the ocean can change at any moment.* One minute it can be peaceful and serene, the next moment it can be aggressive and unpredictable. The ocean demands respect. He sets the jug of water carefully on the desk. He picks up a piece of chalk and writes on the board. When he turns around there's only one word written and it's underlined twice for emphasis: Pronouncement.

His deep eyes come to rest on me and I squirm in my seat uncomfortably. The familiarity of those eyes—I *know* it was those eyes. I can almost see them beneath the water's surface before they disappeared. I feel a sharp pain in in the back of my neck and turn around, glaring at Li who smiles impishly. How can you both like and hate someone so much?

Teacher 4's voice causes me to turn back around in my seat. I can somehow still feel him watching me so I concentrate on Diadona's cascade of blonde, perfect curls. "Today, we're going to deviate a bit from the stuff we've been discussing and instead focus on Pronouncement. Your Culmination Exams are coming up, which means so is Pronouncement." There are some delighted *whoops* from the other students. I feel myself sinking even lower into my seat so that my neck rests on the back of the chair and my ponytail is splayed across Li's desk. Teacher 4 begins to meander slowly up and down each of the aisles. "Does anyone want to tell me why Pronouncement is so important?"

"Because we're done with school!" Jedidiah calls from the other side of the room, which gets a few laughs from the other students including Li behind me.

Teacher 4 smiles tightly. "Not quite. Anyone else?" He ignores Ahna who's practically waving her hand frantically right under his nose. "Diadona?"

Diadona shifts in her seat so that she's sitting sideways, facing Teacher 4 who is standing in front of the row of windows, the red light of the early afternoon glinting off the side of his face and creating a sort of halo around his head. She smiles flirtatiously. "Well, Pronouncement is so important because the Elemental we announce will determine our future affiliations and associations," she pauses dramatically, "like for the rest of our lives."

Teacher 4 continues to walk up the aisle. "Yes, Diadona, very good." She beams at the praise then before turning around, looks at me with a smug smirk as if to say: *You can only wish to be as good as me, Loser.* But Teacher 4 continues, "However, it's even more important than that." Diadona's smirk fades into a scowl and she turns back around in her seat. I wonder what her Pronouncement will be. Whatever it is I hope that I'm not part of it. Teacher 4 is walking up the aisle to my left and without even turning around I can feel when he's standing right between my desk and Li's. My heart beat quickens and I feel the urge to sit up straighter. I absent-mindedly wipe my palms down the side of my jeans again. "Ka? Can you tell the rest of the class why Pronouncement is so important?"

My throat has gone bone dry. I could use a drink out of that jug of water right about now. The class is so quiet I can practically hear the clock ticking with the passage of time. Ahna is boring her brown eyes into mine and mouthing something at me—probably the answer to the question—but I can't make it out.

"Aw, come on Teach, you know Ka doesn't know the

answer," Li groans. It sounds mean, but I've known Li long enough to know that he's trying to save me, trying to pass the unwanted attention on to someone else and draw it away from me.

"Ah, Liwald, don't project your own insecurities onto someone else," Teacher 4's voice is light and teasing. Some of the class giggles nervously. I feel a hand—a strong, solid hand—fall onto my shoulder. *Pulling me up from the depths. Saving me.*

"Um," I start and a few people laugh, but their laughter is cut short by a curt glare from Teacher 4. I shift uncomfortably underneath the pressure of his hand. I close my eyes and see the vast ocean all around me. All the choices and the consequences of each choice; drowning me in the weight of their severity. Those green eyes peering back at me from beneath the surface. I can almost smell the salty sea air and feel the cold water against my skin, right on my shoulder where Teacher 4's palm rests. I don't open my eyes. "Pronouncement is so important because it's the biggest choice any one of us will ever make in our entire life. It's not the Elemental choice that matters, although that's important too." I pause and clear my throat, opening my eyes. I turn around and look up into Teacher 4's face which is riddled with a concern that I can't interpret. I focus on his eyes and as I do it's like the rest of the class has slipped and faded away, as if the two of us are the only people in the classroom. "It's the choice between your body and your mind, between your desires and your needs."

Teacher 4's shoulders seem to relax as if a great weight has been lifted. "Very good, Ka. That answer was well worth the wait."

He continues up the aisle back to the front of the classroom. I glance at Ahna and her eyes are wide in her cherub-cheeked face. "It's not just about which Elemental you'll associate with, but about whether you will follow your desire—the desires for wealth, or beauty, or passion." Teacher 4 scans the room as he says this and I can feel Li stiffen behind me at the word *passion*. "Or will you follow your needs—the need to lead, love, or protect." His eyes drift over to me for just a second before he looks away calling on a student who has a question.

The rest of the class passes quickly. When the bell rings I sling my bag over my shoulder and that's when I notice the dampness that lingers on the left shoulder of my t-shirt where Teacher 4 had rested his hand at the beginning of class. As I'm pushed along out of the classroom's door with the cluster of students I feel a prickle on the back of my neck. The unmistakable feeling as if someone is watching me. I turn, glancing behind me. Teacher 4's eyes lock on mine; tempestuous oceans staring back at me. Li throws an arm around my shoulders as we exit into the stream of students in the hallway. I give him a tentative smile. When I turn back around Teacher 4 is sitting at his desk shuffling through some papers. And I'm left wondering if I imagined it all in the first place.

CHAPTER 5

Two more days until Pronouncement. It's after school, Ahna and I are sitting on some swings at the lower school's playground. We swing in silence, pumping our legs and kicking up at the red sky. Whenever I'm forward, she's behind me and we swing in opposite tandem. Just like our lives are about to be. Sure we'll still be on the same swing set, but we'll be swinging in different directions occasionally passing each other by. I reach out and she slaps at my outstretched fingers as she swings past.

I swing higher and higher until I feel like if I leapt off the swing at the very tippy top, right before you start the descent back to the ground, if I leapt off at that very moment that just maybe I could soar into the red and pink clouds and never look back.

The last days of school were awkward. Every time I was in Universal History I felt like Teacher 4 was watching me. Not in, like, a creepy way or anything. Teacher 4 isn't like that. But more in a watchful, waiting sort of way. Yet every time I'd feel the intensity of those green eyes on me I'd glance up, and he'd be looking the other way or facing the blackboard. Maybe I did imagine it all. One time Diadona thought I was staring at her as she was coming down the aisle of desks. "What're you looking at, Freak?" she'd hissed. I just ignored her. What did it matter anyway? Tomorrow was Exams and the following day was Pronouncement and if I was lucky I wouldn't have to deal with Diadona on a daily basis anymore. Maybe I'll select Metal just to avoid Diadona, but I shiver at the memory of the tattooed man and the filth of the Underground.

"Ka, did you even hear me?" Ahna has stopped swinging and I realize suddenly that I have too.

I shake my head. "Nah, sorry. I was just thinking."

"About your Pronouncement?"

I turn in the swing so that the two chains begin to twist together, slowly elevating me as they grow shorter and shorter. "Yeah, sort of." I turn the other way and the world spins by in a blur of pink as the chains unravel. I enjoy the rush of dizziness.

"And...?" Ahna tries to prompt.

"And nothing." I stop spinning and turn to face her. "I don't know."

"You still don't know?" She scowls disapprovingly. "It's only two days away." She pauses. "You should just be Earth with me."

I grin. "I don't think it quite works like that."

"Well, you'd think that you'd have felt something by now."

I shrug. I've never expressed interest in affiliating with any particular Elemental. They each have their good and bad qualities about them. Earths are loyal and responsible like my mother, but if they have too much of it then they can become stubborn and inflexible. They make great doctors, nurses, and teachers, jobs where they can nurture something like the tiniest of seeds growing into a mighty tree.

My father is a Wood. Woods are steadfast, organized, and logical. They make great leaders. In fact all of Xon 9's Leadership Council are Woods. However, when it's out of Balance, Woods can be prejudiced and bias, not always the best for making decisions that can affect an entire planet.

Metal is the most difficult element to control. When Metal is in Balance they are determined and the bravest of all the Elementals. They make the best soldiers. However, as seen in the Underground, when it's out of Balance they can be cruel and destructive to both themselves and others.

My mind drifts easily to Teacher 4: Water. Waters are wise and resourceful, they too make wonderful teachers, historians, museum directors, librarians and the like. However, too much Water and they can become sly and manipulative.

And then there's my name, *Ka*, which means fire. I'm not sure why my parents named me that considering my mother is Earth and my father a Wood. They say it's because I came into the world fiercely kicking and screaming, like I had a fire for life lit within me from the very day I was born. Ironic, I know. Fires are passionate and social, like Li. But the saying about being burned by Fire is true: too much Fire and they can be sweet-talking and short-tempered.

"Maybe…" I begin and Ahna leans so far forward in her swing she practically tumbles out of it. I chew on a piece of my hair. But I shake my head helplessly and give her a weak smile. "Still nothing."

Ahna sighs and stands from her swing. She picks up her backpack and tosses it over her shoulder. "Well, you better figure it out sooner rather than later. I need to study for Exams." She begins to walk away, but she pauses a few feet away and turns, glancing at me over her shoulder. "You're running out of time you know. You can't be indecisive forever, Ka. Sooner or later you're going to have to make a choice: do you want to continue to be nobody or do you want to become somebody?" She purses her lips then turns back around heading in the direction of the library. She's right. I do want to be somebody…just not anybody.

. . .

I don't go home right away. Some time alone may be just what I need to help me figure out my Pronouncement. After Pronouncement you attend University based on your Elemental. Since your Elemental determines your career path it only makes sense. I feel a sense of dread at the thought of spending the next two years of my life in University with Diadona. Maybe I should just choose Earth. At least I'd have Ahna and I could follow in my mother's footsteps, maybe become a doctor or nurse at one of Xon 9's hospitals. Or...

The drowning dream still haunts me and I can't help but wonder if maybe it was some sort of sign. I know that only Metals really believe in fortunes and all that stuff, but maybe my subconscious or whatever it is was telling me to choose Water. I don't know how to explain it, but I somehow feel like Teacher 4 knows about my dream, knows that he saved me. But that's impossible. Someone can't know about your dreams, unless of course you tell them. And I'm pretty sure he's been watching me; I can feel it. *But why?* He's never paid me much attention before. Or have I just been oblivious all this time?

I snap out of my reverie and realize that I've wandered to the alleyway leading toward the Black Bazaar. I glance around. I've missed curfew and I'm at the entrance to the very last place a girl breaking curfew should be. I hear voices drifting up the alleyway. There's a hollow with a door to the right of the alleyway and I climb into it. The sign on the door reads closed and I press myself against the solid wood, trying to make myself as flat as possible.

The voices grow louder as two men emerge from the alleyway. They take several steps forward so that they're almost directly in front of me. They stop. If they were to turn around they'd see me instantly. I find myself holding my breath. The two figures— men from their voices—are wearing long, ruby colored robes that trail across the concrete walkway. They have large hoods pulled up over their heads and because their backs are toward me I can't hear what it is they're saying.

I've never seen anyone dressed like this before; it's like they're wearing some sort of ritual attire. Are they the Council of Leaders? Usually, the Council just wear long, tan tunics without hoods, you know being Wood and all it seems fitting. I still can't hear what they're saying and the man on the right begins to gesticulate wildly. They begin to walk, heading right toward me. I press myself into the door frame trying to render myself invisible, but they're too preoccupied with their discussion to notice a teenage girl hiding in a doorway. They pass me and continue to walk away. "It has to be soon. We can't afford to wait any longer." The voice drifts over to me. But not just any voice. It sounds familiar.

I step out of the doorway and find myself heading in the same direction, the opposite direction from home. I pull my hood up so that it hides my hair and face. Maybe they'll just think I'm a University student heading back to the dorms. I keep several paces behind them; too far away to hear any more of the conversation. But that voice.

I follow them several blocks, heading toward the University complex. The University complex is landscaped with large boulders and silvery-gray shrubs that line the entrance way. There's a large iron archway with the words: *divide et impera* spelled out in elaborate calligraphy. We pass under the archway and I follow them through the complex. The University is extremely large since it hosts all the Elemental Universities. I've only been to the complex once, earlier this year for a school excursion to show us the various facilities and help encourage us in our Pronouncement. I wish now that I'd paid better attention as I follow the two hooded figures through the labyrinth of buildings and walkways.

Eventually we stop at a darkened building—all the others are lit except this one—so I can't read the plaque with its name. I pause by some bushes lining the side of the building as the two figures walk toward the back of the building. I wait until they round the corner and then hurry after them. I can't explain the compulsion to follow them. It's not like me at all, but that voice. I'm sure that I recognize that voice.

The sun is still high in the sky, but now Xon 9's two small moons have flanked it on either side. I'm beyond late for curfew now. I crouch in some bushes as the two figures stand beside two twisted tree trunks. There's no entrance on this side of the building, or even any windows for that matter. One of the figures leans forward and extends his arm into the gnarly branches of the tree trunks. I'm wondering if something is hidden inside one of the trees when I hear the familiar sound of knocking. A door. The trees are hiding another entrance into the building.

As the two figures wait their conversation again drifts over to me where I hide crouched as small as possible in some very uncomfortable, but large bushes that block me from their sight. I find myself frozen to the spot unable to move, anxious to hear that voice again.

"Are you sure it's going to happen?" The unfamiliar voice is saying. The hood casts his face in shadows so it appears as if a voice is emitting from a black abyss.

"I'm sure of it," answers the familiar voice and now I'm almost sure that I know it. "It will happen on Pronouncement. The solar alignment is perfect."

The other voice is skeptical. "And how do you know it's this one?"

The reply is confident. "Trust me. I know."

"Yes, yes. The eighteenth moon on the hundredth solar alignment."

"Exactly."

"And what if you're mistaken?" A long drawn-out pause and I find that I'm again holding my breath waiting for the answer.

"Am I ever mistaken?" Comes the confident reply. There's a muffled sound, the sound of a door being pulled open and a small slant of light spills into the shadows illuminating the hooded face turned toward me, the one with the unfamiliar voice. I see the glint of greenish-gray. A Water. He disappears into the doorway.

I'm caught off guard and for a moment I lose my balance and topple forward into the spindly branches of the shrub, scratching my arms and face in the process. I take in a whoosh of air, frightened. The other figure, the one with the familiar voice turns at the noise, and looks right in my direction. And as he does the light of the doorway sparkles across his scales and makes his green eyes appear like gemstones set inside his angular face. I feel as if he's looking right at me, sees right through the thicket of bushes and right into my startled brown eyes. But he doesn't indicate that he's seen me at all, instead his eyes grow concerned and he bites his lip before carefully adjusting his hood and heading through the doorway, so tall that he actually needs to duck slightly. The wooden door closes with a solid thud behind him.

CHAPTER 6

Pronouncement. I'm sandwiched in between Li and Ahna in the third row from the stage. The Elementals of Xon 9 overflow the back rows and balcony of the school auditorium. Pronouncement only comes around once a year as the current youth transition into adulthood and declare their paths to their friends, families, and colony. The decisions made today will not only guide our career path, but possibly our future spouses—you don't have to marry within your Element, that's too old-fashioned even for Xon 9—but some Elementals fair better than others in particular partnerships. Like my mom and dad, Earth and Wood are complementary elements. However, Wood and Fire would most likely be a stressful, unenduring relationship. Or Fire and Water.

Pronouncement is one of the few times that colonists are

segregated into their elements; that and at University. After the Transition Phase which occurs while at University, you enter into the Static Phase where your element comfortably comes to rest in harmony with your own physiology. Unless of course it becomes Unbalanced.

The Earths sit in the very back rows of the lower floor and I see my mother talking comfortably with others of her element. In the balcony above us sit the Woods on the far left with the Waters in the middle acting as a buffer from the Fires who sit on the far right, the golden scrolls of filigree on the sides of their faces glistening in the red light that filters through the row of high windows at the back of the auditorium, giving them an odd flame-like effect. I find the Fires both beautiful and frightening at the same time. The Metals don't attend Pronouncement.

I glance at the Teachers who are sitting on one side of the stage, cloaked in black gowns and caps of the Old Earth tradition, each adorned with a sort of scarf displaying their Element. Almost all of the teachers are Earth or Water, but there are a few of the other Elements, including Teacher 7 who is a Metal, one of the few I know who doesn't seem like he'd fit into the Underground. I wonder what it's like to be part of an Elemental and yet have nothing to do with them. Is it like being ostracized from your tribe? Or is it more the other way around—is he the one ostracizing them?

On the opposite side of the stage sit the Council of Leaders. Five elderly Wood Elementals dressed in traditional garb of tan-colored floor length tunics. There is only one woman on the Council and she is also the youngest Leader. Council Leaders are nominated and once appointed their term is indefinite, only ended by death. They sit in very elaborate, carved-wood thrones—a symbol of how much we value both our elders and their service to our colony.

I can feel Ahna buzzing excitedly to my right. She leans forward in her seat and taps her foot anxiously for the ceremony to begin. As if in direct contrast, Li sits to my left, slouched in his seat, arm slung across the back of my seat as if he doesn't have a care in the world. Students talk in hushed whispers all around us and Li turns to make a comment to the girl sitting on his other side.

I narrow my eyes and scan the left side of the stage where the Teachers are seated, searching for Teacher 4. He should be seated right between Teacher 3, Earth English, and Teacher 5, Lost Languages, but the seat is empty. I scan the rows of students in front of me and even turn around to scan the rows of people behind me. Diadona scowls at me from two rows back. I ignore her. I scan the faces of the people in the balcony, searching for those mysterious green eyes, but I still don't see him.

My stomach begins to sink with the possibility that something bad happened to Teacher 4, that maybe the other man—the one whose face I couldn't see—did something to him, hurt him in some way. Why were they there? What happens on the eighteenth moon of the hundredth solar alignment?

Teacher 1, the Head of School, steps forward. He raises his hands and the hushed whispers die down into soft murmurs and eventually silence. Teacher 1 is an Earth. He has close-cropped white hair, wears wire-rimmed glasses, and has a kind, fatherly countenance. Even from my seat in the third row I can easily see the green vine-like curlicues that run up his neck, circling beneath his ear and disappearing into his hair line. Small green leaves, like filaments of the most delicate silk, protrude from his sienna-colored skin.

"Welcome to the Hundredth Pronouncement of Xon 9!" At his words there is a scattering of applause and some *whoops* of excitement from the Fires in the balcony. "Today is a very momentous day for the youth of Xon 9." He glances down at us from the stage, peering over the top of his glasses, glancing at each of us in turn as he speaks. "When we first left our Earthly home and arrived on Xon 9 it was a new, undiscovered planet. We were thankful that even when our sun experienced its death, it still provided us with a new opportunity at life in the form of a new habitat, the red planet of Xon 9 with its underground water source, rocky landscape, lush vegetation, and most importantly its oxygen stores that give us breath. We came to Xon 9 with gratitude in our hearts. But over time we soon learned that our new home was much different than our Earth home in one very important way: its effect on our human physiology. As generations passed on it became clear that the exceptional Elemental mix of Xon 9 had a profound impact on our unique chemical composition, resulting in some curious physical changes."

The other Elementals chuckle along with Teacher 1 at this off-handed comment. The physical side effects of each Element are obviously no secret. "However, over time we realized that we did not have to be victims to these changes. With this realization these changes went from an uncontrollable fate, to a choice that we can make for ourselves. Some of you may already feel it, a tingle in your veins or a strange pulsating in your heart." He pauses, contemplative. "You may feel the metallic bravery of Metal; the nurturing serenity of Earth; or the steadfast fortitudinous of Wood." He clasps his hands behind his back as if deep in thought and slowly begins to pace across the stage. "Or perhaps you feel the wisdom of Water or the passion of Fire."

Despite being full, the auditorium is completely silent, not even the Fires clap or cheer. The gravity of the situation is almost palpable. I glance over to the Teachers and suddenly Teacher 4 is right there in his seat, squished between Teacher 3 and Teacher 5, sitting rapt as Teacher 1 speaks, as though he's been sitting there this entire time. As if I'd imagined his absence in the first place. Teacher 1 stops pacing and turns back toward the crowd, without turning I know that every single set of eyes in the whole auditorium is on him at this very moment. Waiting.

"Today, young colonists of Xon 9, you will make a life-changing choice. You will choose an Element that will act as a physical representation of both your personality and your character. There are no wrong answers here, but once the choice is made, it is ever-lasting and there is no undoing. Will you choose the easy path, the path of least resistance that will give you instant gratification, or will you choose the path that challenges you, possibly the very path that you fear and keeps you awake at night with indecision, but that will make you a better person for having chosen it? Ultimately the choice is yours and yours alone. Choose wisely."

. . .

A black curtain at the back of the stage is pulled open and the lights are dimmed except for two spotlights that are aimed at a very tall black box. The box doesn't even appear to have a door, at least not from where I'm sitting. There are hushed, excited whispers from my classmates. Younger siblings are not allowed to attend Pronouncement, so I am not the only one here for the first time. None of us know exactly what to expect. Sure, there were plenty of rumors: they literally throw you into a pit consisting of your Element or they strap you to a chair on stage and somehow insert the Element into your body. What happens at Pronouncement is not something that is discussed, aside from the importance of the choice that you make.

The first student is called to the stage. It's a girl named Yuina. I don't really know her well, but I watch as she tentatively approaches the stage. We were instructed to wear all white to Pronouncement, something about choosing your Elemental from a symbolically pure and untainted state. Whatever that means. The girl slowly walks up to the large black box and glances, unsure at Teacher 1. He smiles warmly and nods, encouraging her. The box must somehow sense her presence standing before it and a door slides open and she steps into the blackness. The door slides closed.

At first nothing happens. There are some confused murmurs around me, including Li. "She must not be able to decide. She didn't look very sure going in." But I quickly hush him, leaning forward in my seat, anxious to see what will happen next. And then it does.

The box illuminates and we shield our faces from the blinding brightness. Suddenly I am looking at a scene of tall, waving blades of grass and clear blue sky. Earth. It looks so real that I feel like I could reach out and touch it, feel the dewy grass beneath my bare feet and the warm breeze caressing my skin. The grass blades waver back and forth for a few more delightful seconds then fade away as the black box reappears, the grass and sky gone. The girl never exits the box. "What the…" Li mumbles.

"It's like magic," Ahna breathes from my other side. "It's so—I just can't…" It's not easy to render Ahna speechless, but the black box has done just that.

We watch anxiously as the next name is called. They're going in alphabetical order by surname so it's not exactly a surprise. Jedidiah. Normally confident and vivacious, Jedidah's posture betrays his nervousness. The door slides open and then closes, shutting him inside. Jedidah was captain of several sports teams, but not necessarily the best academic student. It always seemed like he was biding his time until one of his many athletic practices. For Jedidiah, the choice must be easy, because almost immediately the black box is covered in metallic swirls of gold, silver, and bronze. Metal. There are some anxious whispers not only from the students, but the balcony as well. I try to be optimistic. Perhaps Jedidiah won't end up in the

Underground. Maybe he will be able to maintain the overwhelming balance of Metal coursing through his veins; maybe he'll become a soldier or strategist. Not all Metals end up in the Underground; look at Teacher 7. The metallic images fade away and the next name is called.

And so it continues for several hours until I watch Ahna disappear confidently inside the box, the blades of swaying grass and Earth blue sky dancing in front of me. Li's name is called next and as he gets up he gives me a wicked grin in the darkness and squeezes my hand. He practically skips to the stage. He doesn't even hesitate, he practically leaps inside the box as soon as the door opens and almost immediately the Fire appears, as if it is consuming the box with Li alive inside. Red, yellow, and orange flames licking up its sides. The faces all around me are illuminated in its eerie glow and then almost as quickly as it appeared, it's gone. Extinguished.

It won't be long now before my name is called. I continue to watch as a boy I don't know very well, but had a couple of classes with, disappears inside the box and after what seems like several long minutes, an image of thick, red tree trunks that reach for the sky appears, a green-leafed canopy spreading across the top of the box: Wood.

Diadona is next and I bite the inside of my cheek as she approaches the stage. She doesn't seem as confident as usual. She hesitates in front of the box and Teacher 1 gently urges her as the door slides open. She looks over her shoulder out into the auditorium, but the way the lighting is I can only imagine blackness looks back at her. Blackness behind her and blackness in front of her. What will she choose? Finally, she steps inside and the door slides closed. Several minutes pass and nothing happens. I rock gently back and forth in my seat. *Please don't choose Water* I find myself thinking. And I'm not sure exactly why I have that thought. In the darkness I can't see Teacher 4's face, but I can still make out his familiar lean frame in the row of Teachers. Suddenly, the box is covered in the crystalline, blue sea. Creatures swim and frolic in the image, and the sun—the Earth sun—seems to shine down from the top of the box, kissing the water in a beam of golden light. I feel a pang deep in the center of my chest, a feeling that is a mix of anger and a tinge of…jealousy. But I don't have time to process what I'm feeling.

Because my name is called next.

Chapter 7

It's like time has slowed down. My feet feel as though I am walking through sand as I carefully make my way up to the stage. I am one of the last remaining students. I climb the five steps up to the stage and my heart pounds in my ears. Teacher 1 smiles at me encouragingly as I near the black box. As I cross the stage, I am facing the other Teachers now and despite the dimness of the stage I see Teacher 4's fathomless green eyes watching me. His mouth is set in a grim line and his eyes harbor an emotion that I can't quite interpret. I turn slowly toward the black box. My heart thumps wildly against my rib cage. I wipe my hands down the sides of my white pants. I glance to my right at Teacher 1 who peers at me with his piercing blue eyes over the top of his glasses. He smiles broadly. It must get tiring—smiling for so long. I glance to my left, directly at Teacher 4, whose eyes I am pretty sure have not wavered since I first came onto the stage. Almost imperceptibly, he nods. I turn back toward the black box. The door slides open. Blackness. Blackness in front of me. Blackness behind me. I could turn around right now. Be the first person ever to say: *NO! I refuse to choose! Why do we have to choose? What purpose does it serve?* Surely, I'd end up in the Underground. But I know better. I'd never want to disappoint my parents like that…or Teacher 4. I close my eyes and take a deep breath. My shoulders relax as I exhale slowly. The unknown. I close my eyes and step inside the box.

. . .

In front of me are five large silver buttons. Each button has an engraving on it representing each of the Elementals: Earth, Fire, Water, Wood, and Metal. Above the row of buttons is a small screen. The screen illuminates and a beam of blue light encompasses me, scanning me up and down from head to toe. "Ka Waylon." An automated female-sounding voice surrounds me from all sides. I never really cared for my name. It doesn't sound like it fits. It doesn't fit together and it doesn't fit me. The automated voice continues, "Female, aged eighteen." *It's my moon*, I think. "Personality Strengths: above average intellect, highly observant, and extremely loyal. Personality Weaknesses: stubbornness, indecisiveness, and the inability to speak one's mind. Calculating recommendation." There's a pause and then, "Recommendation: Water." The voice fades away and the buttons illuminate with a white light emitting from somewhere behind them, making them seem as if they're leaping out at me.

So, this is it. This is the choice. The choice that will determine the rest of my life and who—or what—I will become. Based on the analysis, my recommendation is that I choose Water. *Is that what I want?* I think of my dream the other night and the vastness of the ocean as I sunk to its bottom, only to be rescued by Teacher 4. *Teacher 4.* Those intense green eyes…watching…always watching me. And the night that I followed him and that other Water Elemental to the University. What were they doing there? More importantly, what were they talking about—the eighteenth moon on the hundredth solar alignment?

And then it strikes me, like a bolt of white lightning from the red sky of Xon 9. The eighteenth moon on the hundredth solar alignment. Why didn't I realize it sooner? Pronouncement is held each year on the day of the solar alignment. *Today is the hundredth solar alignment.* Eighteen. *My moon.* I can almost hear the voice in my mind: *And how do you know it's this one?*

My heart sinks at the memory and I look at the glowing button, with its engraved waves cresting and curling over. My fingers hover above it, afraid to touch it in case I accidentally press it. "Recommendation: Water," the automated voice repeats as if I hadn't heard it the first time. My heart pounds, like the wings of a tiny bird trying to escape its cage. Green eyes watching. Waiting. Waiting for what? Water is a dangerous Element: it can sustain life, but it also can take life away. I can feel tears beginning to burn in the backs of my eyes. Seconds seem like hours. Will you choose to follow your head, Ka, or your heart? What do you desire? I feel the memory of strong hands pulling me to the surface and my heart does a little dance inside my chest. I try to think clearly. What do you need? The word comes almost instantaneously: Adventure. I close my eyes and press the button.

After all, my name means Fire.

. . .

The floor drops out from beneath me and I am falling through the nothingness. Okay, well, maybe falling isn't exactly the right word. More like *gliding*. Or better yet *sliding*. I'm sliding down a dark, tube-like slide. So that is the reason why none of the other students came out of the box. There's no sense of direction or time, so I just slide quietly through the darkness feeling my body twist and turn, nothing but blackness all around me until I reach the end.

My feet hit the ground and I scooch out of the bottom of the slide. There's no one there. I slowly stand up. No other Fires, no other students. I appear to be in some sort of tunnel network. The walls and floor are packed dirt. The tunnels are illuminated with torches that are placed sporadically along the wall. Well, this must be the place. I can't imagine Waters having some sort of medieval style tunnel. I walk over to the wall, standing on tiptoe and pull down one of the torches. The flame flickers as I swing it around looking for some sort of sign as to which direction to travel in. These Fires sure don't make it easy.

And that's when I see it. On the floor are red-painted arrows pointing to the tunnel leading down to my right. My nervousness has returned and my heart pounds softly as I follow the direction of the arrows, down the winding tunnel. I hold the torch in my sweaty palm, arms-length from me so that it acts as both a light and a source of protection from the unknown. There's an unidentifiable noise somewhere in the tunnel and I wonder if it's too late to try and crawl back up the slide. Jump out of the black box and say—*Nevermind! I changed my mind!* to a shocked audience. But I know that's not a real possibility. At least the image makes me laugh to myself, even if the laughter is lost before it even passes my lips.

I round a corner and reach the end. There's a large wooden door. I use the torch to illuminate it and I see that it's smudged in black. I glide my fingertips over it lightly. Not smudged, *charred*. I lean in closer and realize that it's not just charred, but it's actually a design, an intricate pattern of swirls that seem to mimic the actual dance of a flame. There's a large metal latch on the right. *Do I knock?*

I think how just a little bit ago Li stood in this exact same spot. He practically leapt into the black box to declare— pronounce—his choice. Would he have knocked? I smile. *No way,* I think. With shaking hands I lift the latch and thrust my shoulder into the giant door, pushing it open enough to step through its arched entrance way. I bring the torch around and inch the door closed behind me. The red arrows continue only a short distance and I reach a small stairwell leading up with another door at the top. However, this door is different. The stairwell is lined with more torches and I can clearly see that this door is made of a grayish-brown metal. Iron. Its handle is a ring and unlike the first door, this one pulls open instead of pushes. The handle is cool to the touch and I use my free hand to pull it toward me.

Red light spills out of the opening and illuminates my white Pronouncement clothes in a pink cast. I step through the opening, holding my torch up above me more out of fear than for the need of light. The room is alit with a huge fire pit in the center. This room too is packed dirt and is very large and circular. The fire seems as if it could lick the dirt ceiling. Above the fire is a large iron grate and the smoke of the fire ebbs and swirls into it. Men and women stand, surrounding the fire, its light dancing off the golden filigree that adorns each of their faces. Fires.

A man approaches me. He's wearing a black tunic that is tied at the waist. I glance around. They all are. But I know this isn't all the Fires of Xon 9 because some of them were upstairs in the auditorium. This must be something special. The man's face is angular. His hair is black speckled with white. He's probably about my father's age. He smiles at me and the fire glints off the whites of his teeth and casts his face in shadows. The effect is an odd combination of beautiful and grotesque. "Ka," he says. He gently takes the torch from my sweaty palm, steps forward, and tosses it into the fire which crackles in response. "Welcome to Fire." He gestures at the other men and women who smile back at me. They seem friendly enough. So why does my heart feel like it is going to be ripped from my chest?

I realize that he's waiting for me to reply. I shift nervously from one foot to the other. What would Li have said? Probably something witty and fantastic. "Um, thanks." It comes out meek sounding and I feel the flush creep up my neck to my cheeks and I'm thankful that they can't see my face in the dim light of the fire.

He begins walking and turns indicating that I should follow him. We enter into a narrow doorway to the right of the giant fire. It's another room. I never even knew all these tunnels twisted and wound beneath my feet, beneath the ground that I walk on every single day. It's like a completely different world that coexists within mine, a different plane of existence.

The room we enter into is circular and it's lined with candles on the floor around its perimeter. Shadows dance on the walls and ceiling. The man leads me to the center of the room. Several other Fires have followed us in, but I still don't see Li. I wonder if he's here. I wonder if he felt scared or excited about what happens next.

The man turns from me and addresses the people in the room. "Let us begin the Ritual of Fire." I feel my stomach dip as if down to my toes. The others respond back to him. "Let us begin the Ritual from the Dawn of Time."

"Before Fire man was cold, hungry, and frightened. With the discovery of Fire man learned that he could be warmed by its flames." Someone hands the man a black cloak and he drapes it over my shoulders as he speaks. "Man learned that with Fire he could be well-fed." Another person hands him a small dish and he dips his thumb into the dish. His thumb comes out black and I realize that the dish is full of ash. He drags his thumb in short strokes across my forehead. Six strokes. My name: KA. "And with Fire man was protected." A third person begins to drop some sort of powder in a circle around us as the first man continues to speak. "Fire is passion. Fire is energy. Fire is lit from deep within. You have chosen Fire, Ka. But be warned: Fire is insatiable." The man bows slightly and steps out of the circle. He pulls out a single match and strikes it. "Fire can give us life and yet, if not carefully controlled, it can consume us."

He tosses the match into the circle of powder and it ignites in a flurry of red and orange.

My eyes grow wide in panic, but as the flames arise around me I find that I'm also filled with a sense of awe. The colors dance around me and light the faces of the people in the room, grossly exaggerating their features. It reflects in their eyes, waving, beckoning. It is both mesmerizing and frightening. A ring of fire. Almost as soon as they started, the flames begin to recede, having run out of the limited fuel given to them.

I stand frozen to the spot, surrounded within the circle of ashes. Any sense of fear seems to have died out with the flame. I no longer feel afraid. I feel an eerie sense of calm as I stand here among these strangers. A woman steps toward the man with a velvet pillow. Tucked into its center, is a small syringe. Somehow I instinctively know what the syringe is for—the rumors at school. It's what induces the Change, the physical manifestations of your chosen Element, by suppressing the body's natural Elemental inclination. The liquid in that syringe is what will forever be your symbol, your reminder, your label of who—of what—you are and what you will become. *Choose wisely.*

"We have bestowed you with the Ritual of Fire, Ka Waylon," he's saying as he takes the syringe from the woman and she steps back, still holding the pillow, to join the circle of Fires surrounding me. He moves to stand in front of me. "And now if you'll repeat these words: I have seen the Light of Fire."

My lips move as if not of my own accord and my voice fills the room surprisingly solid and assured: "I have seen the Light of Fire."

He continues, "I am Passion. I am Energy. I am Life."

I repeat, "I am Passion. I am Energy. I am Life." As I reiterate his words he's preparing the syringe and I know what's about to happen, and yet I am not afraid. I should be afraid.

"I am Petulance. I am Untamed. I am Death. This is the Balance of Fire." He waits for me to repeat his words, brown eyes expectant. The cloak is heavy across my shoulders and I can feel the soft ash on my forehead. The man holds the syringe. Waiting.

I repeat, "I am Petulance. I am Untamed. I am Death. This is the Balance of Fire." I feel the pinch of the needle in my neck and the warmth—*like liquid fire,* I think—spread through me. My knees grow weak and I feel myself tumbling to the earth, but strong hands catch me. Not familiar hands. Not the hands that belong to Teacher 4. Yet, those green eyes are all that I can see, those green eyes watching me. Following me.

That's the last thing I remember before the light fades and the darkness settles in.

Fire gives life.

Fire consumes.

Choose wisely.

CHAPTER 8

When I wake up I'm in some sort of common area. The edges of my vision are still blurry and I put my hand to my forehead. I feel like I was drug around the colony by my ankles. When I pull my hand away it's smeared with ash.

The common area has a few sleek gray sofas upon which I am seated. There's a fluffy maroon colored rug in front of a sleek metal fireplace that is suspended in the air from a tubular pipe running from the ceiling.

There are a few windows that line the opposite wall and I can see the two moons flanking the sun. I have to get home.

"The grogginess will wear off in a few minutes," a female voice slices through my thoughts and I turn, glancing over my shoulder because I hadn't realized I wasn't alone. A girl dressed in all white with a brown, curly ponytail is sitting in a circular black chair that is suspended from the ceiling similarly to the fireplace. "I'm Rhian."

My mouth feels like it's been stuffed with cotton. "Ka," I reply pushing myself up to a more seated position. I look at her wearily. "What was that?"

"Don't worry. Everyone passed out from it. The serum they use to induce the physiological change is quite strong." *Smart*, I think. I don't know this girl from anyone—have never seen her before— and yet I can tell that she's already much more informed than I am. She reminds me of Ahna which makes me wonder about Li.

"Where's everyone else? My friend…" My voice trails off because I'm not sure what to say next.

Rhian shrugs. "Around." She climbs out of the chair and comes around the couch. She sits opposite me pulling a velvety pillow that matches the rug into her lap. Her cheeks are smudged with soot and her forehead is smeared where her name had been written. "We're at the University Complex. This is where we'll find out our career placements and begin our studies."

"I thought that we'd, you know, go home first." I can feel my vision beginning to sharpen and my voice is starting to return, the grogginess fading.

She shrugs again. "I guess not. At least not yet."

There's the sound of a door opening and closing. Then footsteps. "Hey, Fire Girl." Li.

"All of us are Fire now," I grin. I turn to Rhian. "My name, Ka, means fire." She nods and looks at Li wearily as he plops down right in between us.

"Well, this is rather unexpected. I have to say you're one of the last people I expected to see here."

"Yeah me too," is all I can think to say. Mostly because it's true. I had no idea which Elemental I'd end up in, if anything probably Earth or even Water. But why not? My name means Fire after all.

I don't think I've made the wrong choice—at least not yet. Rhian seems nice enough and I'll have Li with me. Maybe it's good to push myself out of my comfort zones. And away from Teacher 4. I wonder what he thinks about my decision. My heart sinks. I wonder what my parents think of my decision. My mother an Earth and my father a Wood. Would they think my decision was impulsive and foolhardy?

I continue. "I guess I was just looking for a little *Adventure.*"

Li grins and raises an eyebrow slightly. "Oh, I think we can take care of that."

Rhian interrupts, "I'm sorry, but do you two know each other?"

I blush. "We're friends. Sorry, I don't know where my head is at. Still a bit groggy I guess. Rhian this is Li; Li this is Rhian."

Li smiles one of his charming, luminous smiles. "The pleasure is definitely all mine."

Rhian rolls her eyes. "Whatever." Suddenly her eyes grow wide. "Look at that!"

We follow her extended finger over to the fire place. Inside the firebox the flames have turned blue and they seem to waver and dance. Slowly a woman's face appears in the flames. "Greetings New Fires. There will be a meeting in the lower level symposium in fifteen minutes. Please find inside the sleeping quarters fresh clothing for you to wear." The woman's face crackles along with the flames. It's hard to tell whether it's a hologram within the flames or something else. "Do not be late. Fifteen minutes." She smiles and then her image slowly absorbs back into the flames.

"Well, that was a bit weird," Li shifts uncomfortably and I realize that he's actually nervous. Normally, cool, calm, and collected Li is a bit unnerved by the newness of the situation. It makes me feel a bit better to know I'm not the only one. He continues, "I mean seriously, what if I don't like the clothes they picked out?"

I roll my eyes and Rhian sighs turning to me. "Is he for real?"

I grin back at her. "Unfortunately."

"Ouch, Ka. After all those years of friendship I've given you that's how you treat me?" He puts a mock expression of hurt on his face, sticking out his lower lip and widening his eyes.

I throw one of the maroon colored pillows at him, hitting him square in the face. His forehead is still smeared with ash. "You heard the woman in the fire. Don't be late."

. . .

Luckily, we aren't late. The clothes they left for us are simple denim pants, a t-shirt, and a black jacket. I happily discarded the white, sooty clothes from Pronouncement and slipped into the fresh clothes. How did they know our sizes? There was a basin and I scrubbed the soot from my face letting the invigorating feeling wash over me. I ran my fingers like a comb through my collar-bone length brown hair trying to get out any of the knots and tangles from the day. Good enough, I'd decided and met up with Li and Rhian back in the hallway.

A few other new Fires had appeared and I wondered how they'd gotten the message from the woman in the fireplace. Then I remembered that there were fireplaces everywhere—in the sleeping quarters, common areas, even a few hallways had fireplaces. And here I'd always thought fireplaces were primarily for a source of heat, but apparently the Fires use it as communication as well.

The building is sleek and modern. The walls are painted a steel gray color with crisp white trim. The floor is carpeted in a neat, tightly woven black fiber that muffles our footsteps. The seven of us cram into the sleek silver elevator at the end of the hallway. The buttons in this elevator are different than any I've ever seen before. Instead of basic numbers indicating the floor, they're all sorts of weird symbols.

Rhian peers over my shoulder. "How do we know which one is the lower level Symposium?"

Another girl with frizzy auburn colored hair studies the buttons. "This one," she says indicating a button that is a circle with other smaller circles surrounding it. Almost like a sun with its rays.

"How did you gather that?" Li asks dubiously.

The girl shrugs. "It looks like a table with people surrounding it, like some sort of conference room." She presses the button and the elevator drops smoothly as it takes us to the lower level.

The other new Fires besides myself, Li, and Rhian are the girl with the red hair, a dark-skinned boy with what seems to be a permanent scowl on his face, another boy with piercing blue eyes and blonde hair in a short ponytail, and one more girl who is a bit taller than everyone else with short black hair—shorter than Li's—and eyebrows that knit together in such a way that her face is very unfriendly. What have I gotten myself into? I inch closer to Li seeking the comfort of someone familiar.

The doors slide open and we step out into a non-descript hallway with a set of double doors at the end. The floor is a fiery red marble interspersed with sparkly golden swirls. The lighting is odd: spots of golden light illuminate the floor making it seem as if it's alive, while contradicting spots of darkness cast shadows against the gray walls. We stop in front of the door.

We look at each other uncomfortably. Do we knock? Just go in? The tall girl with short black hair and stormy gray eyes, pushes past, knocking me in the shoulder roughly and Li catches me carefully, sending her a glare which she ignores. She raps on the door.

As if in automatic response the doors swing open and we step into a large conference room, the lower level Symposium. A large round mahogany colored table takes up the majority of the room. In the center of the table is a giant fire pit. A large fire with yellow-orange flames crackling is in its center and the smoke is being drawn up into a platinum hood that disappears into the ceiling. The table is surrounded by chairs and in them are five adult Fires, the filigree on the sides of their faces reflecting the enigmatic light of the fire.

I immediately recognize the woman who delivered the message in the fire. She has shoulder length blonde hair and sits beside the man from the Ritual earlier, the man with the salt and peppered hair. They're no longer wearing the black tunics, just regular clothes. "Come," the woman says and smiles tersely. "Sit."

We make our way to the open seats and I sit flanked by Rhian and Li. "Welcome to Fire. I am Tristen and these are the members of the Fire Leadership Committee." She nods toward the other adults sitting around the table. "We will be in charge of you during your Transition time from being a non-Elemental into a Fire Elemental."

Immediately the angry-faced boy interrupts. "*In charge of?* I thought that choosing an Element meant you've entered into adulthood?" His voice is tinged with contempt. He taps his hand on the table's surface as if bored by this entire ordeal. Suddenly there's a hissing sound, a frightened look replaces the flippant one on his face, and he yanks his hand quickly away from the surface of the table. Where his hand had been moments before a small spire of smoke appears and then immediately dissipates as it is sucked up into the hood above the fire pit. He looks at his hand, eyes wide. "You-you *burned* me." His voice is aghast and he uselessly shakes his hand to relieve the sensation. He narrows his eyes, shooting daggers at the woman who harmed him. *Is this how Fires keep control? Through pain?*

Not that the boy didn't deserve some sort of reprimand for his blatant show of disrespect to the people in charge. But a *physical* reprimand? Physical reprimands haven't been used since the Old Earth Days. Or so I thought. I shift uneasily in my seat.

But Tristen just continues to smile, ignoring his accusation, acting as if nothing out of the ordinary has happened. "Indeed, Doran, it is a marker of adulthood, but surely you didn't think once you chose that you'd simply be left to your own devices?" *Doran.* For some reason the name seems very suiting to his scowl face, just the way it rolls off the tongue and is left abruptly hanging in the air, as if it is undecided on how to proceed. She continues. "I suppose you could say that we are here to guide you, if you take offense to the words *in charge of you.* Either way, soon you will undergo testing for your Career Placement. You will also begin your studies in the Element of Fire. Tonight you will return home and in two days' time, you will begin your first day of studies. It is expected that you will arrive the evening prior with your belongings and not be tardy for testing the following morning. A schedule will be left for you in your sleeping quarters upon your arrival. We kindly request that family members not of Fire do not enter the facility." She pauses glancing at each of us to see if there are any more questions or interruptions, but we all remain silent. "Very good. You have chosen Fire and we feel that you will find you have chosen wisely. But remember that Fire takes work and dedication, if you do not feed and tend to the Fire, its flame can die out. The consequences for letting the flame die out are dire," she glances wearily at Doran, who wordlessly peers down at his injured fingers. "Are we understanding one another?" We nod numbly at her words: it's the first instance since Pronouncement that a hint of true darkness has permeated the festivities. She turns to the man from the Ritual. "Eoin, will you see our guests out?"

We rise and follow Eoin out a doorway behind the table and fire pit, another entrance besides the main doors through which we'd entered previously. We walk down a short hallway and enter a room that has three platforms encased in what looks like a sort of open tube. "What are these?" The frizzy red-haired girl asks. I still don't know her name.

Eoin smiles gently. His smile is much different than that of Tristen. He seems to actually care about our curiosity and not consider it an inconvenience. "These are your way home, Bryn."

"Teleportation Portals?" The blonde pony-tailed boy asks. "I thought those were out of use on Xon 9?"

"That's right, Pierce," Eoin replies. *Pierce.* What an appropriate name for the boy with the cool blue eyes. "They are out of use for the general populace. We can't just have people popping in and out of any random location unexpectedly. Indeed they were quite difficult to regulate." He looks mischievous for a moment. "But there are still a few that you'll find to be in use. Alright then, who's first?"

The unfriendly girl with stormy gray eyes steps forward. Eoin smiles. "Wonderful, Jielle." Eoin directs her to step onto the platform and instructs her to begin visualizing her destination in her mind. "The teleporter will scan and analyze your destination then deliver you within ten meters accuracy. They're quite amazing machines really. It's a pity that people couldn't utilize them properly for their intended purpose." He presses some buttons on the outside of the machine. "Now before you go, I must remind you all that your Pronouncement will not and should not be discussed. It is considered a private matter especially during the Transition Phase. The majority of your friends and family, having been through it themselves, are aware of this implicit rule and should respect it. Otherwise it is a matter best left unspoken." We nod our understanding. It's true. Besides the rumors at school, Elemental Pronouncement and the process of how it works are not discussed. Not ever. "Alright, Jielle, whenever you're ready." Eion looks at her expectantly.

Jielle closes her eyes and a beam of white light emits from the top of the open-faced tube and encompasses her inside it. In a matter of seconds there's a blast of brilliant, blinding light that causes me to close my eyes and throw my arm up to block my face from its brilliance.

And when I open my eyes again Jielle is gone.

Eion smiles satisfied. "Alright, who's next then?" Pierce, Doran, and Bryn each step into one of the three portals and the same process happens again. There's a brilliant white light and then they're gone as if by magic.

Rhian, Li, and I are all that's left.

Li quickly squeezes my hand before stepping onto the platform. "Tomorrow then, right, Ka?" There's a nervous edge to his words as he lets go of my hand and I realize that he's just as worried as I am about what lies ahead for both of us. *Choose wisely.*

I grin tightly. "Right. Tomorrow." I hurriedly step onto the platform and close my eyes. I want to be home. Away from this place, away from Tristen. I imagine my room with its old, familiar frayed bedspread and the purple colored paint that is peeling where the walls meet the ceiling. I think of my mother and her warm brown eyes the color of soil, the green vines forming a curlicue down her cheek, around her neck, and disappearing into her hairline. Somehow I know that she's waiting for me. Waiting for her only daughter to return home, if only for a little while. I hope that I haven't disappointed her. *Head or heart.*

Desires or needs.

Have I chosen wisely?

Too late now.

I feel the warm light surround me and I know that it's beginning. There's a quick burst of heat, so warm that it's almost suffocating and then I feel a cool, squishy softness beneath me.

My bed.

I'm home.

At least for one more night.

CHAPTER 9

I was right.

Almost as soon as I realize where I am the door to my room is slowly pushed open. "Kata?" My mother's voice. "Kata, is that you?" The whisper has a slight sense of panic just beneath its surface and I wonder, *who else would it be?*

I reply, "Yes, it's me." She pushes open the door. No light spills in. We've lived in this house my whole life; it's easy to navigate in the partial night of the red sun. She closes the door solidly behind her before coming to sit on the edge of the bed. She reaches out and softly strokes my brown hair, inspecting me carefully in the dim light.

"Oh, Kata. What have you done?" she whispers. I've no idea what she's talking about. Is she talking about my Pronouncement? Discussion of my decision is strictly prohibited. That's why there's always so much speculation prior to Pronouncement. While it is okay to discuss the significance of the event it is *not* okay to discuss the actual decision-making—the decision needs to be untainted, pure to the owner without outside influences.

I'm beginning to feel sleepy. The day was long, blending into the next one only to start all over again tomorrow. I mumble, "What do you mean?" At first she doesn't reply, just continues to gently stroke my hair as if she has all the time in the world. But she doesn't. Even in the pink light of the night, I can see the clouds of worry in her eyes.

"It doesn't matter now, Kata. What's done is done. The decision cannot be unmade. I only wish you had heeded my advice." She pauses, stopping stroking my hair. She bites her lip and turns away. I can feel the heaviness of sleep fighting my waking mind like two competitors both yearning for victory. "You must be careful, Kata. Fire is dangerous and if you are not vigilant it will consume you until you burn up and there is nothing of yourself left." My eyelids grow heavier. "Sweet daughter, you have chosen dangerously." Sleep beckons. "And, Kata," as she whispers my name she lowers her voice so that it's almost barely audible, "they must never find out who you are, who you *truly* are." My eyelids slide closed and I hear my mother's voice coalescing inside my dreams. "My Impossible Girl."

. . .

I'm in the black box. Again. I'm staring at the silver buttons with their meticulously engraved icons. *But I've already chosen,* I think.

The mechanical voice infiltrates the box. "Ka Waylon, female, aged eighteen." My moon. That's right I almost forgot. It's my moon. The eighteenth moon on the hundredth solar alignment. "Scanning," the beam of light encompasses me as the box gathers its data. "Personality Strengths: above average intellect, highly observant, and extremely loyal. Personality Weaknesses: stubbornness, indecisiveness, and the inability to speak one's mind. Calculating recommendation." There's a pregnant pause as the box continues to analyze my data. I hold my breath even though I already know the answer. Even though I've already lived through this moment. "Recommendation: Water."

My fingers hover over the button with its engraved scroll of flames. *Kata, what have you done?* My mother's words seep into my mind. *Choose wisely.* Before I can change my mind, I hurriedly move my fingers pressing the button with its crests of waves. The floor drops out beneath me much like before and I'm sliding down and down, deep below the surface of Xon 9. I twist and turn through the darkness until something cold and wet creeps up my legs dampening the hems of my white pants. Water.

I splash into the coldness, holding my breath and closing my eyes. I'm sinking much like in my previous dream. A voice. "Ka, open your eyes." Teacher 4. I open my eyes slowly afraid of the sting of water to come. But it never comes and I find that I can see clearly through the water. Teacher 4 is swimming in front of me and he holds out his hand, and despite that he frightens me and that I don't know what it is that he wants from me, I take it anyway. He pulls me along toward a tall underwater mountain with a large opening like a doorway. We don't speak as we swim toward it.

When we enter it is filled with golden light, like Old Earth light, not the red light of Xon 9. He leads me deeper into the mountain and I have the sensation that we are swimming upwards. We reach a small cavernous area and continue to swim upwards until we break the water's surface. There's a small chamber of air. The cavern is dark, but I can still make out his green eyes which are piercing in the darkness. I cough trying to clear the water from my lungs.

"Why am I here?" I sputter.

He looks confused. "You chose Water."

"No," I reply narrowing my eyes. Afraid he somehow manipulated my choice. "I didn't. I chose Fire."

"Well, the fact that you're here with me right now would indicate otherwise."

"I already chose Fire. I remember the Ritual of Fire and everything." My voice is insistent, but I can feel the doubt creeping in. *Did I choose Fire?*

His eyes soften. "We don't have much time, Kata." My mother's nickname for me. How does he know it? More importantly, why does he use it? "You must be very careful. They must never find out who you truly are." He echoes my mother's words. For some reason hearing them from his mouth irritates me.

"Who's they?" I demand.

He presses his lips and shakes his head. "It doesn't matter.

You've chosen and it can't be undone. I will do what I can to help you."

I scowl and even as I say the words I find that I don't mean them. "I don't need your help."

He reaches out tentatively and pushes a strand of wet hair off my cheek. "You will."

I press further. "Why do you watch me?"

He shakes his head. "You'll find out soon enough. But I can tell you that whatever you think is the reason; it's not it." He tries to cup my cheek, but I push his hand away angrily.

"How do *you* know what I think? You're just my teacher." I'd never in a million years talk to a teacher in this way, but I've never had a teacher like Teacher 4 before. I feel the burn beneath my skin, the angry breath of Fire beginning to course through my veins. The Change.

He smiles at me like I am a petulant child and it just angers me even more. "You really are impossible, you know that?"

And with that he disappears into the pool of dark water beneath us, leaving me alone in the darkened cavern.

I startle awake. I am clutching my pillow to my chest and my breath comes short and fast. *It was just a dream.* I try to take long, slow, deep breaths. *Just a dream*, I repeat.

But, if it's just a dream, then why is my pillow damp? I reach my hand slowly up to my hair, my heart pounding anxiously in my chest.

Wet.

. . .

"Do you have everything you'll need, Ka?" My father asks at breakfast the next morning. We're sitting around the small round table in our kitchen. My mother made toast and eggs this morning. Sometimes we just take one of the food pills—all the nutrients we need compressed into a swallowable form—but this morning my mother insisted on making a proper breakfast using food items from the colony storehouses. Each family gets a weekly ration. It isn't much as it's difficult to grow crops and raise animals on Xon 9. "It's our last breakfast as a family all under the same roof," she'd said.

"We're still a family," I'd argued, but even as I said the words I knew that it was only partially true. Things are changing; it's all changing.

Now, I turn to my father. "Yeah, I think so."

"You'll be gone for a while," my mother points out.

"But I'm only a short walk away," I say.

"Yes, but during the Transition Phase you aren't permitted to leave the University Complex."

"Why?"

My parents exchange a look, a look that I know means they don't want to tell me the truth. My father takes a deep breath. "The Change can be quite, um, what's the word, Novea?" He shoves a piece of toast into his mouth.

"Tumultuous," my mother offers.

90

"Ah, yes. Thank you, dear. Tumultuous. So it's best that new Elementals stay at the University Complex until the Transitional Phase is over. It's also a time to get to know your fellow Elementals, if instead you spent all this time just living your regular life you'd never get to learn the significance of your choice." He glances at my mother over the rim of his clay mug.

She clears her throat. "Yes, exactly, and you'll also get your Career Assignment. Isn't that exciting?" Her voice inflects at the end with a false tone of excitement.

"Yeah, exciting." I think of Tristen and how she burned Doran when he was rude. I mean, I guess I can't be surprised, it is Fire after all and he did sort of deserve it for his poor attitude. But a physical reprimand? I debate whether or not to inform my parents of this, but the words of Tristen stop me: *A private matter.* Besides, maybe other Elementals have physical reprimands too and we just don't know. *Kata, what have you done?*

It's like we're engaging in a kind of dance: my mother, father, and me. It's like we're twirling around the room, dodging, and slipping past the fact, afraid to speak the truth of what my decision means. A horrific thought suddenly strikes me. *Will I ever see my parents again?* I immediately push the thought aside, that's ridiculous. But I can't help but wonder if there's a tiny bit of validity to the thought.

I put my dishes in the sink and turn to head back up the stairs and to my room to finish my packing when my mother stops me. "Oh, Kata, this was left for you yesterday while you were gone." She pulls a folded up envelope from the pocket of her sweater coat and hands it to me.

I take it. "Who's it from?"

"I don't know. It was slid beneath the front door when we returned from Pronouncement." Her eyes lock on mine for a moment and again I see those clouds of worry threatening to burst and flood.

"Thanks." I turn before she can say anything else and dart up the stairs taking them two at a time.

I pull open the curtains letting the red light flood into my room, making the lavender walls seem as if they're glowing from within. Next to my window is a bench with some pillows. Growing up this was my favorite spot to sit and read or do my homework.

My bags are packed and sitting on my bed. I'm only taking two bags with me. Some clothes and wash things take up the larger duffle bag, and the smaller bag contains some pictures of me with Ahna and Li, a few of my favorite books, and a wood carving my father gave me on my tenth moon. It's of an elephant; an Old Earth creature that was considered both majestic and wise. He said it was from his own Transitional Phase, something that I didn't understand until now. It seemed important that I take it with me.

I slowly unfold the envelope. At first I think that it is from Ahna since we didn't get to see each other after Pronouncement, but then I see the familiar handwriting, half-cursive and half-print. I run my fingertips over it nervously. I don't want to open it. *I should open it.* I'm afraid to open it. *I need to open it.*

Ka,

I know that I am the last person you would probably expect a letter from, but the things that I need to tell you are vital to your survival in Fire.

Vital to my survival? What does that even mean?

As you've probably noticed I've been carefully watching you. I'd hoped that you'd choose Water because then my job would be a whole lot easier, but as you read this we both know that is not the decision that you've made.

His job. What job is he talking about?

Right now the details aren't important, but there are some things that you need to know because although I want to help you, you've made it much more difficult for me to do so. First, you should trust no one. And, I mean no one, not even Li or Rhian.

Yeah right. If there's someone I'm not going to trust, it's you. Only you. Well, and maybe Tristen.

Second, always remember that even though your name means Fire and you chose Fire, you are not Fire. It is crucial that you remember this.

But you're wrong. I am Fire. I am Passion. I am Energy. I am Life. I feel the burning just beneath the surface.

Lastly, you may feel the burn of Fire, but if you pay attention you will also feel the wisdom of Earth, the strength of Wood, the bravery of Metal, and the fluidity of Water. It's not impossible if you choose to make it so.

Yours,

Sloan (Teacher 4)

With shaking hands I set the letter down carefully. So Teacher 4's name is actually Sloan. Despite the weird feeling deep in the pit of my stomach—a mixture of fear and curiosity— I find that I like the name. It's a strong name; a protector's name; the name of a warrior. But why is it that I need a protector? Why is it Teacher 4's job to protect me? More importantly, *what is it that I need protection from?*

I hug my knees to my chest and look out the window at the pink landscape, the few trees and shrubs with their gray-green foliage, the white hot sun burning in the blood-stained sky. Tears burn the backs of my eyes and I squeeze my eyes shut, letting the pinpricks of light dance against my eyelids.

You are all possibilities and yet you are impossible. You are the Impossible Girl.

My Impossible Girl.

It's not impossible if you choose to make it so.

What have I done?

CHAPTER 10

Luckily for me when I returned to the University Complex, after a tight-lipped hug from my parents, I found out that my roommate is Rhian. When I walked back into the sleeping quarters she was already there unpacking her belongings—a single bag. I let out a silent sigh of relief that it wasn't Jielle. Maybe I could have handled Bryn, but I'm glad that it's Rhian because I feel like we bonded a little on the day of Pronouncement.

That night we received orders that first thing the next morning we had to report to the Common Area for directions regarding our Career Assignment Placement Test. Now, I hastily swallow my ante meridiem pill and throw my hair into a small ponytail. Rhian is already waiting for me when I return from the bathrooms, rocking back and forth on her heels nervously.

"I'm horrible at tests," she explains. "I get really bad test anxiety. Do you think that there will be a lot of arithmetic on it?"

I give her a half-smile and shrug. I really have no idea what to expect. Although something tells me it isn't going to be like a typical test that we'd have in school.

We hurry into the Common Area where some of the others are already waiting. Doran is there with his now-familiar perma-scowl. Bryn, her frizzy auburn hair pulled back into a pouf ball of a ponytail, bites at her nails nervously. She must have the same sort of anxiety that Rhian has about tests. Pierce stands there looking neat in appearance and relaxed in posture, observing and discerning. Jielle appears from the opposite direction as Rhian and myself. Her short black hair is spiked and her clothes are very tight showing off her lithe frame. She plops onto one of the gray couches and looks at Eoin expectantly.

"Actually, we're waiting for one more," Eoin says glancing around for Li. Eoin waits a few more minutes, then shrugs helplessly. I know Li isn't the most responsible person on the planet, but it isn't like him to not show up when expected. I squeeze in between Rhian and Bryn on one of the sofas. Doran drops down next to Jielle. *What a perfect pair*, I think, with their matching scowls. Pierce doesn't sit. "As you know," Eoin begins, "today is your Career Assignment Placement Test. Each Elemental has particular fields of study that are considered strengths for that Element. For example, Woods make excellent leaders as seen by our Leadership Council. Waters and Earths make excellent teachers, nurses, and care-takers of the elderly. And Metals, when in Balance, make excellent soldiers." Doran snickers at this. It's true we all know what happens to most Metals, but still Xon 9 has a strong paramilitary, and that is thanks to the Metals. Eoin shoots him a look.

"And Fires?" Bryn asks. "What career assignments do Fires excel at?" I have to admire her for shifting the focus from Doran and his attention-seeking ways back to the task at hand. Li appears, catapulting over the back of the couch and squishing himself in between Rhian and me. Rhian shoots him a withering look.

"Ah, Liwald. So glad that you found the time to join us." Eoin looks at Li warily. I glance at Li. He has large dark circles beneath his eyes and his black hair is sticking every which way. I wonder what he's been up to, why he looks so disheveled.

"I apologize, Sir. It won't happen again." I've heard the familiar line so many times before when Li was late to class and asked by the teachers to explain his tardiness.

"I should hope not," Eoin smiles, but it's not unnerving like Tristen's. The difference is Eoin's smile actually reaches his eyes, wrinkling them at the corners. He turns to Bryn. "And to answer your question, Bryn, Fires are good at many things, among them is authoring, theater, painting, sculpting, rhetoric, and event planning." His smile widens. "After all, who do you think organizes Pronouncement?"

Doran's scowl fades. "You mean Fires are the organizers of Pronouncement. They're the ones who came up with the black box?"

Eoin nods. "That's right, Doran. Any event in the colony is planned and organized by a Fire Elemental. It's important that everyone receives a Career Assignment that best utilizes his or her talents. For Fires, that includes the gifts of eloquence, passion, energy, drama, and persuasion."

"So," interjects Jielle. Her features have softened slightly and I'm grateful that Eoin was assigned this task and not Tristen. Besides, I'm sure Tristen has more important things to do. "How does this whole Career Assignment Placement Test work?"

"Jielle, I am so glad that you asked. You'll have to follow me for the answer to that question."

. . .

We're on the lower level again. Down a winding hallway and through a set of steel double doors. Li walks beside me, his shoulder pressed into mine, but we say nothing as we follow along with the others. When we enter the room, several other Fires are already waiting for us. I don't recognize any of them as the Fire Leadership Committee and the feeling of relief is almost palpable.

The room is odd and it's the first room I've seen, besides the bathrooms, in this building that doesn't have a fireplace. The room is all white and has a stainless steel counter top with chairs running along one side of the room and a row of stainless steel upright pods lining the opposite wall. Each of the pods has a Fire standing beside it waiting patiently. The harsh light gives off a cold feeling.

"What's this room?" Rhian asks and I admire her courage.

"Ah, yes. This room is where your Career Assignment

Placement Test will be held." As he says these words one of the male Fires steps to the double doors and programs something into the key pad on the wall. The key pad beeps in response and a green halo of light surrounds the doors, sealing us in until it is deactivated. I gulp nervously and I feel Li's fingers find mine and squeeze gently.

"This isn't like any test at school is it?" Doran asks glancing apprehensively at the pods.

"That's correct, Doran. Your Career Assignment Placement Test, or CAPT, as we like to call it, is done virtually via these pods," Eoin explains.

"But-but I actually studied for this test!" Rhian whines and I try to hide my smile.

"Of course you did," Jielle mutters but luckily Rhian is so distraught that she doesn't hear the unkind words.

"Unfortunately, Rhian, your studies won't help you on this test. This is a *different* type of test," he emphasizes the word different oddly but before I can think too much about it he continues. "This is called a Mindscape. You will be put into one of these deprivation pods—no outside sensory stimulus—and you will quickly travel inside your own mind. By navigating your Mindscape much will be revealed about your personality." I find that I involuntarily shiver at his words and I'm happy to have Li's fingers intertwined with mine. Rhian's face looks about as horrified as I feel inside.

"So how exactly does the data from the Mindscape get collected?" Pierce asks. He's been silent this entire time, blue eyes stony, posture erect and I wonder why he didn't choose Metal. He seems like a perfect solider. Then again, there's some madness, an inevitable risk involved, when pronouncing Metal. Maybe he didn't think it was worth the risk. *What does he have to lose?* I find myself thinking. Eoin's response interrupts my thoughts.

"I'm glad you asked. You will be assigned a guardian who will navigate your Mindscape with you virtually." He motions to the other Fires and they hold up their wrists which each have chunky black bracelets clamped onto them. "They will only act as an observer of course; they aren't to interact at all with you or your Mindscape. No judgments. They are simply there to collect the relevant data." He pauses before asking, "Are there any questions before we get started?"

Everyone slowly shakes their head *no*. What questions could possibly be asked? We're about to go inside our own head and navigate through our own thoughts, memories, and choices. Not only that, but a complete stranger will be with us watching as we navigate the darkest and deepest innermost recesses of who we are at the very core of our existence. How do you even respond to that revelation?

"Excellent. Then let's get started. The process varies for each individual, but this is all that we have planned for you today as navigating the Mindscape can be quite exhausting." He moves toward the pods and starts calling off our names, assigning us to our guardians.

The woman at my pod sort of reminds me of my mother. She's a bit younger, but she has warm brown eyes and dark brown hair pinned to her head in an elaborate mix of braids and twists. She extends her hand. And I grasp it nervously hoping that she doesn't notice my sweat dampened palms.

"I'm Everly. I will be your guardian today." I nod numbly not sure what an appropriate response would be. "Let's just get you set up here." She helps me step into the pod. I put my arms through the criss-crossed harness and she buckles me in. I must look frightened because she says softly, "Don't worry, it's more of a safety precaution than anything. For some people navigating their Mindscape can be a bit intense." I nod as if I understand even though I don't. I realize I haven't even introduced myself. My mother would be so ashamed of my manners.

"I'm Ka," I manage to say as she places a pair of darkened glasses over my eyes.

"It's nice to meet you, Ka." She adjusts the glasses. "There. You can't see anything, right?" I shake my head. Everything is pitch black. "Alright, now I'm just going to place the silencing buds in your ears. Then I'll close up the pod. You'll feel a blast of cool air from the vents followed by a heavy sense of drowsiness. After that it takes about fifteen seconds for your Mindscape to materialize. That fifteen seconds can feel like an eternity with the sensory deprivation so I recommend focusing on the inhale and exhale of your breath. Any questions?"

"Why fifteen seconds?" It's a stupid question and I'm not even sure why I ask it. But I can hear the smile in Everly's words as she responds.

"That's how long it takes for the Mindscape to recalibrate

from all the extraneous stimuli. Okay, here we go. See you in fifteen seconds." She slips the silencing buds into my ears.

The silence is deafening, if silence could be deafening. I hear my blood pumping and pulsing through my body. I can hear my heartbeat in my eardrums. And that's it. Nothing else. I feel a blast of cool air and I remember Everly's advice to focus on my breath. I concentrate on each inhalation—a count of two—and each exhalation—a count of four, trying to imagine the air filling my lungs, my lungs expanding, then decompressing as the air travels back out and through my mouth.

My eyelids grow heavy behind the darkened glasses and I feel my head start to loll forward until my chin reaches my chest. My breath becomes slower and more even.

Inhale.

Exhale.

CHAPTER 11

I'm jolted awake at the splash of cold water against my skin. Not again. But I can see. And I see that I'm in the middle of a vast ocean with no end in sight. I can taste the salt on my lips and the water reflects the stormy gray of the sky above me. Why am I not surprised that my Mindscape would contain water?

I turn in the water searching for Everly, but I need not look far. She's treading water beside me. She says nothing, just smiles, and at first I think that my sense of hearing hasn't been restored, but then I hear the crash of waves in the distance and I remember that Everly is to strictly be an observer only. How exactly does one navigate their Mindscape?

Everly surprises me by calling out, "It will come to you. All of this already exists whether you know it or not. It's your memories, thoughts, and dreams. You're just bearing witness to your own

Mindscape. Sometimes it takes a few seconds for it to gain momentum."

I nod and drag my fingers through the water, creating ripples through its surface. That's when I hear another splash and in the distance I can see someone swimming toward me. *No, not here.* I think. *Please, not here.* But the familiar brown head continues to approach. Teacher 4. Sloan.

He swims agilely and reaches me quickly. He pauses, treading water in front of me. A slice of white light pierces through the gray sky above us. His scales glitter and glisten with water and before I can help myself I reach out cupping his cheek in the palm of my hand, my heart pounding in my chest. His green eyes seem sad. But before I can consider it further, he's pulling me along with him. Down, deeper and deeper into the ocean below, his hand strong around my mine.

I find that I can swim easily and have no trouble keeping up with him. Unlike the other times, breathing beneath the surface isn't an issue. There's no burn in my lungs and I kick my legs gliding through the water. We reach the same cavern as before, the one with the small chamber of air, and we break the surface. This time I can't hide the smile from my face. Teacher 4, Sloan, smiles at me and the color of his eyes shift slightly, making him seem happier. "You're getting pretty good."

"Well," I find myself saying, "I've had a good teacher." I giggle at my own corny words and wonder who is this girl—this witty, flirtatious girl who can swim as well as the Waters.

"For a while there, I thought you were kind of impossible,"
Sloan grins and wraps an arm snugly around my waist pulling me
closer to him so that my chest is almost pressed up against his. And
I—my real self the one bearing witness—can't allow what's about to
happen to go on. It's for me and me only. It's not meant for analysis.
As Sloan leans in I slowly allow myself to sink from his grasp,
slipping back beneath the surface.

Down.

Down.

Down.

. . .

I'm on the swings at the playground with Ahna. We swing
back and forth, higher and higher into the red sky. No words are
necessary. Friends practically since birth, sisters by choice. We
continue to swing silently until Ahna drags her feet in the red dirt
coming to a stop. I follow suit stopping next to her and absent-
mindedly begin to twist the chains of my swing, slowly raising myself
from the ground until I can only reach by my tiptoes.

"You haven't decided yet have you? Ahna chastises.

I ignore the expression on her face. "Yes, I have. I mean, of
course I have." I don't look her in the eyes.

"You're impossible," she says. I twist in the opposite
direction and the swing chains quickly begin to unravel.

And I'm spinning, drunk with dizziness. The world is a blur

of pink, white, and brown whizzing past.

. . .

Li's hand is warm in mine as we walk the Underground. He's tipsy from the forbidden drink, buzzing with *Pleasure,* not that Li needs excess *Pleasure*. "What next, Kata?"

I grin at him wickedly. "Adventure." And we run through the Underground until we stop near a streetlight, standing in its pool of light. He presses his lips to mine and I can taste the bitterness on his lips and I wonder what it is that he tastes on mine. Can he taste the salt of the sea? I don't tell Li it's my first kiss ever. My first real kiss. Sure, Li's tried to kiss me plenty of times, but I've always dodged his attempts. I don't know what's different this time. Maybe it's the Adventure coursing through my veins.

I break away first and we continue our run through the filth of the Underground until we reach the woman with the missing teeth. Suddenly, I'm sitting at the little table in the back of her trailer looking into the whites of her rolled back eyes. Her fingers like icicles locked around my wrist. "You are all and yet you are none. You are Metal. You are Wood. You are Earth. You are Water. And you are Fire. You are all possibilities and yet you are impossible. You are the Impossible Girl."

"NO!" I shout. "NO! NO! NO!"

. . .

"Recommendation: Water."

Choose Wisely.

Oh, Kata, what have you done?

. . .

I'm a little girl. Maybe only about six or seven. It's the same concrete house. The one I always remember growing up in. The one in which my parents still live. I am playing on the floor with my favorite wooden dolls that my father had made for me. I am not alone.

My mother is sitting at the kitchen table which looks out onto the living space where I am playing, lost in some sort of imaginary world. A woman sits with my mother, but she isn't someone that I recognize. Her face is cast in shadows, but I can see the glint of metallic thread as the sun filters through the kitchen window.

"It just started recently," my mother says in a worried whisper. "I don't know what to do." She holds a handkerchief up to her eyes and dabs at them.

"There's nothing ye can do," the woman replies.

"But, surely, I mean, there must be *something*." My mother's voice is pleading. It sounds foreign to my ears. I've always thought of my mother as strong and resilient, patient and kind. This version of my mother sounds frightened. Desperate.

"The child of the eighteenth moon on the hundredth solar

alignment. It's already been seen and once it is seen there is no undoing the Sight." The Sight? Is that what happens to the Unbalanced Metals? That must be why fortune tellers are only part of the Underground.

"*Please*," my mother grabs the stranger's hand and that's when I see it: the strength. I see it in the lines of my mother's face and in the set of her jaw that she won't let go until she has a satisfactory answer.

I continue to play with the wooden dolls. I always found comfort in the solidness of them, the feel of the smooth surface beneath my fingers and the comforting predictability of the wood's grain.

"There is *something*," the woman's voice is hesitant. She reaches into the deep pockets of her shabby gray coat. She pulls out a handful of something that I can't make out in the shadows. "She will need protection. Each one represents the five Elements. On each of five full moons, yeh must take one and repeat this phrase: *Protection, piety, promise*. This phrase must be repeated five times, one for each of the Elements. Then cast the stone during the light of the full moons into the Elemental Abyss." My mother takes the stones, clutching them tightly in her palm.

"And this will protect her?" her voice is full of hope.

"For as long as she needs protecting, it shall protect her."

"And what happens when she no longer needs protecting?" There's a crack in her voice followed by a shuddering intake of breath.

There's a long pause before the Metal woman finally answers. "Then the world as we know it will come to an end."

...

I'm standing in the same room as the Ritual of Fire. But I'm not alone. Everly is there and her face is stark white. This is not a dream or a thought. This is not a memory. My brain is confused as to what's real and what's a fragment from inside my head.

She paces back and forth then turns coming up to me, placing her hands on my shoulders and looking me square in the eyes.

"We must tell no one," her voice quivers as she whispers.

"Tell no one what?" I ask. Nothing out of the ordinary really seems to have happened. I mean who can tell what's dream and what's memory in a Mindscape? Where it's so intricately intertwined like a fastidious umbilical cord linking one plane of existence to another, the conscious to the subconscious.

"You mean... you mean you don't know?" Everly's eyes grow wide. "Oh, dear. This was...this is quite unexpected."

"Did I do something wrong?" Leave it to me to mess up my own Mindscape.

"Oh, goodness, no, Ka." She gives me a small smile. "In fact quite the opposite."

"I'm confused. Is this a dream or a memory?" Her hands still rest on my shoulders and I feel them as though we are standing in the white room outside of the pod, but I somehow know I am still strapped inside.

"Neither. Ka, I am breaking the one rule of navigating the Mindscape by interacting with you. I'll have to alter the data." Her voice trails off.

"Will I still get a Career Assignment?" She's starting to make me nervous. I can't shake the feeling that something went very wrong. Everly's words and her body language are sending two very conflicting messages.

"You have to listen to me, Ka." Her eyes lock on mine and she moves my shoulders so I'm forced to look into her eyes. She's deceptively strong for an older woman. "We must never—and I mean NEVER—speak of this. You must never tell anyone about your Mindscape. You must not speak of your recommendation for Water and how at peace you felt with the Water man. You must never speak of your inability to decide. And you must never, ever under any circumstances whatsoever reveal the words of the Metal woman or the lengths that your mother has gone to protect you."

A sense of dread seems to wash over me as I realize that everything to which I've just beared witness has somehow caused Everly to stop our navigation. "I—I don't understand," I mumble and it's true. I don't.

"The words of the Metal woman in the Underground: *You are all and yet you are none. You are Metal. You are Wood. You are Earth. You are Water. And you are Fire. You are all possibilities and yet you are impossible.* The eighteenth moon on the hundredth solar alignment. The protection of the Five Elements. Goodness, darling, you don't even know who you are!" Her words are incredulous as if she can't believe my own dumbness.

Her eyes grow bright with excitement as she clutches me in a tight embrace, her lips hovering near my ear as she whispers softly, "You are the salvation of so many colonists of Xon 9, including myself. You are a myth, a legend. You are the stories of over five-hundred years, passed in hushed whispers from one generation to the next," she smiles. "And you are very, very real. Ka, *you are the Impossible Girl.*"

CHAPTER 12

As I lay in bed with Rhian's slow, solid breath in the bed beside me, the events of the day replay in my mind, over and over on an endless loop.

Not only my Mindscape, but Everly's words. After we exited the Mindscape we were told our Career Assignments. Pierce was assigned to paramilitary tactical planning, which means he will work closely with the Metals. No one was surprised. Doran and Rhian were both assigned to news reporting, much to Rhian's dismay at having to work more closely with Doran. Jielle was assigned to theater which I think is appropriate considering her aloofness and the fact that she seems to hide her actual emotions quite well; maybe she is better at wearing someone else's. Bryn received art history with an emphasis in sculpture. Xon 9's buildings are adorned with sculptures and paintings that replicate those from our time on Earth, ones that could not be saved. Li was assigned a rhetoric study track. That one surprised me a bit considering he's never been too stellar at school, but turns out he is quite persuasive, maybe a future speech writer for the Leadership Council.

And then that leaves me. My Career Assignment Placement rested solely on Everly's data from my Mindscape, which had to be conflicting at best. I remember how she bit her lip nervously as she presented the data to Eoin. "Ka's data is inconclusive at this time." I liked how she had added *at this time*. I held my breath waiting for Eoin's reply, waiting for him to say we had to navigate my Mindscape again or to say that I wasn't fit for Fire. But that's not what he said.

"Ah, a complicated one. We haven't had one of those in a while." He patted me on the shoulder as the others, including Li, stared at me warily. "It just means you will be following an exploratory track your first semester of study. Then your Mindscape will be re-evaluated. At that time we should have a clearer idea of what Career Assignment would serve both your desires and our needs." Everly's shoulders had softened at Eoin's words. None of the other adults seemed to think it strange, so I just went along with it.

Besides that meant I could take different classes and not be confined to one track of study. When I returned to the sleeping quarters, Rhian had said she felt tainted after navigating the Mindscape and needed to take a shower to wash off "the sense of failure" at having to spend the next two years in close study with Doran.

I'd laid on the bed, shoving my hand beneath my pillow and pulling out the envelope with the familiar handwriting that I had placed there earlier. I needed to tell someone; someone that I could trust. More importantly I needed to tell someone who would understand.

. . .

I wait until Rhian's breath is deep and even. I slip a hoodie over my head and grab my favorite boots. I exit the door slowly and pad down the hallway in my socks to Li's room. Since the new Fires had an uneven amount of males and females, Li lucked out and doesn't have a roommate. I try the knob and it's unlocked. I open the door slowly and duck inside.

He doesn't wake. I approach his bed and shake him gently. He looks so peaceful and innocent asleep. If only. I whisper his name. He opens one eye and a sleepy grin spreads across his face. "And here I thought you were just a dream."

"Shut up," I hiss. "I need something from you."

He laughs huskily. "I bet you do."

"Idiot. Get up." I punch him in the arm until he obeys and slides to a seated position.

"Okay, okay. I'm up. If you're not here for a midnight *rendez-vous* can you tell me what else warrants waking me up from my restful slumber?"

"I need," I hesitate. *Just ask.* "I need *Courage.*"

He cocks an eyebrow in the dimness. "At this time of night? Ka Waylon, what on Xon are you up to?"

Too many questions. I don't have the time—or the willingness—to answer them. "Do you have it or not?" I'm bluffing and he knows me well enough to see it easily. But luckily I've known Li a very long time.

"Alright, alright." He slides off the bed and pads barefoot over to one of the dressers pushed beneath the window. He opens a drawer and rustles around inside, pulling things out and holding them to the dark pink light that spills through the window. Finally, satisfied he comes toward me backing me up against the closed door. He dangles the silver packet in front of my face. "It's gonna cost you, Kata." I try to grab for it, but he yanks his hand away before I can get it.

"You are so annoying," I hiss.

"Am I?" His breath is warm on my neck. And I feel the little fire beginning to rise deep in the pit of my stomach. But indulging Li isn't part of the plan. I only have so much time. His bare chest is pressed to mine and I'm already regretting what I'm about to do. I know that I'll have to make up for it one way or another. I slap him. Hard. "What the—!?" He exclaims flinging his hand to his cheek and in the process dropping the silver packet. It flutters down to the floor near my boots and I pick up my boots and the packet in one fell swoop.

"Sorry, I really am. But I'm kind of in a hurry." I hurriedly kiss his other cheek and he doesn't shrug away which is a good sign. I turn and open the door a sliver, but his words cause me pause.

"You really are impossible, Ka. You know that?" Without turning around I can practically see the wicked smile on his face. Leave it to Li to take it as a good thing when a girl smacks him.

"Thanks!" I whisper over my shoulder as I pull the door shut behind me and run in stocking feet down the hallway. I'm not sure if I'm thanking him for the Patch or for calling me impossible.

. . .

I tear the packet open and stick the patch to my forearm, shoving its wrapper in the pocket of my pants. I take the emergency stairwell down from the third floor sleeping quarters. I don't stop to put my boots on until I reach the ground level. I take a deep breath and slowly slide out the door and into the pink night.

At first I keep to the shrubs and shadows of the buildings. I don't know the consequence for sneaking out, especially so early in the Transition Phase, but I didn't know of any other way. The memory of Doran pulling his hand from the burning table and Tristen's sadistic smile give me a queasy feeling—physical reprimand, but the Courage coursing through my veins quickly puts the kibosh on such thought.

After I exit the University Complex beneath the iron arch reading *divide et impera*, I begin to relax. I hurry along, putting as much distance between myself and Tristen as possible. I don't really have a plan, but my feet seem to know something I don't as they lead me along the sidewalk. Technically, I'm now an adult, having turned eighteen and pronounced an Elemental, but I still find myself anxious at being caught out past curfew.

My feet continue to lead me and I begin to recognize the buildings as they change from the clean, architecturally pleasing buildings of the University Complex and into the run-down, broken-windowed buildings in between home and the Complex. I stop at an alleyway with a familiar wooden sign. Of course. This is where I saw him the other day before he headed to the building at the Complex. The envelope sits heavy in the back pocket of my pants. I don't know why I brought it with me, maybe for comfort. Or maybe for hope—hope that I'd be able to find him: the one person who can hopefully answer my questions.

I head down the alleyway and down the concrete steps. I emerge in the Underground in search of Sloan.

. . .

I've never been out this late past curfew. It's around midnight and some of the vendors have their gates pulled down. The old streetlamps cast a harsh yellow light that lands in small pools on the cobblestone road. A couple sit on a metal bench under one of the lights, huddled close together, a brown bottle shared between them. I can hear the buzz of a tattoo needle as I walk past an open vendor sandwiched between two closed ones.

I don't know where to go or who to ask. Really I was just

counting on good luck, not that I usually seem to have it. I mean what can I say: *Excuse me, have you seen a Water in a hooded cloak wandering around? Oh, by the way he has really amazing green eyes.* I chide myself, *Stupid. You're here for information. Strictly business.* But for some reason I can't shake the secure feeling of Sloan's arm around my waist in my Mindscape. Somehow it felt so right. *Desires versus needs.*

I hear the sound of laughter drift down the alleyway and I head in its direction. At least it's a place to start. On the left is a small cantina-style vendor. The door is slid up and there's a young, burly man with short, spiky black hair behind the counter. There are tables that wrap around the front and the side of the vendor and little strings of lights are strung across wooden posts. I guess it is supposed to look ambient and inviting, but I find that it has the opposite affect: it looks creepy and foreboding.

A couple of the tables in front are occupied and when I round the corner I see Sloan sitting at one of the small tables—no cloak or anything weird, except he's with a woman. She's pretty maybe a couple years older than he is with long blonde hair. He doesn't see me.

At first I feel panic, but then I'm overcome with a sense of boldness. The Patch. I may have *Courage*, but I'm not crazy, so instead of approaching them I sidle up to the bar, sliding carefully onto one of the metal stools. The man gives me a leery look before approaching me. "What can I get you?"

I swallow nervously. "Um," *Don't say water, anything but water.* "Just a water." The man rolls his eyes and walks away. At first I think he isn't going to give it to me, but he surprises me by returning with a filled glass. He sets it on the counter in front of me.

"Anything else?" I bite my lip and shake my head and the man walks away. I take a big gulp of the water, eyeing Sloan and the woman out of the corner of my eye. And that's when I realize my mistake. I didn't notice the smell.

I'm coughing and sputtering before I can help myself. My eyes are tearing and I can feel the burn all the way down my throat and into my stomach as if whatever I just drank is intent on setting me aflame from the inside out. I glare at the man who has a small smile on his face.

"Sorry. We don't have water." He hands me another smaller glass. "Here, drink this. It will take the edge off." The smaller glass also has a clear liquid, but it's sweet smelling. So I narrow my eyes, taking it anyways. "Here, I'll have one too." He pours himself one right on the counter and then clinks his glass with mine. "Bottoms up." And he downs the liquid in one big swallow. I close my eyes and do the same. Almost immediately the burning sensation in my stomach subsides and my sinuses seem to clear out.

"Thanks," I mumble even though he tricked me with the first drink.

"Ka?" I recognize the voice immediately and realize too late that my coughing fit probably attracted some attention. So much for discreet. I swivel around to face Sloan. He's standing behind me alone, but I can see the blonde woman walking past, the glint of metallic thread glinting in the light as she passes by. A Metal. I wonder if she lives in the Underground and that's why Sloan comes here.

"Yeah, um, hi."

"What are you doing here?" He pauses. "Did you get my letter?" I feel the letter in my pocket, a solid reminder of my purpose tonight, the sole reason that I've chosen to break so many rules.

"Yeah, I did." *Courage, Kata.* "There are some things I wanted to talk to you about."

He nods as if he'd expected as much. "This isn't a good place." He tosses a few bills onto the counter and the bartender nods at him. "Come with me." As I rise from the barstool he places his hand softly on the small of my back, guiding me back onto the cobblestone street and further down the alleyway, in the opposite direction of the Black Bazaar.

This is already totally different than any of our other interactions. He seems so un-teacher-like. He seems so *normal.* The alleyway dead ends into another set of stairs which we ascend in silence. We exit into the night onto a sort of rocky ledge. The ledge looks out over the town, but we're higher up and combined with the distance the town just appears as teeny tiny dots of light—a miniature-sized town, like one my wooden dolls would have lived in.

He leads me down a narrow pathway, teetering along the edge, until we reach a little alcove. I wonder if he takes the blonde woman here, but I scold myself pushing the thought aside. *It doesn't matter.* He sits down on the edge, feet dangling in the air and pats the spot next to him. I hesitate. *Courage.* I sit down.

His shirt sleeves are rolled up to the elbows and he picks up a small red pebble from the ledge and tosses it out into the air where it's immediately swallowed by the night. He seems relaxed, easy-going. "You seem different," I find myself saying.

He looks at me sideways, grinning. "So do you."

"I just mean, well, I…it's just that…"

"I know. Teacher. I get it." He stares into my eyes for a beat longer than is comfortable then turns back to stare into the night. And I realize he really isn't much older than me. I'm eighteen, he's probably twenty or twenty-one at the most. I try to recall if Teacher 4 was in our school last year and I can't seem to remember.

"No it's not that. You seem more relaxed." He glances at me but doesn't acknowledge my words. I realize that he's just as wary of me as I am of him. But then why does he want to bother protecting me? "How do I seem different?"

The night is comfortable and the warm breeze ruffles his hair. "I can sense the Change in you. You seem more confident and more…" He scrunches up his face as he tries to think of the word. "Fiery." He turns toward me and his eyes sparkle.

"Yeah, well, the whole Fire thing and all." I pause. *Remember why you're here.* "I had my Career Assignment Placement Test," I offer.

He turns his body toward me, so that one leg is back up on the ledge curled beneath him and the other is still dangling against the side of the rocky formation. His eyes don't sparkle and his face has gone a little pale, even his scales look more white and less green. "Tell me."

And before I can help it, I'm explaining to him my entire Mindscape with Everly. Meticulously leaving out certain details, the intimacy of the moment I shared with him, but careful to emphasize my ease in the water. Leaving out the part about kissing Li, but retelling my fear at the fortune teller's words and my mother's apprehension during her visit with the Metal woman. When I'm finished he just stares at me, an unreadable expression on his face. "That's why I'm here. You said you were protecting me."

He gives me an impish smile. "You don't make it easy that's for sure."

I forge onward, the Courage flowing through me. "I've seen you, you know, watching me."

He looks down at his lap where his hands rest folded. "You're easy to watch," he mumbles and even in the light of the moons and dim light of the sun, I can see the flush creep up his neck.

"Why? Why are you protecting me? The Metal woman told my mother I'd need protecting and when I didn't need it anymore the world as we know it would end. What did she mean?"

"Oh, Ka. I wish I could tell you everything, but there are some things you need to find out for yourself, unfortunately. Don't think I'm a bad person because of it. I'll help you in any way that I can, but my help..." He searches for the right word. "Right now my help must be limited. There are certain things with which I cannot interfere."

I pull out the letter from my pocket. "So, your stupid tips, it says to trust no one. Does that include you too?" I can feel the surge of anger beneath the surface. Typically, I'm not quick-tempered and am extremely non-confrontational. I wonder if it's the Change or if Sloan just seems to have that effect on me.

"Of course not." He actually looks hurt at my words, as if I'd slapped him just like I slapped Li earlier, but instead of a smile his lips are downturned at the corners.

I get up hastily. "I thought that I'd be able to trust you. That you'd be able to help me understand what this all means; how I can keep myself safe!"

"I am trying my best to keep you safe," he says slowly rising to his feet. "But there are certain restrictions. I told you, Ka, I wish I could explain it to you, but I can't. In fact, I'm forbidden to explain it to you. There are certain things you have to do on your own. I can only do my best to protect you from afar."

"Well, it's not good enough," I find my anger flaring and I toss the envelope at him. The white envelope lands in the red dirt. He bends to pick it up. "Maybe I don't need your protection after all." I turn on my heel and begin to walk away, but he grabs my wrist, yanking me back to face him.

"I wish you wouldn't be so stubborn." I glare at him and he lowers his voice as if anyone could hear us out here on the edge of space. "The one thing I *can* tell you is that the answers you need lie in the stones."

"And how can I find them? They were tossed into the Elemental Abyss." I try to pull my hand away, still angry at his refusal to actually help me in any real way.

124

But he shakes his head. "The Mindscape has the answers." His face is sad and I realize that there's so much he wants to tell me, but that for whatever reason he really truly can't. "Oh, and another word of caution. Stay as far away from Tristen as you can."

I nod. That much I already knew. His grip around my wrist loosens. Our conversation is over. It didn't go exactly as I'd planned. At all. I don't know whether to thank him or just walk away. I feel more confused than ever before. I turn to head back down the ledge, but his voice stops me. "It wasn't Courage that you needed tonight." When he grabbed my wrist he must have seen the Patch on my forearm.

I pause, closing my eyes. "What then?"

"Patience."

I feel my breath catch in my throat, the sting in the backs of my eyes. I don't turn around, fearing if I turn around and see his face I'll be drawn into his arms, seeking the comfort from my Mindscape. Instead I simply walk away with more questions than answers.

CHAPTER 13

I am not a planner. Sure, some Fires are good at coordinating and event planning. But not me. Because if I was then I would have thought of a way back in before I ever even left. When I arrive back to the Elemental Fire building at the Complex, the door I exited earlier is locked. All the sleeping quarters are on the third floor and even so I wouldn't be able to figure out which window belonged to Li's room.

Besides, Li is one of the last people I want to see right now. As I walked home my stomach roiled with all the conflicting emotions. Excitement to see Sloan; anger that he wouldn't help me; jealousy of the blonde Metal woman; fear at retrieving the stones from the Elemental Abyss. The cauldron of feelings stirred and percolated the entire walk home.

Now I'm half-hidden in the shadows as I creep around to the

other side of the building hoping that there's another door, or maybe a first floor window that I can somehow open from the outside. Yeah, right. But much to my surprise when I round the corner there is another door. I try the handle. Unlocked. I quietly close it behind me. I'm in a stairwell that only leads down. I can see the dance and flicker of the torches lining the walls. This must be where the Ritual Room is located, where the slide dumped me out rather unceremoniously. Muffled voices drift down the hallway, but I can't make out what they're saying.

My choices are to either go back outside to find another entrance or to head in the direction of the voices. I feel the fading pulse just beneath the Patch on my forearm. Courage. Sloan's words come flooding back to me and I shake my head as if I could actually shake those words right out of my ears.

I follow the stairs and they open on to the torch lit hallway. The voices float toward me. The torches are placed far enough apart so that spaces of darkness rest in between. They cast odd, menacing shadows on the stone walls. As I walk the voices grow louder, arguing. Someone is having an argument.

I quicken my pace and come to the end of the passageway. I can either go left or I can go right. To my left I can see a sleek black elevator, but to my right I can hear the angry voices. And then—a scream pierces through the silence, a sound filled with anguish. Before I can help myself I'm running down the hallway toward the voices.

I stop just outside an open cavern-like doorway on my right, the hallway continuing to what I suspect is the Ritual Room at its end. I press myself flat against the wall and listen.

"You are not being truthful," a voice chastises. I immediately recognize its annoying lilting quality: Tristen.

"I am!" sobs the reply and my heart sinks when I realize I recognize that voice too: Everly.

"Liar! You're no better than the heathens in the Underground. Tell the truth, Ev-er-ly. What did you see in the Mindscape?"

"I told you what I saw. Check my data!" hisses Everly. I'm afraid to peer into the doorway, afraid of what I may see. My heart pounds in my chest and I concentrate on the cold stone pressed against my back.

"Her results were inconclusive. We haven't had an inconclusive CAPT in decades. It seems…well, it seems *impossible*." She emphasizes the last word and my heart catches in my throat. They're talking about me. Does Tristen know about what happened in my Mindscape?

"Nothing is impossible, Tristen," Everly replies tersely.

"Quite the contrary. I'll let you go for now, Everly, but I will not be made a fool by you. Consider tonight a warning." There's a clicking sound and then soft footsteps. The footsteps grow louder and Everly emerges from the room at my right.

At first she doesn't notice me and I don't want to startle her, but then she catches sight of me out of the corner of her eye. Her eyes grow wide and she immediately grabs me by the arm, silently ushering me down the hallway and back toward the elevator. We hurry beneath the torchlight and she impatiently presses the elevator buttons with shaking hands. After what seems like an eternity, with her nails pressed into the flesh of my arm, the elevator doors slide open and we get inside.

In the dim light of the elevator I can see that she's been crying. Her eyes are puffy and her nose is red. Her hair in disarray. She presses the button for the sleeping quarters and as soon as the elevator passes the second floor she hits the emergency button and the elevator comes to an abrupt stop.

"You shouldn't have been there," she says but she doesn't look at me.

"I didn't mean to—I was—was she talking about me?" Everly still doesn't look at me as she nods. She seems small and fragile in this moment, her arms wrapped tightly around her own waist in a sort of hug. I ask the question to which I don't really want the answer. "What did she do to you?"

She sneers, "Oh, Tristen. She's all for the fun and games."

"No, really. Everly, please tell me."

She turns carefully lifting up the back of her sweater and I can see what looks like a tattoo, black flames creeping up her spine. Except. "That's—those are—that's *charred* into your skin."

Everly drops her sweater back down and swipes at her nose. "When you don't follow the rules there are consequences."

"Oh, Everly," I feel nauseated. "I-I'm so sorry."

Her expression turns fierce and she grabs me by the

shoulders. "No, Ka. Never sorry. I will not—not ever—be the one to betray the Impossible Girl. My loyalty always has and always will lie in where my heart guides me. I falsified your data and, even now knowing the consequences, I would do it again given the chance."

I take a deep breath and slowly exhale unable to shake the image of the blackened flames. "Wasn't physical reprimand banned centuries ago? Someone should report her or something." I feel so angry and so helpless.

Everly scoffs, "Surely, you are not so naïve as to think that no one breaks the rules? Myself included. Tristen does what Tristen wants and she's the Chief Fire. There are certain people for whom misdeeds fall on blind eyes, so there's not much anyone can do to stop her." Her face softens. "I'm afraid I've put you in a dangerous situation, Ka. By changing your data I thought that I was helping you, but Tristen has only grown suspicious. You must be very careful." I nod numbly and Everly presses a button and the elevator continues its ascent.

My body feels heavy, like it is full of lead, as if I have been awake for days and could fall asleep right in this very spot. Only days ago, my life seemed so simple, so ordinary. And now, everything is…different. I think including me. I can feel the Change pulsing just beneath the surface, making its way slowly through my veins.

The elevator slides open and I take a hesitant step forward, then turn around before the elevator doors can close. "I don't deserve such loyalty. I'm just an ordinary girl. Really."

But Everly smiles softly and shakes her head. "No, Ka, you

have never been ordinary. You may think so, but not a day in your life have you ever been ordinary. Only extraordinary people perceive themselves as ordinary."

The elevator doors close before I can thank her, thank her for her suffering in order to protect me. *Another protector.* What could be so valuable that it needs protected so vigilantly? Who—or what—is it exactly that I am becoming?

. . .

All I can think about the next few days is avoiding Tristen and how to retrieve the five stones out of the Elemental Abyss. I sit in my classes and stare out the window at the pink landscape, at the other Elemental buildings that make up the University Complex. Ahna is in one of those other buildings. I bet she'd have the answers and would be able to help me. She doesn't know that I'm the Impossible Girl, just that I'm her best friend. And maybe that's just what I need right now: someone who remembers me as simply, wonderfully ordinary.

The bell rings and I practically dash out of the Physiology of Fire class, plowing into Rhian in the process. Her face looks worried as I bend over to help her pick up the books and papers that scattered all over the hallway when I ran into her. All of our classes are on the fourth floor. New Elementals' sleeping quarters are on the third floor. The second floor is reserved for the second year Fires still attending University. The fifth floor is where the Fire Leadership

Committee resides. And, well, we know what kinds of activities the lower level is used for.

Rhian gives me a funny look. "Are you doing okay? You've seemed really distracted lately."

I nod vigorously. "Oh, yeah. I'm fine. Doing great!"

She continues to study me, reading my face for clues, but our friendship is still too new. "Too bad we don't have more classes together, but I guess since your results were inconclusive you get to take a little bit of everything."

I try to put a sympathetic expression on my face. "I know our schedules are totally out of sync."

"Well, I better get going before Professor Twenty-One starts his lecture. See you later. Maybe we can hang out or something?" Her face looks hopeful.

I nod vigorously again, not quite paying attention to the words that I'm saying. "Yep. Sure, sounds great. See you later!" Rhian disappears into the classroom and I head back to the third floor.

I need more time to think. I really don't want to sneak out again, but new Elementals are not supposed to socialize with one another. Something about ensuring loyalties and promoting bonding amongst the new group. I toss my messenger bag onto the floor and flop onto my bed. My bed is messy and unmade, dirty clothes dangling off the bedposts. Rhian's bed is neatly made. None of her clothes are on the floor; her desk is organized with not a single pen or piece of paper out of place. My desk doesn't even look like it's been used. Namely, because it hasn't. It's the first week of classes, I tell myself. No real work has been assigned. It's mostly been lectures anyway.

Normally, I'm not so messy. Actually, I'm a very neat and tidy person. It's just I don't have time to think about anything else. My conversations with Sloan and then with Everly repeat in my head like they're on some sort of an endless loop. I could probably ask Everly about the Elemental Abyss, but I feel like she's risked enough for me already. I can't get her screams from the other night out of my head; they echo in my mind each evening as I try to fall asleep and then follow me into my dreams.

No, it has to be Ahna, but I don't know how. There's a knock at the door and my heart seizes in my chest, fearing that it could be Tristen—although I doubt that she'd bother with knocking. But it's not Tristen; it's Li. He takes one look at me and lets out a low whistle.

"You look like crap."

I scowl at him. "Gee, thanks." He doesn't sit, just stands in between Rhian's and my bed with his arms folded over his chest.

"So, are you going to tell me what's got you so rattled? First, you ask me for Courage and then the next time that I see you you're totally distracted and erratic. What gives?"

I sigh. How easily I've forgotten that Li has known me as long as Ahna. He may be a pain, but he's just as much a friend as she is. But he doesn't have the information that I need. Although…
"Do you know how I can talk to Ahna?"

He shrugs. "I'm sure there's a way."

I push myself up, kneeling on the bed excitedly. "Do you think you could find out?"

"Sure, but you still haven't answered my question."

I sigh flopping back down. I don't want to answer him; don't even know how to answer him. The things I've seen in my Mindscape, the Metal Woman's words—both the one in my Mindscape and the one in the Underground, my mother's fear, Everly's sacrifice, and of course Sloan. I don't want to put another person I care about at risk; it's bad enough I'm going to have to ask Ahna for information and she too will ask questions that I don't want to answer. So instead of answering Li, I just continue to gaze silently at the ceiling.

After a few moments he lets out a long sigh. "I'll see what I can do." I hear the door open and then close behind him. I get up after him and turn the lock. I clean up some of the clothes that are strewn about, carefully hanging them in the closet. Then I make the bed, careful to tuck in all the corners and smooth out the blanket. Next, I pull some books out of my bag and set them on the desk, so that it at least looks like I care about my classes. Although I'm not sure who exactly I'm fooling.

When I'm done I crawl back onto the newly made bed, rest my head on the pillow and close my eyes. In the silence of the room, almost immediately, Everly's cries fill my ears. I stick my index fingers into my ears and whisper senseless words over and over again to try and drown out the sound of her cries, the image of the charcoal flames on her back fill my mind and I put my fist in my mouth to stifle my own sobs. I fall into a fitful sleep, tears still wet on my cheeks.

. . .

I'm jostled awake by Rhian shaking my shoulders gently. "Ka, you have a visitor." I groan and open one eye. First, I see Rhian's dark hair and big brown eyes riddled with concern. Then to the left is Li looking at me expectantly. Crap. I probably look like a wreck. "Here," Rhian thrusts a dampened washcloth at me and I smile thankfully as I rub its coolness across my cheeks. I scooch over and Li sits beside me.

"Well?" I ask and I run my fingers like a comb through my hair, trying to untangle it.

"Hi to you, too," he mumbles but he's grinning. "I found a way."

"How much is it going to cost me?" Our heady conversation regarding the Courage Patch replays in my mind. But he surprises me by shaking his head.

"No cost. If—" He raises an eyebrow and I realize this is going to be a very big *if*. "You tell me what's going on."

"Nothing is going on!" I exclaim and the words even ring false in my own ears.

Rhian scowls at me, picking up the washcloth and tossing it into a laundry basket. "You aren't fooling anyone, Ka."

Li nods in agreement. "She's right. Whatever it is, let us help you."

It's so tempting, to unburden myself with the weight of the last week, but where do I even begin to explain? And worse, what if I put them in danger? I've already inadvertently put Sloan and Everly in danger, and now needing Ahna's help, I'll be putting her in danger too. The turmoil must be evident on my face because Rhian puts a hand on my shoulder and looks at me with such an imploring expression.

"Please, we're your friends, Ka. And whatever it is that you seem to be dealing with we can help you. At night...I can hear you. You think I'm asleep, but I can hear you crying, the tossing and turning." She turns away embarrassed. "And I know you snuck out the other night. I don't know why, but seriously, let us help you. Please."

It's not because I need someone else to know. I decide to tell them because they look so tormented by the fact that I haven't told them yet, haven't sought out their friendship and their help in my time of need. Because that's what friends are for, right? They're supposed to be there for you, not out of obligation, but because they *want* to be there for you.

I leave out the unnecessary details about Sloan, but I am sure to include the bit about Tristen and what she did to Everly.

Rhian's face is shocked and at some point she had sat down on the edge of her bed, eyes wide. "So that's why your test results were inconclusive." I nod.

"I still don't get it though. What does it all mean? So Teacher

4——" Li begins.

I correct. "*Sloan.*"

He rolls his eyes. "*Sloan* has been trying to protect you, but from what?"

I shrug. "I'm not sure yet. From Tristen maybe?"

"Sounds like Everly's got that down," Rhian says.

"And why didn't you tell me about the Metal woman? I was there with you that night," Li chides.

"It didn't make sense to me at the time. It still doesn't, not really."

Rhian's nodding. "What if, I mean it's probably a stupid idea, but what if the Metal woman in the Underground and the Metal woman who visited your mother are the same woman? Then wouldn't she know where the Elemental Abyss is and how to retrieve the stones?"

I hadn't thought of that. "It's possible," I find myself saying. In my Mindscape I hadn't gotten a good look at the Metal woman who had visited my mother. Her face was cast in shadows as she sat in the kitchen trying to assuage my mother's fears. I just remember the distinct glint of the metallic threads on her face. "That was twelve years ago. I can't be sure."

"There's only one way to find out," Rhian replies.

"Maybe it isn't a trip to visit Ahna that you need," Li says in agreement. "Maybe it's another trip to the Underground."

CHAPTER 14

I'm going to have to go alone again, but this time there's a plan. The three of us sit in a circle as Li explains each of the devices he found after my earlier request. The first device he pulls out is a sleek silver wristband. He demonstrates how it works by slipping it over his own wrist and pressing a button on its underside. Almost immediately he seems to disappear: completely gone from sight. "It's a cloaking cuff," he explains, his voice emanating seemingly out of thin air. "I'm not really invisible of course, it just messes with the perception of others who are not wearing the cuff. If we each had one on, we'd be able to see one another. It just changes the visual frequency." He slips it off and he materializes back in front of us.

"I've heard of those things," Rhian says slipping it over her own wrist and disappearing from sight. The door opens and closes as if on its own, then opens and closes again as Rhian returns. She removes the cuff and hands it back to Li. "These things cost way more than even you could afford." She raises an eyebrow and Li shrugs sheepishly.

"So I happen to know a guy." Li's one of those people who always happens to 'know a guy.' He pulls out the next item. It's white and flat. He taps the top and a three-dimensional image of a smiling Li doing a ridiculous dance appears in the middle of the room between my bed and Rhian's. It's the right height and weight, everything down to the distinct freckles scattered across his nose. He taps it again and the other Li pixelates and disappears. "It's a holographic recording. What we'll do is record an image of you sleeping soundly and then place the disc so that the image is projected onto your bed. That way if anyone happens to show up, they'll see you sleeping soundly." He turns the disc on again and the dancing Li returns. I reach out and swipe my hand through it, causing the image to pixelate before correcting itself. "That's the only real issue. If they try to touch the image it will clearly reveal that it's a hologram. We'll just have to hope it doesn't come down to that."

"Okay, so we know how I'll get out of and into the building, as well as have a decoy if needed. Anything else?" I'm anxious at another trip to the Underground, and rightfully so. The last two trips didn't exactly turn out wonderful.

He hands me the cuff and I slip it over my wrist, but don't press the button. He pulls out a silver packet from his pocket. Another Patch. "I don't know if you'll need it, but just in case." He tosses it onto the bed in the space between us. *Deceit*. I think of Sloan's disapproving look at the patch I had worn the last time I went to the Underground several days ago. I hesitate, but take the silver packet and carefully slip it into my own pocket.

Just in case.

. . .

That night when the twin moons are high in the sky, Rhian and I place the holographic disk in a little nook just beneath her mattress so that the hologram of a sleeping me that was recorded earlier appears on the empty bed across from hers. I don't put the Deceit patch on, but it sits heavy in my pocket as a reminder. We'd discussed the best method for me to enter and exit the building without causing suspicion so I don't have a repeat of what happened last time.

After much debate we decided that I'd cloak myself in our sleeping quarters, then Rhian would go to the bathroom. As Rhian heads to the bathroom, Li would be returning from the bathroom. When Rhian opened our door I'd slip out and when Li opened his I'd slip in. Then I would exit through the window in Li's sleeping quarters. Unlike the window in our room, Li's window opens up on the roof over the entrance to the lobby. So I'd be able to climb onto the roof then use one of the supporting steel beams to help me slide down to the ground below. When I return, the same process would happen, more or less. I'd have to climb back up to Li's window and then a similar bathroom routine would be repeated once Li sends a communication signal to a small, box-shaped device that he gave Rhian earlier.

Rhian throws her arm around me in an awkward hug. "Good luck," she whispers in my ear.

"Thanks," I whisper back. We pull apart and I hit the button on the underside of the cuff. Rhian opens the door and light spills in from the hallway. We exit together: one of us seen and one of us unseen. She heads toward the bathroom just as Li exits. He gives her a small smile and I fall in step beside him, following him into his sleeping quarters. So far this plan is already better than my previous one. I could have been caught the last time and I'm sure the consequences would have been dire if Tristen is the one administering them. I can only imagine the consequences if I get caught this time. I shudder and Li closes the door behind us.

I press the button so that Li can see me. "Ready?" he asks.

I nod. "Yep." My heart pounds nervously in my chest as I step over to the window which is already open, a cool breeze drifting in, pinkish white light from the sun and moons cast shadows on the floor.

I render myself invisible and then stick one leg out of the window so that I'm straddling the window sill. "Wait." I feel Li's hand on my shoulder.

"But you can't see me," I reply not understanding how his hand found my shoulder quite so easily.

"Just because I can't see you doesn't mean I can't *feel* you."

His lips find mine and he kisses me quickly. "Be careful." I nod even though he can't see it and slip out the window.

The roof is about half a meter down from his window and I land softly without a sound. I make my way to the edge. I'm now about a story and half from the ground. I inch myself closer then carefully dangle my legs over the edge at an angle so that I'm lying on my stomach. My legs kick in the air until they find one of the metal support beams. When I find one, I wrap my legs around it tightly. I let my fingers slip from the edge of the roof, grasping around the beam and slowly shimmy my way to the ground below.

I sigh in relief. I'd like to think that this means the hardest part of tonight is over, but I know better than that. I take off at a half-jog, half-walk anxious to get my visit to the Underground over with.

When I feel I'm far enough away from the University Complex, I press the uncloak button, rendering myself visible. Just like the last time, my feet lead me without much guidance from my head. Thoughts flutter in and out like a lost bird. What if I can't find the Metal woman? What if I see Sloan again? Worse, what if that blonde-haired Metal is with him again?

I reach the wooden sign pointing down the alleyway sooner than I'd like. I hurry down the alleyway and down the steps into the Underground. The smell always reaches me first. It's not that it smells *bad*; it just smells different. It's the weekend so a lot of the vendors are open, their owners leaning out and shouting at passersby. I hear the familiar buzz of the tattoo vendor as I step onto the cobblestone street.

The Metal woman's trailer had been near the entrance that much I remember, but I can't remember which one it was. The first few to my right actually have their gates drawn closed. Unless I want to waste the entire night trying to figure it out, I'm going to have to ask someone.

I follow the hypnotic buzz of the tattoo needle. I've never actually been in a tattoo vendor before. It's always seemed so intimidating, but I find myself drawn to the sound and it's only a few vendors from where I think the fortune teller's shop was located. Blue and red neon lights shine from around the doorway. From the window I can see a man sitting backwards in a chair, the tattooist hovered over his bare back. A woman sits beside the man who is getting tattooed, her hair is wild and I can see the glint of metallic thread against her dark skin.

I tentatively approach the few steps leading to the entrance. *Act confident,* I think. *Act like you belong here. In fact, if what they say is true, you do belong here. You are all Elements and yet you are none.* I wander through the doorway, but no one acknowledges me. The walls of the trailer are covered in white papers filled with colorful designs. Some sort of rhythmic drumming music plays softly from somewhere and I can hear laughter drifting from the back of the shop. I let my eyes scan over the images on the walls: mythological creatures, skulls, all different types of flowers, half-naked women, suns, and moons…almost anything you could imagine and I bet it's somewhere on these walls. That's when it catches my eye, small and in the corner, somewhat away from the rest.

It's not very large about the size of the bottom of one of the brown bottles so prevalent in the Underground. It's a five-pointed star: each point of the star representing a different Element: the sleek silver glint of Metal, the curling green vines of Earth, the solid ridges of Wood, the crashing wave of Water, and the flames of Fire. Only one word stands out in my mind: Mine.

"That's not a particularly popular one," a woman's voice slices through my thoughts. I turn and it's the dark-skinned woman I saw earlier.

"I'm not one for what's popular," I reply.

"You interested? I could take you right now." An offer. She must also be a tattooist.

"I don't have much money," I say, but can't seem to take my eyes away from the intricate design.

"I'm sure I could make you a deal," she coaxes, but it doesn't sound deceiving like my usual experiences with the Metals in the Underground.

"Actually, I came to ask about a woman, a fortune-teller." I tear my eyes from the tattoo and turn to face the woman.

"Oh, you probably mean Bina. She went out for a bit, but she usually comes back. You know some herbs can only be collected by the light of the moons."

"Herbs?"

"Yeah, she's into all that woo-woo stuff: crystals, herbs, and all that." *Magic stones* I think. "So how 'bout it? It won't take long."

And before I can even debate whether or not it's a good idea I find myself answering, "Sure, why not? I have to wait for Bina either way."

"Good. Follow me."

. . .

I follow the woman to the back of the trailer. She's tall and thin, her shirt rides up revealing a sliver of dark tattooed skin above the waistband of her pants. We enter a room that has a torn red vinyl chair. There's sketch drawings covering every single inch of wall space. And there's a table covered in little bottles of ink with some hand-held devices, which look like medieval torture machines from my Earth History textbook, set on top of it.

She follows my eyes. "We do our tattoos the Old Earth way. With the advent of the color laser technology it's kind of made it an unconventional choice, but it's like a dying art, you know?" She smiles and when she does so it brightens up her entire face. "Where do you want it?" she asks.

"I-I'm not sure. I've never done this before," I say nervously as I shrug off my jacket tossing it onto the red chair.

"Ah, virgin skin. My favorite kind," her smile turns wicked for a moment, but quickly fades. This woman isn't like any other Metal I've ever encountered. She turns the design over in her hands as if she's studying it. "How about…" she comes over, pulling the back collar of my t-shirt down and pressing the damp paper to my skin. She presses firmly then pulls the paper away. "Here, take a look." I hold up a hand-held mirror and peer into it and the reflection allows me to look into another mirror behind me where I can see the purplish outline of the Elemental Star right in the middle of my neck; it's center over my spine. Most of the time my hair will cover it. No one will even know it's there. Except me.

I grin. "It's perfect."

"Great. Then let's get started." She has me sit on the red chair backwards with my chest pressed into it, my hair pushed to one side. "It's going to feel like a bad scratch, but trust me it will be over before you know it. This particular design isn't too large." The buzz of the tattoo needle fills my ears and I hold my breath anticipating the first painful scratch. I gasp as the needle penetrates my skin. "The outline is the worst," she explains.

I close my eyes trying to focus my mind on other things and away from the burning sensation in my neck. "You seem young. Have you been a tattooist long?" I ask.

I can already feel myself getting used to the rhythmic sensation. "Long enough," she replies after a moment. "I didn't always live in the Underground. But…" she pauses, "things changed." I think about what my parents told me about unbalanced Metals. They can be deceptive, merciless and destructive. But a balanced Metal, I remember my father saying, is a force to be reckoned with; they are the bravest and most determined of any Elemental. "For a while I was a soldier, but it"—she searches for the right word—"changes you. I saw some things I'd rather have not, learned some things I couldn't unlearn." I can almost hear the contempt in her words. The buzzing stops as she switches from outlining to filling in the colors of the design.

I know what she means. I've seen things, learned things that I too wish I hadn't. "Couldn't you just have, I don't know, switched assignments?" I ask.

She chuckles. "There aren't many other assignments for a Metal, besides those in the Underground. But it's okay. I like it down here, most of the time."

For a long while there is silence, just the buzz of the tattoo needle. After a while the sensation in my neck has gone numb and finally the buzzing comes to a stop. The whole process probably only took about thirty minutes. She dabs at my neck with a rag and then smears some kind of ointment on top of my neck. "Take a look," she orders.

I hold up the mirror again and what I see pleases me. *You are all and yet you are none.* The fresh colors look as though they could leap off of my skin and into the air around us. "It's beautiful," I say.

"Well, it's yours now," she grins pulling off her black latex gloves and tossing them into a bin.

"What do you mean?"

"Once a tattoo is given to someone, it's taken off the wall. House rules."

"I thought you said it was unpopular?" I ask.

"Unpopular in that most people wouldn't even consider it in the first place. Not many people want a tattoo representing an

Element besides their own. I think in the several years I've been here only one other person ever even considered it."

"But they didn't get it?"

"Nope, otherwise it wouldn't have been there for you today," she smiles. "Call it fate."

"How much do I owe you?" I fish around in my pocket for the little money that I brought with me.

"No charge," she waves her hand at me.

"What?" I ask incredulously. It's not like a Metal to refuse money. Most Metals are greedy and manipulative in their dealings.

"Just be sure to come back and visit. The conversation I've had with you is more stimulating than what I usually get around here," she nods indicating the front of the trailer where the two men were earlier.

"Zora," she extends her hand and I shake it, catching a glimpse of a tattooed feather that shifts into tiny birds flying away on the inside of her forearm. I feel like my tattoo represents who or what I am becoming, what then does Zora's tattoo reveal about her: who she was and who she's become?

This woman isn't like any other Metal I've ever met before. I could easily see Zora as a Fire, her passion for art and her own craft are sure signs of a Fire Elemental. Maybe we can't be categorized so readily. Perhaps we are all a little bit of each Element. If so, then why must we choose? "I'm Ka," I reply slipping back into my jacket.

We walk back to the front of the trailer and Zora peers out the open gate. "Right there," she points to a vendor, its gate isn't open but the light is on above the door. "Bina's returned."

"Thank you," I say as she walks me to the doorway.

"I hope you find the answers that you seek," she smiles. Her words catch me off guard, but when I turn around Zora's already disappeared back down the hallway.

. . .

My biggest fear isn't that Bina won't remember me, but that she *will* remember me. And that she'll refuse to see me. I approach the door tentatively. The skin on the back of my neck feels scratched raw. I nervously grasp the small tube of ointment in my pocket that Zora gave me before I left.

I climb the couple steps up to the door and knock. There's no answer. The light above the door is still on and the gate is closed. I knock again this time with more of a sense of urgency. It has to be now. I can't risk this elaborate plan a second night and I need to know how to retrieve the stones out of the Elemental Abyss, more importantly I need to know what it means to be the Impossible Girl. Everly said she is the stuff of myth and legend—but then how come I have never heard of such a tale?

After several long minutes the door opens a crack and a steely eye appears in the darkness. "We aren't open for business tonight!" Then a pause. *"You!"* An accusation. The door opens wider and it is the woman with the missing teeth. Her gray streaked hair is pulled back into a haphazard bun. She wears a housecoat sweater and slippers. "Come in, quickly."

I slip into the doorway confused by her unexpected hospitality. The last time I was here she seemed less than pleased. "Are ye alone?"

I nod. She hastens around the room lighting various candles. There's a shabby green couch, a banged up wooden coffee table, an overstuffed blue armchair and a large bookshelf filled with books. Actually the room is overflowing with books: on the floor, beside the couch, scattered across the table. There are stacks almost to the ceiling. I wonder how I didn't notice before and then I see that there's a partition separating the hallway to the back room for patrons from the actual living space.

"Sit," she orders and I do, moving some books so that I can fit onto the couch. Bina sits in the armchair. "Ye've returned. I told ye to never come back."

I swallow and nod again. "I-I know. But I think you're the only one who can help me." She looks at me waiting for me to continue. "You know who I am, but I don't. Tell me who or what I am."

"Tis a long story," she replies.

"I've got time," I retort. She lets out a long sigh then gets up and disappears in the back of the trailer. I can hear the bang of cupboards and the running of water. Bina returns with two mugs and hands me one. I sniff at it unsure of whether to trust that it's not poisoned or something.

"Ye came here for my help and yet ye suspect that I've

tricked yeh. Why then would ye trust anything I have to say?" she asks.

As she watches I raise the hot mug to my lips, take a tentative sip, and swallow it down. Chamomile tea. She nears the front door and flips the switch, turning off the light outside indicating that she's not home. Finally she returns to the armchair.

"Yer mother came to me years ago," she scrutinizes me, "from the looks of it about thirteen or so years ago. The other day when you came, I didn't know who ye were. Not until much, much later when I thought about what I'd seen did I make the connection, but it was too late. I'd already sent ye away."

"Why did my mother come to you?" I ask.

"She was worried and rightfully so. Ye were exhibiting some...peculiar...behaviors." I wait hoping that she'll elaborate. "Conflicting personality traits; often when one is very young yer drawn to one or two Elements in particular, but ye...ye were not. Yer mother said ye were determined like Metal, wise like Water, bold like Wood, loyal as Earth, and passionate like Fire."

I recall a time when I was very small, maybe three or four, and my mother was sad. I don't remember why, but as she tucked me into bed for the night I could see the tears on her cheeks. I'd reached up my pudgy little hand and wiped them away. "Don't be sad, Mama. Sorrow is finite, but happiness is infinite. Soon you will be happy again." She had given me a strange look and replied, "Why, Kata, what makes you say such things?" But I remember simply smiling back at her as I snuggled down beneath the covers. *Wise like Water.*

And then there was another time when I was with Ahna. We were maybe nine or ten and some of the boys in our class were making fun of her, calling her a Brainbox because she was so smart. Their shrill prepubescent voices taunting; Ahna's eyes brimmed with tears. "Ignore them," she'd insisted. But I hadn't. I went right up to the loudest boy and shoved him. He fell flat on his butt and began to cry. "Pick on someone your own size, you vermin!" I'd hollered, my small hands clenched into fists. The boys had run away after that to tell our teacher. But I didn't care. *Loyal as Earth, passionate like Fire.*

Even more recently, my decision to not choose Water even though the Box so clearly recommended it as the best choice for me, anything to avoid Teacher 4's watchful eyes. *Determined like Metal.* Instead I'd chosen Fire, probably the choice least expected of me. *Bold like Wood.*

"You said I am *all possibilities and yet I am impossible.* What exactly does that mean?"

Bina looks right into my eyes. "I bet ye had a difficult time choosing an Elemental, am I right?" I nod. She is right. "Tis because ye are not meant to decide, not meant to choose fidelity to one, because ye have all of them running through ye."

I slowly lower my mug. "But I did choose. I chose Fire."

"I know that. I can see it in yer eyes, the burning. And I see that ye can feel it in yer veins just beneath the surface. But tis not who ye are. Ye can say ye are anything, but deep down ye know that ye are not these things."

"The Box recommended Water."

She chuckles. "The Box has to make a recommendation. It is a simple analysis of yer most dominant traits. Nothing but an algorithm. Like anything, it has its flaws."

"So some people choose wrongly based on the recommendation?"

Bina narrows her eyes. "Ye've met Zora?" I nod. "Zora is an example of a wrong recommendation." I think of the drawings covering the walls and her passion for the art of tattooing. Then I think of her unhappiness as a soldier. Zora would have made a wonderful Fire, instead she is in the Underground with the other unbalanced Metals.

"Who is the Impossible Girl?"

At this Bina smiles. "The Impossible Girl is the stuff of myth and legend. She is a story told to sleepy children at bedtime, a fairy tale."

"I don't know it."

Her smile fades. "Of course not, Child. Yer mother was no fool. She did all she could to protect ye." She takes a sip of tea. "The legend goes that a girl would be born who could not be categorized; who would exhibit traits of all the Elements of Xon 9, which as we know is impossible, everyone must choose. No exceptions. But on her eighteenth moon of the hundredth solar alignment, the Impossible Girl will be asked to choose."

I shift uneasily in my seat. "And what happens when she chooses?"

"The world as we know it, here on Xon 9, will cease to exist."

"But I've chosen, haven't I? And nothing has happened."

Bina's gray eyes turn stormy. "Yet. Yer mother took the proper precautions to protect ye. She threw stones into the Elemental Abyss. No easy feat mind ye."

"I was told that I need to retrieve the stones."

"'Tis true."

"And what happens when I do?"

"The world will change."

"But what if I don't want the world to change?" Even as I say the words, I know they aren't reflective of how I truly feel, not deep down. Something tells me that things need to change. I just don't know why yet. "What happens if I don't get the stones?"

Bina's lips downturn into a frown. "Then the Imminent Darkness will continue to grow stronger."

"I've never heard of the Imminent Darkness." I say incredulously. This all sounds almost too ridiculous to be true. A girl who exhibits characteristics of all the Elements, one who must be kept a secret because she has the power to end the world as we know it. It is a legend, just that. A fairy tale. It can't possibly be true. It sounds impossible, because it *is* impossible.

"Of course ye haven't. Tisn't like they go around announcing their presence. There are people out there, living beside yeh and me, who want a different vision for the future: one of dominance and control."

"But that can't happen. The Council of Leaders would never allow that to happen."

"Wouldn't they? Did yeh pay attention in Earth History class?" I bite my lip. I'm pretty sure that I paid attention. "Haven't you ever wondered why in our Old Earth days our society was so advanced and yet when we came here we seemed to have regressed? Why are we living much as they did thousands of years ago? We establish life on another planet, yet we are little more than primitive apes."

I hadn't ever thought about it. I had just accepted it for what it was. Is this why I'd never heard of the Imminent Darkness? Because of my own complacency?

"*Divide et impera:* an ambiguous phrase at best," she continues. I picture the elaborate arching entrance into the University Complex. "In Latin it means *divide and conquer.*"

"That doesn't seem so evil," I say. It's simply a harmless phrase. Isn't it?

"Another meaning is *divide and rule,*" she pauses. "Or yet another is *divide in order to conquer.* And just who do ye think decided to use that particular motto? They categorize and group us like specimens. Specimens who fit neatly into various careers, who are predictable and unoriginal. Forced to share in a sort of sameness, a society of limited choice. But what if—and tis a big what if—there was someone who could change all that? Someone who could prove beyond a reasonable doubt that we are all, in fact impossible, we are not so easily defined. Life as we know it on Xon 9 would be forced to change, to evolve. We could come into our full glory as a knowledge-filled, technologically-rich society, as it should have been all along."

"And why me?" I want to learn more about this Imminent Darkness, but I sense that our visit is coming to an end.

Bina shrugs. "Do we ask why the sun died? Some things simply just *are*. And we decide to either accept it or to reject it."

"What happens if I retrieve the stones?" None of this is making sense. The Impossible Girl could be anybody—I can't be the only one to have turned eighteen on Pronouncement, or could I have been?

"If ye accept who ye are, in its truest form and capacity, that ye are indeed the Impossible Girl, then each stone will give you great power."

"What kind of power?"

"Didn't ye notice how ye often feel unsure and indecisive? Not particularly brave, nor very smart, nor passionate? Simply ordinary?" My eyes grow wide at her words. How does she know that I've felt those things? "Tis because of the stones. When each stone was cast into the Elemental Abyss with your mother's affirmations, they took with them a part of yer identity. In essence ye are almost a shadow of yer true self. Yer strongest Elemental traits were taken away in order to protect ye."

"So as I retrieve each stone that trait will return to me?" I'm shocked. Everly had told me I am extraordinary, but did she truly have any idea to what extent? All these years, I've been but a dim light of my true, magnificent self. A shadow self. My heartbeat quickens at the thought.

"More or less, but mind you tis not easy to retrieve the stones," she sets her mug onto the coffee table and reaches for my hand. "Ye must go to the Elemental Abyss. Far off in the mountains of Xon 9 you will find a cave. Inside the cave are five portals, each portal corresponds to an Element. This is the Elemental Abyss. Ye must enter into each portal in order to find and retrieve its stone. Once ye have each stone ye must destroy it."

"How do I destroy them?"

"I cannot tell ye because I myself am unsure. But once each stone is destroyed ye will feel that fractured Element of yourself return." It all seems too surreal to even be fathomable. "The journey will not be easy and there are many who will be keen to stop ye from succeeding; however," and she puts emphasis on the word *however*, "there are also many who are prepared to help ye, who see the Imminent Darkness and crave Illumination." Sloan. Everly. Bina. Mother.

"Which stone do I destroy first?"

"The stone with the most power will be the one containing the qualities ye lack the most." Her words are cryptic, but I think it is no coincidence that I chose Fire. Fire represents all the things I am not and wish that I was: the qualities that Li has always exuded that I always felt I couldn't be: energetic, sentimental and full of a passion just to live and breathe each and every day. Fire is what I lack the most which is why I chose it.

Bina gets up and wanders to the back of the trailer and quickly returns with a small, burlap bag. "I see ye already have a cloaking cuff, but perhaps these will help ye as well." She hands me the bag and I peer through the draw-string opening. Inside is a pack of matches, a small vial of a clear liquid, a tiny multi-faceted crystal, and a speckled feather. I look up at her confused. How will this random compilation of items help me on my journey? "Ye will know the meaning of each item only when the item is needed." She looks up at the clock. "Tis getting late. The moons will be setting soon, ye best be on yer way now, Impossible Girl."

I stand up with her, gripping the bag tightly, as if it is a lifeline to my true self. "Ka," I say, "My name is Ka."

For the first time Bina smiles and when she does the ominous look in her eyes lightens. "Yer mother calls ye Kata, no?"

I nod. "She does."

"And do ye know what the name means?"

I nod my head. I do, but I simply assumed that Kata was a pet-name my mother had made up for me as a small child. "It means 'pure' in one of the ancient Earth languages."

Pure.

And then it dawns on me. English is one of the few classes in which I excelled. Pure. Definition: without any extraneous or unnecessary elements. Synonyms: Untainted. Clear. Genuine. Real.

Kata is the sacrifice my mother made when she fragmented my personality, taking tiny pieces away and throwing them into the Elemental Abyss in order to protect me, keeping me safe. It was her reminder of who I had the potential to become. Ka may be my name, but Kata is who I am.

In actuality, Bina is right. I am all possibilities and yet I am impossible.

And here this entire time I thought I was simply ordinary.

Bina walks me to the door and as I step out onto the stoop she leaves me with some final words. "Go, Kata. Go and find out who you truly were meant to be. Save us all from the Imminent Darkness that has scarred our civilization and which has become a blemish on the history of our World. Go, Kata, and become the stuff of which these legends were made."

CHAPTER 15

I make the return trip without incident. I lay awake in my bed thinking about the night's events. I don't have classes tomorrow. However, I did promise Rhian we could hang out since tonight we had a change of plans. I rub my hands absent-mindedly over the bandage on the back of my neck, the one covering my new tattoo. I smile into the darkness. I still can't believe that I did it. It's something that I can't explain: the inexplicable pull to the Elemental star design. And now it's mine; Zora said no one else can have it now that I do.

My mind is a tornado of thoughts rushing around, darting in and out. According to what Bina told me, I need to get to the mountains which are west of the University Complex, but it's a day's trip easily, unless…my mind drifts to the teleportation portals that sent us home the night of Pronouncement. You just imagine you're where you want to go and—*bam!*—you're there. You only need a portal on the transporting end, not the receiving one. That would save not only a lot of time, but also a lot of planning. I could simply wear a cloaking cuff and sneak into the lower level at night to send myself to the mountains. I could just get some coordinates to help me better visualize where I need to go. If I visualize the coordinates maybe I could still get there, since I don't know what the Elemental Abyss is exactly. Bina had been vague only saying it was a portal in a cave. I mean, how do you picture something if you've no idea what it looks like?

But how will I find the coordinates? Definitely not anywhere in Fire. Now that Tristen's grown suspicious I'm sure I'll be watched that much more closely.

I do still need Ahna, after all. She knows everything about anything. And she won't say no. She's the most steadfast person in my life besides my parents, which is why she chose Earth. Earth's are honest, loyal, and responsible. If I'm making a huge mistake searching for the Elemental Abyss she will be the first to tell me. I *need* her help; I won't be able to do it without her. She'll help me figure out how to find the Elemental Abyss, the rest will be up to me. Friends help one another, how Li and Rhian helped me tonight, and like I know Ahna will too. Then why has Sloan—who knows more than anyone else—refused to help me at all?

I finally fall asleep when the sun has risen high into the sky, red light pouring through the window. Today I will pay a visit to my best friend.

. . .

During the day it's much easier to exit and enter the buildings of the University Complex. There's a constant ebb and flow of people leaving from and returning to buildings. I slip the cloaking cuff over my wrist and press the button. Knowing that Tristen suspects my data is fake, I can't afford to be seen breaking any rules. The last thing I need is to draw unwanted attention to myself.

I head to the lobby and easily slip out with a group of people headed out the main doors. People are sitting on the stone walls and on benches throughout the complex. A group of Waters kick around a ball in an open space and I feel a pang in my gut, half-expecting to see Sloan's sparkling green eyes looking back at me, forgetting that I'm invisible. But he's not here.

I make my way down the winding sidewalk, past the Waters Building where I saw Sloan and the other cloaked figure enter, which was only several nights ago, but feels so much longer. Unlike the sleekness of the Fires Building, the Waters Building is more classic in design, simple stone architecture. I continue past the Woods Building, which is built around a massive Red Oak tree. Red Oaks were one of the only Old Earth trees that seemed to thrive on Xon 9. They were some of the tallest and sturdiest trees on Earth, so I figure if a tree had to make it, it's a good thing it was the Red Oak. The Woods Building is like a giant tree house and as I walk past I try to imagine my father going about his studies in that building.

Further down is the Metal Building. It too looks sleek and

modern, but it has no windows. Instead it looks like a giant steel box, a soldier-producing factory. I can't imagine Zora inside its walls. Lastly, I come to the Earth Building. The building isn't like any I have ever seen. The entrance is a small, non-descript dirt mound with a wooden door and then the rest of the building is underground. Behind the mound is a giant glass dome that provides natural light to the building beneath.

The University Complex was literally created to help you get into your Element, to understand your Element at its very core. I think of the stone walls and torch lights of the unmarked level in the Fires Building, the level below the lower level, and of the giant fire pits. In contrast to the rest of the building's design it seems almost primitive. I'm not sure what that says about Fire.

As I approach the Earth Building two girls exit through the door and I run to slip in before it can close. That was almost too easy, but I don't have time to dwell on my good fortune because I am completely taken with what lies before me.

A compact staircase built into the packed dirt walls leads me down to the main part of the building below. The effect of the glass dome is dazzling. Red light catches and sparkles off specks of stone packed into the dirt walls and floor. Roots push through the earthen walls in some spots and I slide my hand along a wooden hand-railing as I make my way invisibly down the dirt steps. It's worn and smooth beneath my palm.

There are vines hanging from the ceiling of the building and in the center, beneath the glass dome is a large sturdy tree, native to

Xon 9, its silvery leaves reaching for the light above. I reach the bottom of the stairs and am unsure where to go from here. In the distance I can hear the steady flow of a waterfall. Water doesn't flow freely on the surface of Xon 9, only below. I think I could spend all day here, in this building; it is like I've entered another world altogether. I can imagine my mother navigating these pathways, sitting at the base of the tree beneath the glass dome, the crush of the waterfall humming in her ears as she went about her studies.

I look around and notice that although the Earth Building is all one level, besides the entrance, there are several tunnels leading off the main atrium. A boy passes me, tiny green vines starting to creep up the back of his neck, inching toward the curl of his brown hair. His arms are full of books and I decide to follow him. We turn down one of the tunnels to the right of the tree. There are arched doorways with small wooden doors and tiny plaques: the office of so-and-so. At the end of the short hallway is another curved doorway, but this one is a triple set of wooden doors; however they are closed. The boy frowns as he looks from the stack of books in his arms, to the closed doors, then back to the stack of books. His glasses slide slightly down his nose, and I really want to help him. But if I open the doors, won't he know that someone is there, even though he can't see me?

We wait several beats and I quickly grow impatient—impulsive like Fire—and I grab one of the cast iron handles and pull the door open, holding it for the boy to enter. His blue eyes grow wide in his face and then dart from left to right and back again.

"Hello?" he whispers.

"*Shhhh!*" I hush.

"Oh-oh, right," he stammers. Then chortles to himself, "It is a library after all." I follow him through the door; seemingly lost in his mission he's probably already forgotten about the mysterious opening of the door.

I wander up and down the library stacks. Although English was my best subject, I was never really interested in reading or books, and unfortunately that meant I never made many trips to the library during my school years. Earths are right up there in wisdom and intelligence with Waters so it's no surprise to me that their library is gigantic. I'm scanning book spines when I suddenly smash into someone, the side of my face into their chest.

The person reels backward and to my horror—or to my luck—it's Ahna. I kneel in front of her. "I'm so sorry!" I whisper.

She looks confused, brown eyes suspicious. "Ka?" she whispers back. "Is that you?"

"Yes, it's me!" She gets to her feet dusting off her khaki skirt and picking up the books that went flying when I ran into her.

"How come I can't see you?" she asks.

"Cloaking cuff."

"You've been hanging around Li too much. I knew it was a bad idea when I heard you'd pronounced Fire."

"Very funny," I scoff. "Listen I need your help finding something."

"Well, we can't stay here in the stacks like this. If I see

someone I know they'll really think I've lost my mind if they see me talking to thin air. Here, follow me." She leads me to a long table where some students have books out and are reading or studying. She sets the books down then takes a seat. Carefully, she opens a notebook then taps her pen a second before writing down:

Tell me what you need.

I smile. *Oh, Ahna, you sneaky thing you.* I lean over her shoulder, wrapping my hand around hers and write:

I need to know about the Elemental Abyss.

Why??

Long story.

Indulge me.

Isn't there somewhere we can go to talk?

She bites her lip considering my request then nods.

There is. Let me pull a few books first then follow me.

Thanks ☺

She rolls her eyes, but gets up from the table, slipping her notebook into her bag which is strapped across her shoulders and, leaving her other books behind, proceeds to wander around the stacks pulling out seemingly random books.

When she's done I follow her back out the main library doors and down the tunnel back to the atrium. "Are you there?" she mumbles and I reach out and place my hand lightly on her arm. She shivers. "Don't do that! It's creepy." I laugh to myself and resist the urge to annoy her further.

We walk together across the atrium and down into another

maze of tunnels. In these tunnels the plaques have room numbers. Eventually we stop—this time I'm careful not to run into her—and Ahna slides a card through a reader beside the door. The lock tumbles and she opens the door, waiting for me to enter, before following me through herself. She closes the door behind us.

We're in her sleeping quarters. There are two beds, except they are bunk style. There's two desks, a bureau, and tall bookshelves already overflowing with books. There are no windows but every inch of the ceiling is covered with hanging incandescent light bulbs that give the room a soft, warm feeling. The floor has a mossy looking rug in the center of the room.

"My roommate, Mabry, is scheduled for a shift in the nursery today, so she'll be gone a while." She drops the stack of books onto the bottom bunk, shrugs her bag over her head and tosses it onto the dirt floor. "So are you going to tell me what's going on?"

I press the button on the cloaking cuff and flop down onto her bed. "Ah," I sigh. "it's good to be seen again. It gets a little weird being unnoticed."

"And may I ask why exactly you need a cloaking cuff in the first place?" She grabs my wrist, turning it over in her hand, examining the sleek silver cuff.

"Like I said it's a long story."

She flops down beside me. "I have time."

And so I start at the beginning, more or less, about how I came to choose Fire, despite the Box's recommendation of Water. I tell her about Tristen and Doran, Everly and my Mindscape, as well as my meeting with Sloan.

"Wait—you mean to tell me Teacher 4's name is Sloan? And he sent you a letter because he's some sort of protector for you?"

I blush. "Something like that."

"That is so romantic!" she coos excitedly. "I always thought he was kinda cute. And he's definitely smart…and calm. He'd be a perfect balance to you and your impulsive, irrational nature, Ka."

"It's not like *that*," I object. "He's just like a guardian or something. Besides I'm not impulsive. I'm just a bit impetuous."

She snorts at that then changes the subject. "So what does it mean, this Impossible Girl thing that Everly called you?"

"That's where it gets a bit crazy. The woman in my Mindcape, I had actually met her in the Underground before." She gives me a disapproving look. "Anyways, her name is Bina and she had told me the same thing: I am all possibilities, yet I am impossible."

"Did she explain what it meant?" I relay my visit with Bina including the stuff about the Elemental Abyss and how I need to retrieve and destroy the stones.

"But if you destroy them aren't you, in theory, destroying your own personality?" Ahna looks skeptical as she flips absent-mindedly through one of the books on the bed.

I shrug. "I don't think so. It sounded more like it would release that part of my personality and give it back to me. Remember my mother did it to protect me."

"I've never heard of the Imminent Darkness before," she

looks thoughtful for a moment. "I'll see if I can do some research on it. It will be fun and give me something to do when class isn't in session."

"You have a funny definition of fun," I joke. "But thanks, that would be helpful. So have you ever heard of the Elemental Abyss?"

"I have, but, well, Ka, I've heard the legend of the Impossible Girl before too, you know as a kid." She looks reminiscent. "My mother used to tell Li and me about her as a bedtime story."

"Little did you know she'd end up being your best friend."

"This whole time your mom knew who you were and yet she never even told you." There's a tone of disbelief in her voice.

I counter, "How do you protect the ones you love the most?" I think of Sloan, not so much his omission, but more his refusal.

Ahna's lips form a grim line and she nods in understanding. "You lie to them."

"Exactly."

. . .

We spend several hours flipping through the books Ahna pulled from the library. She feverishly scribbles in her notebook. Finally, we close the last of the books. I tell her of my plan to use one of the teleportation portals.

She gives me an acerbic look. "Li really is rubbing off on you! The teleportation portals leave a record of destinations after it scans your mind. All it will take is for Tristen or someone else to look into the log and see exactly where you've gone."

I sigh exasperatedly. "What other choice do I have? It's either that or hike and somehow I think if I hike off to the mountains of Xon 9, I'll be gone so long surely the fact that I'm missing will be noticed that much sooner."

She bites her lip deep in thought. "True. I concede, I guess you're right. It's the most logical plan. According to the map the cave is approximately 6.92 D by 13.4 W."

I mentally commit the coordinates to memory, just in case.

"One thing still concerns me though," she picks at the edge of one of the books, its dark blue cloth cover already fraying at the corners. "What if it doesn't exist?"

Her words catch me off guard and I feel my heart sink. "What?"

"The Metal woman said so herself that the Impossible Girl is a legend. What if the Elemental Abyss is just that too, a legend?" She scrunches up her face lost in thought.

"Well," I begin thinking of the memory of my mother, sitting with Bina in the kitchen while I played oblivious to their discussion, the look of anxiety and sadness in her eyes. I consider the great risks that she took to ensure my safety: five trips to the Elemental Abyss, not to mention the lies she must have had to tell over the years to protect me. I can only imagine how she must have felt, deep down inside, as she watched me for years, unable to choose an Elemental, not drawn to any of them, struggling to figure out who I am.

Only, the entire time she knew exactly who I was, but couldn't tell me. I can't hardly fathom the doubt and fear she must have felt. "Every legend has to start with some element of truth, doesn't it? Legends are just stories that have grown and expanded, become larger than life, but that doesn't mean that they can't be true. Maybe you're right and I'll get there and there won't be an Elemental Abyss, just an empty, lonely cave…and maybe…maybe I'm not the impossible girl, perhaps I'm just an ordinary girl who was meant to do something extraordinary. Or maybe I wasn't meant to do anything special at all. But, Ahna, what good will it do to just sit here and wonder? If I'm lucky I'll go out there and even if none of it's true, I'll have the greatest adventure finding out. Every story, every legend, even every lie has to begin with some grain of truth and I'm intent on finding out what that truth is."

My words shock me because they don't sound like they're mine. They sound as if they've come from someone wiser, stronger, and much braver than I could ever be. But Ahna smiles and throws her arms around me. "I'm so happy to see you make up your mind about something. For so long, Ka, I've watched you be insecure and unsure of yourself, but now…even if none of it *is* true, this change that I see happening in you, it's worth all the risks you're willing to take to find out." I smile and wrap my arms around her too, my best friend since before the time I could remember.

She's quick to add, "And just for the record, I've always thought you were quite impossible."

CHAPTER 16

I wish I didn't have to go alone. The one person that I want to take with me on this journey is the one person who's refused to help me. If Rhian or Li went with me they would be noticed. Not that my absence will go unnoticed, but three new Elementals missing is a lot more obvious than just one.

I decide to leave the night before classes start again. Maybe if I'm lucky and don't return quickly they'll just think I snuck away to be with my family, the result of homesickness. I am an only child after-all, very close to my parents and not used to being away from them. It's as good an alibi as any. Except that my parents don't know about it. I also decide not to tell Rhian or Li that I'm leaving because I don't want them to have to cover for me. I do, however, leave Rhian a note that I carefully slipped under her pillow earlier this evening, simply telling her everything's fine and not to worry about me. The less she knows in this case, the better.

In the middle of the night, I carefully press the button on the cloaking cuff and, despite our past plans which were carefully orchestrated, I slip out the door as quietly as possible. Luckily the cuff cloaks you and anything on your person, so I take my messenger bag with me. Inside it I have the small burlap bag from Bina, a book from the Earth library that has some maps in it, a few nutrient pills, some water, a flashlight just in case, and the envelope containing the letter from Sloan. I don't know why I took it—a reminder of his betrayal?

I haven't been to the ritual room since the day of Pronouncement, but I recall the night I discovered Everly and my suspicions that the level was the same one. I skip the elevator and head for the stairwell. I make my way from the third floor to the lower level, where I first met Tristen, using the flashlight to guide me in the darkness. I come to a stop. There are no more steps down to the lower level. Do I have to go outside just to get to the level below? I bounce the flashlight's beam around the stairwell and that's when I notice a covering in the floor.

It's like a manhole covering, but it's painted to blend in with the coloring of the floor. I carefully use my hand and, as quietly as possible, slide the covering over and off to the side, trying not to scrape the floor, and allow myself just enough space to lower myself down. I peer down into the opening first and I can see the bounce of torchlight, flickering below. Jackpot. I lower myself feet first into the opening. I don't bother to pull the cover closed after me.

A short metal ladder leads down, stopping about three feet from the dirt floor. I drop the rest of the way and land in a crouched position. I look around trying to get my bearings. I need some kind of landmark in order to know which way to go. That's when I hear the voices. This time though they aren't angry—or scared—like before. Just a muffled conversation drifting down the tunnel.

I follow the direction of the voices figuring it would lead me nearer to the room where Tristen harmed Everly. I recognize the end of the tunnel: right to the voices, left to the slide and then another right to the ritual room. That's the direction I need to go. But I find myself drawn to the voices. I want to know who's speaking and of what. I walk slowly toward my right and stop when I near the entrance from which the voices drift, no need this time to press myself against the wall because no one can see me anyways, but as I peek around the corner I'm still careful.

What I see is an odd room. The light is dim like all the things on this level, and attached to the floor are thick black chains, anchored with giant black rings. I think of the sounds I heard before Everly rushed out the door that night. Chains unlocking. What is this room? And that's when I see the people in the room. Eoin and Tristen are standing off to the side and in a set of chains is a boy, a dark-skinned boy with his head bowed and immediately I know who it is. *Doran.*

What's going on here?

"Don't you think you're being a little melodramatic, Tristen?" Eoin is asking.

"Oh, Eoin, if I don't make a demonstration regarding the price for disobedience how will they ever learn?" Tristen chastises.

"It's only been a week, don't you think you're little episode at the first meeting was sufficient?" Eoin's brow is furrowed in concern.

"This one is disrespectful and indolent. He is a poor reflection on Fire. I'm afraid if he doesn't learn now, that he may never learn." Tristen walks nearer to Doran, sticking her long pale fingers beneath his chin and slowly raising his head so that he is forced to peer into her eyes. The vicious look in his own eyes is gone and what looks back is blank, a void of nothing. His cheeks are dirty and tear-stained and his lip is bleeding.

Tristen continues, "I fear this one may end up in the Abyss." The Abyss? What does she mean? A shiver runs down my spine and suddenly going to the Elemental Abyss has taken on a newer, more disturbing possibility.

"Come," Eoin puts his arm around Tristen's shoulders. "We have other, more important work that needs our attention."

Tristen doesn't turn away. "Have you learned your lesson, Sweet Doran?" She coos and my stomach roils in disgust.

There's a long pregnant pause and then finally Doran nods his head ever so slightly. "Good boy. After I am quite sure you have learned your lesson, you will be released tomorrow in order to attend classes." Eoin's face shows no emotion and I can feel my blood boiling in anger as he guides Tristen away, as if he's ignoring that Doran's even there, and leads her toward the doorway. I instinctively press into the wall even though I cannot be seen.

The awkward pair wander down the hallway in the opposite direction from which I plan on going. Eoin keeps his arm around her as they walk, disappearing down the hallway. Tristen I know is pure evil, but Eoin's indifference surprises me. I wish I could warn Rhian and Li, but there isn't time. I have to get to the Elemental Abyss and retrieve the stones. And I need to find out what Tristen meant when she said Doran may end up in the Abyss.

I take a few tentative steps away from the doorway and then stop cold in my tracks. *Crying.* First softly, then loud racking sobs. *Oh, Mother of Xon*, I think. *Damn you, Conscience.* I spin on my heel and make my way into the torturous room. The hair on the back of my neck immediately prickles as I step carefully around the chains on the floor.

I look around for a moment. How did Tristen burn the fire into Everly's back? Did she brand her? Tattoo her? I look around but don't see anything. Maybe Tristen prefers to keep her weapon of choice close by her side. I hurry over to Doran who is done crying now but snuffling something awful.

"Hey," I whisper.

He looks up, eyes growing wide, then quickly replaced with a fierce look. I get the feeling Doran would have done well in Metal. "Who's there?" He growls softly. I quickly press the button on the cloaking cuff, revealing myself to him. He sniffs arrogantly. "What do you want?"

His words anger me. No wonder Tristen was quick to punish him—not that I agree with it, but he sure doesn't make it easy to want to help him. "I was going to help you, but if you want to stay here all night be my guest." I shrug and am about to press the button to render myself invisible again.

"Over there." He juts his chin in the direction of the nearest wall. "That's where the button is to unlock the chains." He's kneeling. His ankles are wrapped in short chains and his arms are in longer ones. "They lock and unlock using radio waves." I arch an eyebrow at him, but hurry over to the button on the wall and press it. There's the familiar click and his chains are unlocked. He rubs his wrists and his ankles then stretches and arches his back. The blood on his lip is caked and dry; I realize that he literally bit through his lip.

"What did she do to you?" I ask.

"Like you care," is the instant response.

"I do. I've seen things, Doran. You aren't the only one." His reply is silence. "Well, I better be going. Things to do," I say grimly and head toward the door.

He quickly falls in step beside me. "Where are you going? Why aren't you upstairs? How did you know I was down here?" *Suspicious.*

"Oh, you can ask me fifty questions, but I ask you one and you refuse to answer?" I head in the opposite direction of that horrible room, toward where I know the ritual room and where I hope the teleportation room are located.

He smirks at my words. "Fine. But it doesn't matter does it? It's over. She's already won." I stop, turning to him.

"No, she hasn't. And she never will, do you understand?

People like her don't win." I continue down the hallway and he jogs to catch up with me.

"So where are you going?" I turn left. "To the teleportation room."

"Oh," then, "well, you're going the wrong way."

I stop. "No, I'm not."

"Yes, you are. The room is that way." He points down the hallway and I can see the confidence returning to his eyes.

"Are you sure?"

He rolls his eyes. "Of course I'm sure." So I head in the direction he indicates. We take a couple of turns and then we arrive at the teleportation room. "It's one of the secure areas." He points to a DNA scanner located on the wall. I can't hide my disappointment. I hadn't noticed that the last time. I feel like a balloon from which all the air has been let out: deflated. He studies me a moment, brown eyes scrutinizing. "You want to get in that room that badly?"

I give him a beseeching look. "No, I was just taking a nightly tour of the darkest and creepiest places Fire has to offer."

He smiles at that and it really does change his face, in a good way. "Well, you did help me back there." He takes off his zippered hoodie and inspects it and then plucks something invisible off of it. Next, he presses a discreet button on the DNA scanner. A tiny tray slides out. And he places what he plucked onto the tray and then it slides closed. Within seconds the light turns green and the door slides open. We step into the room and the door slides shut behind us.

"What was that?" I ask.

"DNA. All that long blonde hair from Tristen. I knew it was bound to be on my clothes somewhere."

"You're a genius," I say and he smiles.

"Maybe a little. Do you know where you're going?" I pull out the book flipping to the map and recite to Doran the coordinates that Ahna and I had found earlier. He carefully activates the teleportation portal and a little screen lights up on the side of the machine as it conducts some basic diagnostics. "Where's that?" He asks referring to the coordinates.

Tristen's words about Doran ending up in the Abyss float back into my mind. I could lie. But what purpose would it really serve? I've helped him and now he's helping me, some sort of understanding has passed between us, having witnessed Doran in such a fragile state only moments ago. "The Elemental Abyss."

He pauses, fingers hovering over the activation screen, and his eyes cloud over with darkness, but it quickly dissipates. "Take me with you."

"You don't even know why I'm going," I point out.

"Does it matter?"

I consider this. Really, it doesn't. I had wanted someone to go with me, but didn't want to endanger anyone. Doran has already seen Tristen's dark side. "What if you get in more trouble?" I ask.

"Who said I'd come back?" For some reason his words don't surprise me. I adjust my bag nervously.

"Doran, why did you choose Fire?"

He smirks at me. "Why did you?"

"It could be dangerous," I say.

"At this point, I don't think many places are much more dangerous than staying here, at least for me."

I nod. I expected as much.

"I need to find something. Something very, very important."

"Well, it's just your luck that I happen to be most excellent at finding things," he grins and an unfamiliar playful look shines in his eyes.

In a short amount of time he has proven himself both extremely helpful and resourceful. He could be just the person I need to accompany me on this journey.

"I'm not sure what we'll find there," I say, my last ditch effort to deter him in case he may be looking for a way out, but I know that he isn't.

"Geez, aren't you just a barrel of fun. Seriously, why did *you* choose Fire?" This time he's still grinning when he says it.

He heads over to the next teleportation portal and presses the button, the activation sequences begin. We each step onto a metal platform. "What happens when they see that the teleportation portals were used? Can't they run a diagnostic to see where the last person was sent?"

He shrugs. "They could. And if they do, well, we'll pretty much be screwed." I blow out a sigh. Well, that's reassuring. "So since we don't know what exactly this Elemental Abyss looks like to picture it, are we just focusing on the coordinates?"

I nod even though he can't see me. "Yes. The only thing I

know is that it is located in the mountains of Xon 9 deep inside a cave."

"Good enough for me."

Then I have a dreadful thought. "What if we land in different places?"

"Seriously, you need to relax. If we are both focusing on the same coordinates we should be fine. Are you ready?"

My voice is small and nervous. "Yes."

"Ka?"

Again. "Yes?"

"Thanks." And in front of me I can see a blinding white light and I know that Doran is already gone. I realize then that he easily could have gone home, but instead he wanted to go with me. *Why? What is he running away from?*

I've ran away. My entire life I think I've been running and I didn't even know it. Running from who I was, running away from growing up. This entire time I've been trying to elude the unknown. I think deep down I've known all along, that I was different. Felt the call of the fragmented pieces deep in the very core of my being, calling for me to retrieve them and make myself whole again. Only I didn't understand. I misinterpreted it for indecisiveness, for fear. But the reason I couldn't decide is because I truly was never meant to decide. The decision had already been made long ago. We can all run away from our fears, but eventually they will catch up to us because really they never leave us. Our fear is part of who we are, a whisper, a dream. It is our constant companion and it reveals to us the darkest corners of our existence just as much as the things that we love and honor illuminate everything else. Just as much as the things we cherish are representative of who we are as a person, so too are our fears representative of our truth, of who we really are at the core of both our collective and individual worlds.

There will be no more running.

I imagine the mountains of Xon 9 in my mind. Their jagged red peaks and ledges. I try to picture a cave, a large spacious cave with stalagmites from the floor and ceiling, water dripping meanderingly down their gnarled shape. I concentrate on the coordinates in my head: 6.92 D by 13.4 W. I visualize my mother journeying through the mountains as a young woman, carrying the stones given to her by Bina, reciting the words: *Protection, Piety, Promise* five times before tossing in the first stone. *Our fears are our truth.*

I feel the warmth trickle through me as the portal scans me to see where it is that I want to go. Even with my eyes closed, the brilliance of the light dances across my eyelids. The heat is almost unbearable. And then I feel myself being torn away, floating majestically through time and space. Last time it was fast and unexpected, but this time I try to focus on the ebb and flow, the sensations happening all around me. And just as quickly as it began; it's over.

I land on the ground with a hard thud.

I open my eyes.

Chapter 17

The first thing I notice is how windy it is wherever it is that I've landed. Dirt whips around in the air and my hair is blowing every which way making it difficult to see much of anything. I still have my bag which I take as a good sign. I hastily pull my hair back into a sloppy ponytail and take in my surroundings.

The next thing I notice is that I'm very high up, which explains the wind. In the distance I can see the pinpricks of light that I know is my colony. The two moons are high up in the air now, the sun a faded red. The palms of my hands burn and I can see tiny scrapes from the sharp rocky path on which I landed. I am quite literally in the middle of the mountains of Xon 9.

I call softly, "Doran?" But there's no reply. Maybe he didn't come with me, perhaps he decided to teleport himself home after all. I turn around carefully, the ledge I've landed on is only about one and a half meters wide. When I turn I'm surprised to see that my imagination wasn't as far off as I'd expected.

Behind me is a large cave opening. In the moonlight and dimness of the night sun, I can only see inside about a half meter, but it's entrance is about three meters wide if I had to guess, and just a bit taller. Is the Elemental Abyss inside this cavern? Honestly, there's only one way to find out. I carefully pull my flashlight from my bag.

I enter into the cavern and right away I notice the dramatic drop in temperature. I zip up my jacket so that my neck is more covered and flick the flashlight on, sweeping the beam of light around. The floor is much like what I landed on just outside the opening. The majority of the ceiling is covered in stalactites and parts of the floor in stalagmites, like gnarled fingers reaching out as I shuffle carefully past.

Somewhere I can hear the faint dripping of water, which is a bit of a rarity on Xon 9. I mean, we have water—how else could we, who were so accustomed to life on Earth, have survived without it?—but it's a diligently controlled and slightly manufactured process, always manmade, like the waterfall I saw in the Earth Building. There aren't many naturally occurring instances of water. It doesn't rain, our atmosphere isn't conducive to it, and thus why our water is primarily manufactured. Drills are used to extract water from within the dual cores of Xon 9. It then goes through extensive filtration and cooling processes before being distributed for its various uses. All of Xon 9's plants and shrubs are native and thrive on low levels of water, drawing what they need from the layers of earth below.

Not sure where else to go or what else to do, I follow the sound of the dripping water, the delicate *plip-plop*. The cave is a reddish-brown much like everything on Xon 9. My boots echo in the silence. The stalagmites and light from my flashlight cast eerie shadows, reminiscent of monsters on a child's wall when he's trying to fall asleep all alone in his room, the covers pulled securely up to his quivering chin. If I hadn't seen the familiar colony lights, I'd have feared that I teleported to an altogether different planet.

The path curves and winds, eventually I come to a point where I must choose a path: left or right. Simple. I close my eyes listening for the increasingly louder sound of water. I turn left and continue down the path, feeling the slight gradient downward. Walking deeper and deeper into the cavern. I pass several large columns where stalactites and stalagmites have merged, forming a thick pillar. The sound of water increases with each step I take until it is no longer a damp-sounding *plip-plop*, but a soft hum and then louder still until it becomes a steady crash. The path curves to the right and my light catches something glistening in the darkness. Water.

The cave opens up onto an actual waterfall emptying into a sort of basin, a small lake. A soft, opalescent glow emits from the water. I swing my flashlight left to right and back again. Is this another water source that Xon 9 taps into? But it seems unadulterated. There are no foot prints, forgotten lunch boxes or drill parts, no indication that humans have visited here. But if all the water sources on Xon 9 come from beneath the planet's crust, then where does this waterfall originate? Before I can ponder the thought I glimpse something out of the corner of my eye. I bring the flashlight over and where the rocky shoreline meets the lake is a small, wooden boat floating, tethered to the shore by a frayed rope and a metal stake.

I approach the boat tentatively, shining the flashlight inside to make sure there are no animals—or people—inside.

"Convenient isn't it? A boat just sitting there?" a male voice startles me, causing me to nearly jump out of my skin. I whip the flashlight around and grab my messenger bag, ready to strike or bludgeon them to death with my water bottle and nutrient pills. "Geez, Ka, you don't need to blind me."

Doran.

"You, moron!" I hiss, afraid to yell and disrupt the tranquil nature of this place. I narrow my eyes and continue to shine the light in his face. Blinding him is the least of my concern at the moment. "You scared me half to death. You're lucky I didn't knock you unconscious with my bag." My heart is still pounding in my chest, but I can feel it slowly beginning to subside. "Where have you been?" I demand.

Doran shrugs nonchalantly. "Guess I landed a bit deeper into the cavern than you did. I must have better visualization skills."

I scoff. "Whatever you need to tell yourself to sleep better at night."

"You never answered my questions," he says walking toward the boat. "It's a lake, clearly manmade. So why is this boat just sitting here? Where would they take it?"

"How do you know it's manmade?" I scowl, agitated that I didn't notice this myself.

"No naturally occurring water sources on the surface of Xon 9. Geez, didn't you pay attention in school?" I stick out my tongue. "The waterfall uses the water from the lake. There's probably some sort of mechanism that drains some of the water, then transports it up and then down the waterfall it goes and cycles back into the lake." Damn. He really is some sort of crazy genius. "But, the question remains: why is it here? Why the boat? Why the waterfall?"

"Because waterfalls are pretty?" I ask, knowing I sound shallow, but unable to help myself. I have no clue why someone would create their own lake, let alone their own waterfall.

"I say let's hop in this boat and see what happens!"

"Are you sure that's a good idea?" I ask nervously. I've never been in a boat. And I sure as heck don't know how to swim. At least not in real life.

"You're looking for this Elemental Abyss aren't you? Do you want to find it or not?" He crosses his arms and looks at me expectantly. I hate the condescending look on his face. And I hate to admit it, but he's right. I'm not going to find anything staying here on the shore where it's safe. This place was built for a reason—what was it?

"Fine. But if we tip over I'm dragging you down with me."

He starts untying the tether. "Get in," he orders. I step tentatively over the edge of the small boat. Inside are two benches and tucked into the sides of the boat are two wooden oars. I sit on one of the benches and watch as Doran wraps up the tether and gives the boat a shove, and then swings his legs effortlessly over the edge as we drift further into the lake. He drops the coil of rope from his arms to the bottom of the boat and then sits across from me.

At first we drift peacefully, but soon we come to an almost stop near the center of the lake. We aren't close enough to the current of the waterfall to keep us moving. He detaches the oars and carefully dips them into the water. He starts rowing, slowly and rhythmically. He does it gracefully and with much ease. I narrow my eyes at him again.

"How do you know how to row a boat? I've never even seen boats except in books."

He smiles mischievously. "My father was a Water." *Was.* I want to ask about his father, to learn more about him and what he meant to Doran, but I'm afraid that it will bring the darker, cynical Doran back and right now I need the resourceful, maniacal genius Doran if I want to find the Elemental Abyss and get out of here in one piece.

We row closer to the waterfall, its crushing sound is soothing and peaceful. Almost involuntarily, I can feel my eyelids beginning to slide closed. And soon I notice that Doran is no longer rowing, the oars hang limply in the green-blue water. My vision is soft around the edges, but I can still make out Doran, his chin dipping closer and closer to his chest as his head lowers. A nap would be so good right now. I've been so tired: all this sneaking out has meant not a lot of sleep. And maybe if I just take a little nap, maybe Sloan will appear to me again, in my dreams.

Suddenly, the boat is jostled and I snap awake gripping the edges, knuckles white, afraid that we're going to tip over. "What the heck was that?" Doran's eyes are wide and his face panicked. He tries to yank the oars back into the boat. He gets in one, but as he tries to pull in the other it's like it is stuck in mud or something. "Help me, Ka. It's like something is pulling on the other end!"

I lean forward trying to help him pull the oar back on board, but I see what he means. There's something strong pulling it away from us. "That's impossible!" I exclaim even though my physical senses are betraying every minutiae of actual sense I may have.

"Impossible or not, it's happening!" he cries.

"Just let go!" I scream. So he does. And whatever is on the end of the oar clearly was not expecting that, the opposing force almost tips the boat for a second time. I grip the sides for dear life, holding my breath and feeling the insides of my stomach slosh from side to side. "What. Is. It."

He shakes his head. "Look!" I shine my flashlight and see a figure breaching the surface several feet away. I cannot tell if it's man or beast. It has a face covered in gray scales and silvery eyes with shaggy green hair. It lifts the oar above its head and waves it at us tauntingly, then turns around and dives back into the water, flipping a long finned tail at us in the process.

"Is that…but…" I can't believe what I'm seeing with my own eyes.

"Unbalanced," Doran says.

"Wait, what?"

"Metals aren't the only ones who can become Unbalanced. *Any* Element can become Unbalanced." He's staring off after the creature.

"So what you're saying is that—that creature is an Unbalanced Water?" He nods. I think of Sloan and how patient, gentle, and kind he seems.

Doran's face darkens. "Too much Water and they become deceptive, tricky, and narcissistic. They become the doers of others' dark work." A stoic look passes through his brown eyes and then quickly fades and I'm left to wonder if maybe that's what happened to his father, why he used the past tense when speaking of him.

Dark work. Imminent Darkness. That means we have to be getting close. "What if," I hesitate because the idea is a little outlandish, even for me, "what if these creatures, these Unbalanced Waters are protecting the Elemental Abyss?"

Doran looks at me and nods slowly, a soft smile playing on his lips. "You make a good point. Why else would this manmade lake be here in the middle of a cavern? Maybe the Unbalanced Waters are a safety precaution of sorts, protecting the Elemental Abyss."

"But we still don't know exactly where it is."

Then his face lights up even more, any thoughts of his father gone, at least for now. "Maybe it's located *behind* the waterfall."

"You can go behind a waterfall?"

"Sure. And it would offer protection, a sort of concealment.

The waterfall is beautiful and its sound distracting."

"And then that thing—that thing that happened to us. Right before the attack." The boat has begun to drift closer in the direction of the base of the waterfall.

"Yeah," he says suddenly seeming to remember. "I felt so sleepy. The sound was so beautiful."

Suddenly, I have a realization. "It's not just a waterfall and not just for concealment, it's an enchantment."

"An enchantment? You hang out in the Underground too much."

"No, seriously. Look at it from an Elemental perspective. First, the Elemental Abyss is representative of all the Elements. The cavern is representative of Earth, the boat Wood..."

Doran nods beginning to catch on. "The lake, waterfall, and creatures are Water."

"So the enchantment would be from Metal."

'That leaves Fire," he says eyes growing wide and he doesn't need to tell me what he's thinking because I'm thinking the exact same thing. All the dark possibilities that Fire holds, especially Unbalanced Fire. "We're getting closer to the waterfall, the current is pulling us closer."

"Doran, what if that creature—what if it wasn't trying to hurt us? What if it was trying to help us?"

"Well, it had a funny way of showing it."

"No, seriously. What if it did that to *wake us up*? If it hadn't grabbed for the oar and shook the boat, we'd still be asleep drifting in the middle of the lake. And now look, we're almost to the waterfall."

He shrugs. "Maybe." But for some reason I think that I'm right. We edge closer to the waterfall and the boat slowly spins and drifts among the foaming and bubbling concussion of water.

I stick my fingers out, mesmerized by the flow of water, its rainbow of blues, greens, and purples. Doran slaps my hand away. "No. If you're right and it is enchanted, there's no telling what could happen if you touch it." He shudders. "What if those creatures aren't Unbalanced Waters, but people who tried to get to the Elemental Abyss?" I pull back my hand and shiver thinking of my mother. She came here five different times in order to protect me. My mother has become a much braver person in my eyes. I say a silent wish to be able to see her again and tell her as much. "Look! We're heading behind it now."

It's like a little tunnel, a safe haven behind the crush of the waterfall. The sound is almost deafening and the right side of the boat sidles up to a rocky ledge. There's another metal stake in the ground and Doran immediately jumps out with the rope and begins to knot the tether. The boat rocks gently as I make my way out and back to the safety of the land. If I am the Impossible Girl, and indeed contain every Element within me, I still fear the water, the things that remain hidden beneath its depths. Water has secrets. What secrets could Sloan be keeping from me?

There's a source of light emitting further down the passageway, reflecting in the waterfall and bouncing back, a sort of blue-white glow. We walk silently following the light's refraction, the cacophony of the waterfall growing dimmer with each step. We round a corner and suddenly the light is blindingly bright after the cavern's dimness.

The passageway opens onto a large open space, clear of stalactites and stalagmites. Hovering in the space are five large doors, black and menacing. In the center is a pedestal with a glowing blue-white sphere on its top. The Elemental Abyss. I take a step forward and am instantly overcome with a searing painful sensation. Doran knocks into me pulling me out of the way.

So hypnotized by the Elemental Abyss I didn't notice the gaping chasm in between where we're standing and the doors hovering impossibly in space. The chasm is about two meters wide. From where we stand, Doran's arm still protectively holding me back, I can see down—and down forever into a fiery inferno. On the other side of the chasm is a set of battlements almost a meter high. We'd never make it over both the chasm and the battlements, even with a running start.

"I think we found Fire's representation," he deadpans.

"How will we get across that?" I groan. "It's at least two meters wide! It's too far to just jump over it with the battlements on the other side."

"Hold on! I'll be right back!" Doran releases my shoulders and immediately runs back up the way from which we just came.

I'm kneeling on the hard ground. We've come so far. I can't imagine that we'd get this far only to turn back. In fact, I refuse to let that happen. I stare at the glowing pedestal and mysterious doors.

How do they open? And what happens once one does open? Is it a one-way trip if you actually step inside? My mother didn't have to go through the doors to toss the stones inside. But I'll have to cross the threshold in order to retrieve them. What will happen to me if I don't make it back?

I hear the pound of Doran's feet and he reaches me panting, his eyes alit with excitement. He's carrying the oar from the boat. "We can use this!" He grins.

I frown. "Isn't that made from wood? Won't it just burn up?"

"Well, eventually, yes. But if we douse it in some water, it will slow the burn time. We don't need that much time. Just enough time to get across."

I shake my head. "It's too dangerous."

"It's our only hope. It's just like anything, Ka. One foot in front of the other and before you know it you'll be to the other side." He sets it on the ground and I open my bag, pulling out the bottle of water and handing it to him. Hurriedly, he pours it over the oar, careful to try and get every part. I shove the empty bottle back into my bag.

Doran takes the oar and carefully swings it across and over the chasm, placing it between two of the battlements. "Ladies first."

But I shake my head. "No, you go first."

"Suit yourself." He closes his eyes and takes a deep breath seeming to muster up the courage and then like a flash he's quick-stepping across the long arm of the oar. In a matter of seconds he's on the other side of the chasm, a victorious smile on his face. "Your turn. Come on, Ka. You've come so far! You can do it."

What a weird night it's been. First, finding Doran, then him insisting on coming along with me on this journey. Then losing him and finding him again right before finding the boat and being attacked—or saved?—by the creatures in the water. The creatures rousing us before we could fall asleep—and for how long might have we slept? Forever? Who knows?

And now here we are.

My father always said, *"There are no coincidences, only truths which we have yet to notice."*

I close my eyes. My pulse is pounding in my ears. I wipe the sweat from my palms onto my pants. I take a deep breath. I open my eyes.

And I carefully step one foot onto the wooden oar. I can feel the sweltering heat of the fire in the chasm, a painful, instantaneous death.

Legends don't die, I tell myself. I lock eyes with Doran, concentrating on the flames reflecting in their brown pools. I tentatively put one foot in front of the other. Not looking down and just concentrating on Doran surrounded by the black doors, the blue-white light like a halo around his head.

Almost there.

Only another step or so.

So close.

And that's when I slip.

CHAPTER 18

A strong hand wraps around my wrist and forcibly yanks me to the other side of the chasm. I fall into Doran knocking him to the ground. As I get up I am still shaking. "Thanks," I mumble.

"Man, you are really lucky I've been here. I mean, what if you hadn't found me and hadn't invited me along with you?" He gets up and begins to dust his pants off.

"I didn't invite you," I point out.

"That's beside the point. How far would you have gotten without me? You'd either be still standing on the shoreline or asleep in the boat floating in the middle of the lake. Or you'd have gotten eaten by one of those creatures. And you'd for sure have been burnt up to a crisp just now," he grins satisfied.

I step closer to the glowing pedestal. The pedestal is sleek and metallic. The sphere on top glows blue, casting excited shadows on the walls of the cavern. This isn't like the cavern that we traveled through to get here. The walls in here are completely smooth as if someone had painstakingly dug out this room. The effect is a globe-like quality. Each of the five doors is closed and painted black, but now that I'm closer I can see that in careful calligraphy each door is labeled:

Fire   Water   Earth   Metal   Wood

I approach one of the doors, Fire, and almost immediately I can feel the hum of energy emitting from it, a sort of ringing in the air and a strange vibrational sensation that seems to spread throughout my entire body. And I haven't even tried the handle yet.

I tentatively reach out for the handle, but Doran swiftly swats my hand away. "Seriously this time, how do you survive?" he asks with a shake of the head.

"I'm pretty sure I did pretty fine before you came along," I retort. But he has a point. I need to be more careful.

I watch as he licks his fingers then quickly touches the handle, tapping it to see how it reacts. There's a slight sizzling sound. "That's what I suspected. That handle is white-hot."

"How do you think they open then?" We look at each other, then at the glowing sphere. "I think it has something to do with this." I look around the pedestal, but don't see anything. The sphere itself however has caught my attention. Not only does it have an eerie glow, but the blue color inside seems to coalesce and ebb as if it is a living, breathing thing. "This thing kind of reminds me of a crystal ball or something," I say. It reminds me of my trips to the

Underground.

Without much thought—or precaution—I reach out and place my hand firmly over the sphere.

Instantly, I have the sensation that my hand is stuck to the cool glass. It's like the sphere is sucking something from me. Memories and thoughts swirl through my head; similar to my Mindscape except much more rapidly and more like flashes than reliving the experience. Faster and faster until my head feels like it's spinning out of control, about to burst. A brilliant white light replaces the steady blue glow and finally I can pull my hand away without fear that I'll leave my flesh still attached to the glass surface.

"I don't know what the heck that was, but look!" I turn at the sound of Doran's voice and that's when I notice the doors are no longer dark and foreboding, each one has a brilliant white light emitting from behind its frame. "Do you think they're unlocked now?"

"Only one way to find out." I step toward the door labeled Fire and glance at Doran who nods encouragingly.

This time I carefully touch the knob, testing the temperature: cool. I take a deep breath and pull open the first door. A gust of wind comes through the doorway and whips my ponytail, blowing dust into my eyes.

And then I'm propelled forward not of my own accord, my feet shuffling to keep up as I tumble headfirst through the open doorway.

. . .

I'm falling in a kind of nothingness. There is no time and there is no sense of spatiality. It just *is*. I feel light, like my body weighs nothing at all. I can't hear anything; I don't know if Doran followed me through the entrance or if the door shut before he could come through. In this weird dimensional space I find that my thoughts are simple and seem to have slowed down. Everything seems easy and effortless. I know that I am falling, but my body feels stationary. I suppose this is what they meant by Elemental Abyss, because that is definitely an accurate word for this place where there is no light nor dark. There is no *is not* in this place, only *is*.

Thoughts drift in and out of my mind like the boat floating lazily on the lake. Sloan in class, his green eyes scrupulously studying me when I'm not paying attention, instead staring out the window at the reddened landscape. The Metal woman—Bina—watching me as I walk past, carefully analyzing me before calling out to me. My mother sitting at Pronouncement surrounded by her fellow Earths, shoving a balled up fist to her mouth to prevent the shocked sobs as the Black Box goes up in flames: her daughter chose Fire. Tristen sharing a knowing glance with Eoin as I complete the Ritual of Fire. Zora noticing me as I wander past the tattoo vendor, completely unawares that she had already marked me for her next great piece of art. Doran's look of panic as he pulls me from the fiery chasm.

It's as if all of these things—things that I was not aware of while living them—have slowed down specifically to come to my attention, but I'm not sure what it could mean. The effect is similar to hovering outside of your body and watching the events unfold from someone else's point of view.

As the last one tumbles away from me I realize that I'm experiencing the sensation of speeding up. Faster and faster until—

. . .

I really have to stop with these rough landings. There's a thud to my left. Doran gets up and tilts his head side to side, stretching out his neck.

"Well, that was surreal."

"Yeah, that's a good word to describe it."

He comes up next to me and we look around. At first, it doesn't seem much different than the landscape of Xon 9. The dirt and soil upon which we stand is the familiar reddish-brown and the sky is tinged with red. But then if you pause and look—really look—you can see how different it actually is from whence we came.

The temperature is sweltering and the air feels thick and heavy. The sky is tinged with red, but also with black and from where we stand in the distance are ominous black mountains with fiery tops. Smoke swirls out of the tops and diffuses into the air. We studied these in school: volcanoes.

I take off my jacket, shoving it into my messenger bag, but it's not much relief from the heat that seems to press in on me from all sides. I can already see beads of sweat forming on the temples of

Doran's forehead.

"So, where do we begin?" he asks.

I shake my head. "I don't know." I scan the landscape and see the swirls of orangey-red coursing across the surface like fiery rivers, veins running through the skin of wherever it is that we've landed. "We're looking for a stone."

Doran laughs, but it's a hollow sound that's immediately swallowed up in the humidity. "Sure, no problem. Find a stone on the planet that's full of rocks."

"You think this is another planet?"

"What else could it be?" We begin to walk with no real sense of purpose, heading in the direction of the largest volcano off in the distance, the one that is spewing red fire into the blackened sky.

I can feel the heat of the ground through the soles of my boots. We walk for what feels like hours, but I'm not really sure because, like when I initially fell through the door, time somehow seems different in this place. It's as if time as I know it, linear, forward-moving time, somehow no longer exists.

My legs hurt from walking on the uneven surface. The closer we get to the volcano, the more uneven the ground becomes, the mercurial cooled lava mixing with the solid red earth. We pause sharing miserly sips of water from one of the remaining bottles left in my bag. I swallow a nutrient pill and offer one to Doran, but he shakes his head. When I return the bottle to my bag, my hand graces the sack from Bina. Not only do I have to find the stone and bring it back, but I have to destroy it as well in order to release that fragmented piece of my personality, to make myself whole again.

White-gray flakes begin to float down from the sky and land at our feet. I hold out my palm and catch some in my open hand. Soft, sooty. Ash.

"It's raining ash," I say looking at the looming mountain ahead of us. "We have to hurry."

We continue onward toward the very place from which we should probably be running. In a place full of rock, how will we find the singular stone that my mother tossed in? I don't know if it's just a regular stone; I don't even know what color it is. This world is red and obsidian, a dark place.

In Earth Literature we once read a story called *Dante's Inferno*. If I had to imagine an inferno, I think that this would be it. I feel as if I'm trudging through a desert that's been set on fire: the smoke stings my eyes and lungs, the sweltering temperature causes each breath to be painful and my head throbs with dehydration. Ash is in my hair and smeared on my skin, mixing with my own sweat. I've heard the saying *through hell and back* before, some Old Earth sayings stuck with us on Xon 9. I just hope that I can get to the 'and back' part.

"There! Look!" Doran's voice shatters through my thoughts. I follow his finger to where he's pointing. At the base of the volcano, even from here, is what looks like an opening. We're standing on a cooled lava shore, a stream of bright orange-hot lava blocking our path. Doran follows my eyes to the fiery river in front of us. "It's not that wide. If we get a running start, I'm sure that we can jump over it."

"I don't want a repeat of earlier," I say nervously. Death by fire is not my preferred option of demise.

"But it worked, didn't it?" He paces excitedly back and forth. "Here, give me your hand. We'll do it together this time."

"Maybe the stone isn't in there. Maybe it's out here somewhere."

"Why else would there be a doorway into a volcano, Ka? We're in the middle of an abyss, literally. We'd never find it out here if it were just tossed in with all the other rocks in the landscape. It's our best, and most logical, chance to find what you're looking for." He reaches out his hand expectantly. "Besides if this stone is as important as you've said it is, then it would be kept someplace special."

He has a point. I hesitantly place my hand in his. We take a few steps back from the banks of lava flow. "On the count of three," he says and squeezes my hand. We get a running start and head right for the river of fire. "One." Would I ever have survived this journey alone? "Two." Probably not. "Three."

We soar through the air and land solidly on the other side. "See?" Doran grins. "I told you we'd make it." He pulls me along toward the opening at the base of the volcano.

The opening is low and narrow, not much taller than myself, and low enough that Doran has to duck. I'm about to pull my flashlight out of my bag, but as we emerge on the other side of the opening I see that I don't need it. The light from the streams of lava is enough to illuminate our way. Rivers of lava crisscross around us and we follow the narrow pathway that runs along them. I can feel the incline beneath my feet, we're steadily heading upward. The path narrows and we have to walk single file, Doran leading the way.

"What exactly are we looking for again?" Doran asks and his voice is swallowed up by the sound of the rushing, cackling lava.

"A very important looking stone."

"Like that one there?" He's stopped walking and I almost bump into him. I peer over his shoulder. The narrow pathway opens into a small raised area. There's an iron railing around a pedestal, much like the pedestal with the glowing sphere in the Elemental Abyss. On top of this pedestal though, instead of the sphere that opens the doorways, is a shiny, oblong, obsidian stone protected in some sort of glass bubble. My eyes grow wide.

We've found the first stone.

In my excitement I push past Doran and up the rocky path to the raised area which seems to hover and float in space, pools of lava bubbling beneath eagerly in its push to get to the surface. I reach out and press my fingertips to the glass which, despite all the heat, is still cool to the touch just like the blue sphere.

Doran is behind me, paused at the railing. "How do we get it out?"

"I'm not sure. Last time I just put my hand on the sphere and it was like I couldn't let go until it took what it wanted—or needed—from me." I tap the glass carefully. But still nothing happens.

"What exactly did you say these stones were for?" Doran asks. And I realize that I never did explain to him what they're for, why I need them, or why it's so important.

"It's kind of hard to explain, but the basicness of it is that in order to protect me as a child my mother was told to throw five stones into the Elemental Abyss. The stones were given to her by a Metal woman named Bina and within each stone is a fragment of my true personality." Even as I tell the story I know how unbelievable it all must sound, but when I turn and lock eyes with Doran, there is no doubt or ridicule looking back at me.

He gives me a half-grin. "Makes sense. Personally, I never would have pegged you for a Fire." He doesn't ask why I need protecting, nor does he ask why my personality needed to be fragmented.

I realize I was very quick to judge Doran. I assumed he was a trouble-maker, some sort of delinquent looking for a way to challenge authority by becoming a Fire. But I don't think I could have been more wrong. Doran is the way he is because it displaces his own hurt to act out at others, but Doran thrives in adventure and escape, constantly searching for ways to ignore the causes of his own pain. Doran isn't a trouble-maker; he is trustworthy, brave, and selfless. If I hadn't found him in such a vulnerable position, I never would have learned these things about him and I surely never would have made it this far.

"Thank you." The words tumble out before I can stop them. Doran stops leaning on the railing and approaches the pedestal.

"Now, don't go getting all girly and emotional on me," he smiles. "We're not done yet. We have to figure out how to get this stone, and then we need to figure out how to get out of here and back home." He pauses before saying the word home. Where is home for Doran? He inspects the glass bubble, looking beneath it, and tapping the glass gently. "How exactly did the sphere that opened the doors work?"

I close my eyes recalling the odd sensations. "Well, when I put my hand on it, it felt like it was alive and was grabbing me so that I couldn't get away. Then it seemed like it was going through my head, sorting through my memories. And then all of a sudden it just let me go and the doors were unlocked."

"Strange." He peers at me curiously then turns his attention back to the enclosed obsidian stone. "Maybe this works similarly. But instead of it sucking out your memories like the sphere, maybe you have to consciously think of something. Like putting the memories in. Here." He takes my hand and places it carefully over the glass. "You said each stone is a fragmented part of your personality, right?" I nod. "Then close your eyes and think of what it means to have Fire. Why do you need it back? What does it feel like it? Why does it matter?"

I obey and close my eyes. Fire. Fire frightens me. I think that's why I chose it in the first place, not only was it so different from Water, but it scared me too. Fire is passion and lust. Li. It's not thinking something through before doing it. It's a knee-jerk reaction. Doran. But Fire is also kindness and fierce loyalty, like Rhian. All of us have Fire coursing through our veins, but it scares me when Fire is out of control, when it's used to dominate and manipulate. Like

Tristen. Fire is a short fuse, quick to temper.

"It's working," Doran whispers and I can feel the glass somehow softening beneath my fingers. "Keep thinking. Why do you need it back? Why does it matter?"

My mother appears in my mind, the frightened look in her eyes as I played in the living room oblivious to who I was or what it meant. Then my mind takes me to Bina and her words about the legend of the Impossible Girl and how the Imminent Darkness has seeped into our society and deprived the people of their true selves, forcing them to choose and categorize themselves, limiting their full potential to thrive. That's why it matters: to me and to everyone. We all have Fire within us. We can be passionate and loyal, but we can also be angry and manipulative. Why then must we choose only one if we are truly all of these things? That is why it matters.

I can feel the glass softening to liquid beneath my palm. I need it back because this is who I am, who I was meant to be. I am passion. I am anger. I am dark, but I am light. I am aggressive and manipulative, but I am also loyal and kind. I need it because it is me. I am Fire.

There's an itch and a burn in my veins. *Yes, yes. You are Fire.*

Finally, fine particles of sand shift in my palm, trickling through my spread fingers, and I open my eyes.

"You did it!" Doran cheers. I carefully pull the smooth obsidian stone from the pile of sand which only moments before was the glass orb.

Suddenly, there's an angry rumble and the ground beneath

our feet shakes menacingly. I stick the stone into my bag, burying it deep in the folds of my jacket. Rocks begin to tumble from above us. We throw our arms over our heads and run back down the narrow pathway which begins to crumble away behind us.

I pound down the path as the walls of the volcano shake around us. The rivers of lava seem to jump and splash beside us. The air is oppressive and a rumbling, sizzling sound buzzes in my ears. We dash back through the opening at the base of the volcano and thick swirls of ash greet us outside.

"It's erupting!" I shout.

"Maybe we made it angry by taking the stone!" Doran shouts back. We run toward the lava river. He grabs my hand and without counting or thinking, we leap over it landing roughly on the other side.

The sky lights up with white lightening and there's a loud crash. The ash is coming down faster now making it almost impossible to see. It sticks to my eyelashes and to my cheeks. We run, still holding hands, stumbling over the cooled lava and jumping over the smaller streams of lava that crisscross the landscape. The ground shakes beneath our feet and the heat that permeates the soles of my boots is almost painful. We continue to blindly run along.

When we arrived it seemed as if we had simply fallen out of the sky. How then will we get back? Is there a doorway on this side as well? There has to be. Doors are two-way. Whoever heard of a one-way door? I hope I am right.

My head throbs, my legs ache, and my lungs burn. Rocks

begin to pelt at us from the sky. Lightening streaks across the horizon of the blackened blood-red sky. I trip on a misshapen piece of cooled lava, sending me sprawling forward.

I use my hands to break my fall. Doran doubles back, helping me up. I check to make sure that the stone is still wrapped safely in my bag. I'm dirty and my pants are torn. My hands and knee are bleeding and my hair is matted and covered in ash. I think of how when we first arrived I'd thought we were in an inferno and how now with the angry volcano spewing ash and fire into dark sky, it seems even more like we are running through a nightmare.

"There!" Doran coughs and I see it. A swirling black mass hovering enigmatically above us. We stop beneath it, but it's too high to reach it. I'm so hot and so tired. I just want to sit, only for a minute. But there's no time. "Here, help me stack some rocks so we can reach the opening." We look for loose stones and boulders, anything that we can move and stand on to better reach the portal.

There's a crashing and a deafening roar. I look back toward the volcano and it's as if the entire top has just blown off. Fiery orange lava overflows from its top, oozing down the sides. Thicker rocks begin to pelt down from the sky hitting my shoulders, arms, and head.

"Here!" Doran yells over the rush of noise. He pushes me toward the pile of stones and I stand shakily on top. The portal is above me. A black and golden swirl of time and space, a gateway back to the Elemental Abyss, the only way back home. If I stretch my fingers I can just barely reach. Last time it almost seemed to suck me up and in. I can only hope that the trip back works in the same way. "Hurry!" Doran cries.

"What about you?" I say looking down at him. His hand rests on the small of my back ready to help push me into the portal if need be.

But he shakes his head. "Don't worry about me, Ka. You have to go." My eyes grow wide as I notice the rush of lava which seems to be approaching, an angry flood of fire heading right toward us.

"I can't leave you, Doran. Not now." I pull him up onto the pile of stones with me. "Together!" I yell over the crashes of thunder and angry roar of the lava flow. He clasps his hand with mine and together we reach out toward the portal. Doran is taller than me and his fingers reach easily. There's an irresistible pull upward and I feel the pile of stones slip out from beneath me as the hot lava kisses the toes of my boots.

Doran's fingers are tight around mine as we're pulled into the portal and back into the nothingness. Floating through the empty space in between the world of Fire and the constructed world that is the Elemental Abyss.

Again there is no passage of time. But there's the same sense of having an out of body experience. Except this time it's not people that I know. I see Tristen studying Doran from the doorway of a classroom, her hazel eyes dark and calculating. I see a woman with similar features to Doran, the wide nose and deep chocolate-colored eyes, watching him with concern, her hands wringing nervously, and

213

the silvery metallic threads on the side of her face reflecting in the light.

And then I see a man who looks like a much older Doran, but with the familiar silvery green scales on the side of his face. The man is smiling and laughing, while playing with a smaller, much younger Doran. The Metal woman looks on smiling. The scene then changes quickly and I'm seeing an older Doran, maybe twelve or thirteen. The man from before is no longer laughing and smiling, anger creases his face and his eyes are cloudy. He is yelling and gesticulating wildly. And then it happens.

A slap to the face.

The look of shock and hurt on Doran's young face. And then. Anger. The look of Fire in his eyes.

Time flashes forward and I'm seeing a much older Doran with a tired-looking woman beside him. The Metal woman, his mother. I recognize the familiar trailers around them: the Underground. His father is not there. His mother watches anxiously as Doran serves something in bottles and items wrapped in brown paper to the customers who approach their small shop. I can see the worry etched on her face and the hope too, that there is something better for her son out there somewhere. Something better than what she's been able to give him.

As we continue to hurtle through the emptiness I wonder if Doran has seen my life much as I've seen his. Does he know who I am now and why I'm here? Does he know my secrets as much as I now know his?

Secrets may push people apart, like with Sloan or my mother, they can create a void, a separation between the two people, pushing them farther and farther apart until the chasm is so wide that it becomes virtually impossible to cross.

But secrets too, can create closeness. There's a sort of peace in knowing that someone else has secrets to hide and there's a kind of unspoken comradery that only comes from knowing the deepest, innermost parts of another person.

I won't share Doran's secrets or the things that I've seen. And I can only hope that if he's seen the same as I have, that he will choose to not share mine.

Secrets are powerful. They have the ability to both divide and unite.

The familiar sensation of time speeding up washes over me and even though I can't see Doran in the nothingness I can still feel his hand solid in mine as we hurtle together toward the other side, back toward the Elemental Abyss, and back toward Xon 9. Both now marked by the things we've experienced and seen together, an unspeakable bond now forged between us, rendering us both changed forever. Life can never seem the same again. I feel like I've just been scratching at the surface this entire time and the real experience, actual life, is really much, much deeper.

This time I can see a light beckoning us through the void, pulling us like magnets toward it faster and faster.

The light grows brighter and brighter, until it is so bright that it's almost blinding. It is like a living, breathing thing that is swallowing us both whole.

Faster and faster.

Brighter and brighter.

Eventually it flings us up and tumbling through the opening, back to the Elemental Abyss. We hit the ground with a roll and the door slams shut behind us.

Chapter 19

Everything hurts. My head is spinning, my hands are scraped, and my knee is bleeding.

"Is it just me, or was the return trip significantly worse?" Doran coughs, slowly getting to his feet.

I groan as I stand up. "Definitely way worse." The blue sphere glows dimly casting eerie shadows. All the doors are black and ominous again, including Fire. One stone at a time, one fragmented part of my identity at a time. Pieces of the puzzle that is my life.

Doran cautiously approaches the chasm. The oar is no longer there providing a makeshift bridge, it probably dropped into the fiery depths.

"How will we get across?" I'm so tired; the trip into the Fire portal was almost more than I can stand. And we cut it a little close, what with the eruption of old Mount Vesuvius or whatever it was.

"Very carefully?" he suggests. "It's too wide to jump, not like the lava river." He inspects it further. "Do you have anything to help us get across?"

"Don't you think I would have mentioned it the last time?"

"What kind of packer are you?"

I sigh. "Apparently not a very good one. I didn't think I'd be leaping across fiery chasms and rowing through enchanted lakes."

"Maybe," his face lights up with an idea, "the chasm has a protector like the lake."

"You mean you think that there's some sort of hideous Fire monster inside the chasm?" I reply dubiously.

"Seriously, after the things we've experienced today, would it really surprise you?"

"Where was it before? We got across fine with the oar."

"Fine?" He raises an eyebrow.

"Well, more or less. So where was it then? How come it didn't come up and attack us?"

"Remember, the creature in the lake didn't attack us, you pointed it out yourself," Doran points out. He's right. I had said that the creature had helped us; it had shaken the boat just as we were falling asleep to the waterfall's enchanting lullaby.

"So," I say finally catching on, "maybe the creatures only appear if we need help."

"I'd say we could use some help about now."

"The question is how do we summon it? We didn't call for the Water creature; it saw what was happening and came to us." I frown.

"Should we try and jump across?" Oh, the impulsiveness of a Fire.

"No!" I exclaim. "That's a horrible idea. And what happens if we miss?"

"Maybe the creature of the chasm will rescue us."

"And if it doesn't? Are you okay with burning up to a crisp?"

"Good point." Doran falls silent as he thinks about what to do next. And then I remember something very important: I am Fire.

We are Fire.

"We've both participated in the Ritual of Fire. And we've both been injected right? With that serum that induces the Transitional Phase?" Doran nods as if to say *So?* Clearly not following my line of thinking. "Well, if we're both Fire then essentially we're summoning our own essence."

I see the shift in his eyes, from confusion to understanding. "You're right. We're basically calling on our own Element for help. But how can we tell it who we are and why we need its help?"

I pace back and forth beside the chasm as I think about the situation. We are Fire. Fire is now coursing through our veins. Fire is in our blood. "That's it! We need to show it that Fire is in our blood!"

Doran digs in his pocket and pulls out a small pocket knife. He kneels beside the chasm and before I can stop him, he slices quickly and cleanly through his own skin. I watch wide-eyed as several drops of blood fall into the chasm with a sizzling sound.

"Creatures of Fire, we call on you as your brethren. We need your help." He looks over at me and I shrug. It sounds as good as anything. He wipes the blade on his pants and puts it back in his pocket.

At first nothing happens and I'm worried that I just let Doran slice himself for no reason. But then a dark plume of smoke comes rushing out of the chasm. It swirls and ebbs, causing Doran to stumble back in surprise, bumping into me. I'm thankful for the unexpected protection and peer cautiously over Doran's shoulder, gripping his arm tightly.

We watch as the smoke contorts and distorts until it forms a sort of face and I'm reminded of when Tristen made an announcement through the Fire. I'm now realizing that the Elements are much more complex than I'd initially realized; they can be manipulated and bent to our will. We are the Elements. The Elements are us.

Glowing orange eyes look back at us.

"Some help here," Doran hisses backing into me as the smoke comes toward us as if it's inspecting us.

"Um, uh. Hello. We, uh, we were wondering if you could help us cross the chasm," I stammer nervously.

The smoke continues to swirl, orange eyes discerning. Then suddenly it pulls back from us, hovering over the chasm, and I think at first that it didn't work, that Doran cut into his own flesh in vain. But then carefully the smoke shifts and adjusts itself, continuing to hover over the chasm until it makes a sort of path, a bridge over the gorge.

"It made a bridge for us," Doran says in disbelief.

I feel a sense of urgency. Fire is temperamental; it could change its mind at any moment. I grab Doran's hand and drag him toward the bridge. I step a foot tentatively onto it, and even though my mind knows that smoke is not solid, merely a vapor, the bridge feels substantial beneath my sole.

I don't wait to see if it will last. I yank Doran on and over the bridge, running quickly across and just as Doran reaches the other side we turn and watch as the bridge dissolves, taking the shape of the intimidating face once more. Its orange eyes burn bright. It blinks twice then twists into grotesque swirls before disappearing back into the chasm.

We don't have time to process what we've just seen; we hurry down the tunnel and back in the direction of where we'd left the rowboat. It's still there staked to the ground, floating restlessly in the calm waters behind the waterfall.

The familiar rush fills my ears, a cacophony of drums that virtually drowns out everything else. I climb into the boat and Doran untangles the tether, wrapping it around his arm before climbing into the boat as well.

We don't have any oars now, so we're at the mercy of the waterfall's currents. Doran uses his hands to guide us along the rocky ledge before giving us a good shove away and around to the other side of the waterfall.

I can see the shoreline of the manmade beach when we

emerge from behind the waterfall. The current pushes the boat toward the middle of the lake, turning the boat this way and that before we practically come to a stand-still.

The soothing song of the waterfall makes my eyes grow heavy and the weight of our adventure presses in from all sides.

I feel a sharp pinch. "Ow!"

"No!" Doran hisses. "You have to stay awake!"

"But I'm so tired," I whine.

Doran's face sinks. "I know. Me too." He gives himself another pinch, but his eyes are slowly sliding closed. My head begins to lull toward my chin and I feel myself sliding off the wooden bench and onto the bottom of the boat. Yawning, I pinch my forearm, but it doesn't have any effect.

The world grows fuzzier and fuzzier.

But we can't fall asleep, I think. I hear Doran slide to the bottom of the boat with a thud as his head softly hits the edge of the bench.

With each cognizant thought I can feel the dream world seeping slowly in and coalescing with reality. I fall gently forward, resting my cheek against Doran's chest. His breath is slow and even. My eyes close.

Where is the Water creature? Why aren't they coming to help us?

What if we never wake up?

. . .

"Ka."

The voice is soft and gentle. Familiar.

"Ka, wake up."

I reluctantly open my eyes. But I'm not awake. At least not in the real world.

I'm curled up on my side, in the fetal position. I feel the grainy sensation of sand beneath me. I'm wearing the same clothes as I am in actuality, but I'm soaking wet and can feel my hair dripping streams of water down the back of my neck and over the raw skin of my Elemental Star tattoo.

I recognize the voice, but I'm not sure where it's coming from. I sit up slowly. My head is throbbing.

I'm sitting on the shore, a vast gray-green ocean is in front of me. Obviously, not something that exists anywhere on Xon 9. There's a light breeze and I can taste the salty air on my lips. I look around for Doran, but he's not there.

I'm alone.

There's a bright golden orb in the sky and it makes the ocean sparkle and glisten. That's when I notice the brown head bobbing in the water. I crawl to the waters' edge until I'm kneeling in the surf and the head comes closer until it's in focus, but still several feet away.

It's Sloan.

"What am I doing here?" I ask.

He doesn't swim any closer. "This is your safe place. It's where you go when you're frightened or nervous, anytime that you need comfort." I'm reminded of the Box's recommendation that I choose Water. Perhaps I do find comfort here.

"Where's Doran?"

Sloan shrugs. "In his own place of comfort. That's what the waterfall does. It's an ancient Water enchantment. It lures you to sleep and takes you to a place where you won't want to leave." He swims on his back, floating from side to side as he talks. "You could be here indefinitely, never waking up. Essentially dying in that rowboat. And no one would ever know."

"You'd like that," I cringe even as the words tumble out.

He stops swimming and peers at me, tilting his head to the side quizzically. "You dying? Surely not." His voice sounds hurt.

"No," I correct. "Me never leaving here."

He laughs and it sounds different than it does at home; it has a tinkling ringing sound like the most beautiful of bells. Everything seems more beautiful here. Softer, gentler.

"Yes, I suppose I'd like that. But it can't happen. I woke you up so I could tell you how to break the enchantment."

I sigh. "But what if I don't want it broken? I like it here. Everything seems…"

"Fascinating?"

"Yes, fascinating," I agree.

"That's because that is exactly what this is: a fantasy, a figment of your imagination."

"Oh."

He laughs again. "Don't sound so sad."

"I thought you said you couldn't help me? That I had to do all of this on my own."

"I did. And you do."

"Then how are you here right now?"

"I'm not."

"You're not?"

"That's why I can't come any closer. I'm part of the fantasy, a conjectured part of your imagination. If I came any closer you may enjoy the fantasy world too much and not wake up in the real world."

"You wish," I mumble.

"And I'd very much like for you to wake up in the real world," he adds. There's a splash of water and even from the distance between us I can see those piercing green eyes. Persuading, assuring.

I sigh. "What do I have to do?"

. . .

It's not going to be pleasant. Sloan's directions were very explicit. In order to end the fantasy and wake up I need to die. Obviously, I wouldn't die in the real world, only in the imaginary one. But still. Once I end the fantasy and wake up back in the row boat, Sloan said the creatures in the lake will have pushed us safely to the shoreline. Then I just have to drag Doran as far from the sounds of the waterfall as possible. Once he can longer hear the song of the enchantment he'll wake up.

Dying isn't easy. Especially when your instincts are to survive; to live. But Sloan assured me it was the only way. He hasn't lied to me yet; maybe that's why I brought his letter along with me even though it really served no purpose, a reminder of what is true. Sloan is true and he's vowed to protect me. I don't know to who or when, or even how. I just know that it's so, just as I know that even in this fantasy world his words ring true.

And so after Sloan has disappeared I walk slowly deeper into the water. I hold my breath and duck my head underneath. Even as my lungs burn for air; I don't dare break the surface. I float, watching the golden orb cast rays of light across the water's surface. Black dots appear in front of me and I know that it's close. My mouth slowly slides open and my lungs begin to fill with water. I begin to sink.

Down. Away from the golden light.

Down and down.

Down into the ocean's depths.

I wake up coughing and sputtering.

I'm perfectly dry.

I'm in the rowboat and the boat is pushed onto the shoreline just as Sloan said it would be. Doran is fast asleep, snoring softly in the bottom of the boat. I climb out of the boat and then lean over the edge, leaning in to wrap my arms beneath his armpits and clasp my hands around his chest. I unceremoniously drag him up and over the edge of the boat and to the ground. His legs are splayed out in front of him. He does not wake.

This is going to be a lot of work. Doran is several inches taller than me and fairly thick in size. I have to drag him down the tunnel and back into the cavern, away from the sound of the waterfall.

I take a deep breath and begin the slow process of dragging Doran down the tunnel, but I quickly realize that hunched over walking backward isn't going to work. My back is aching on top of everything else. He's too big to toss over my shoulder, and besides his body is deadweight at this point.

And that's when I have another idea. I jog back to the boat and unknot the rope that acted as a tether. I wrap it underneath his armpits and around his chest, knotting it securely and giving it a tug for good measure. Then I unravel the rope and wrap the other end around my waist. It isn't going to be easy, but at least this way I can walk forward instead of backward.

I trudge slowly down the tunnel and toward the cavern, just concentrating on putting one foot in front of the other. Doran's sneakers leave two parallel lines in the dust and dirt as I walk. I round the bend toward the cavern.

The waterfall is now a soft hum in the distance, but Doran still doesn't wake. I'm so tired that I feel like I could collapse right here in this very spot. But I push onward. Doran helped me successfully retrieve the first stone, the least I could do is drag him to safety.

As I plod on, I wonder what Doran's place of comfort could be. Is it somewhere with his parents? Probably not, considering what

I saw traveling in the Abyss. I wonder what happened to Doran's father. Did he become one of those Water creatures? Or is there something else that happens to Unbalanced Elementals? It isn't common for Elementals to be Unbalanced, besides Metal, of course. And that's because Metal is extremely invasive and hard to control. That's why they stay in the Underground; if they didn't who knows what could happen. What havoc they would inflict on our society.

According to Bina, the Imminent Darkness is already taking care of that. But who-or what—is the Imminent Darkness? Is it a group of Unbalanced Metals—or something else? And worse, what are their reasons for doing it?

I stumble forward tripping over my own feet, catching myself with my already badly scraped hands. I physically can't go on anymore. I rest on my knees, head bowed. We're so close to the entrance to the cavern, but I just can't do it by myself any longer. I swipe angrily at the frustrated tears that streak my dirty face.

"Why the long face?" Doran groans, his voice hoarse.

I turn and grin through my tears. "When did you wake up?"

"Sometime around when you fell. That was quite the jostle," he rubs the side of his head. "What the hell was that?"

"The enchantment."

"That's one hell of an enchantment. I was in the best place…my parents were there…and…" He shakes his head. "Nevermind. How did you wake up?"

"A friend told me how to break the enchantment."

"A friend?" he raises an eyebrow.

"It's complicated. But the important thing is we're here now, right? And we're both awake and going home."

He laughs bitterly. "Home. You may be going home. But that's not where I'm going." His face flashes with sadness. "At least not yet."

"Then come with me," I say helping him to untie the rope around his chest.

"What about Tristen?" he asks.

"I don't know. I have other friends still at Fire too. Li and Rhian. But we can't go back there. It's dangerous." I explain, recalling Doran's words about my packing skills and shoving the rope inside my messenger bag in case we need it later.

"We can't just leave them there with Tristen. You've seen what she does and no one seems to stop her. Who knows what she's capable of?" He pauses. "Or what she's done since we've been gone."

I nod slowly and think of Everly. He's right. We can't just leave them all there. I can't leave my friends behind, especially after all the things they've done for me.

"Okay, so we go back to Fire. But how do we get there?" I ask. "It's not like there's a teleportation portal hanging out in the mountains somewhere. We're far away from civilization."

He nods, helping me slowly to my feet. "Well, we've gotten help from both Water and Fire."

"Who are you suggesting we get help from? There's no time travel Elemental."

"Isn't there? I really am concerned about the education you've received, Ka." I give him a playful shove. "Didn't you say your mother is an Earth?" I nod. "Well, Earth isn't just the ground we walk on. It's everything. It's where we came from, like the planet. Earth is one of the most powerful Elementals for that very reason: Earth is all encompassing. It's the dirt and the sky, the sun and the moon. It's the trees—Wood—and the minerals in the soil—Metal— the magma beneath the surface—Fire—not to mention Earth was mostly covered by oceans—which is Water—and of course Earth includes Earth itself, which just so happens to include one of my favorite natural occurrences, the wind."

"And how do you suppose we harness the power of the wind to get back home?" I question.

"Well, it worked the other two times back in the abyss. And it seemed rather simple. I say all we have to do is ask."

Chapter 20

We make our way back to where I originally landed just outside the cave's opening. The wind whips at my ponytail as I stare at the twinkling lights off in the distance that are my colony. The two moons are high in the sky, but it feels like days have passed since I first entered the cave alone. Is it possible that it's only the same night? Stars shine dimly in the pink sky.

"Are you ready?" Doran asks.

I stick my hand in my messenger bag, feeling around for the smooth obsidian stone and once my fingers brush against it I nod.

"So how do we summon the wind? The Water creature showed up when we needed it and the smoke creature came when it was summoned with the blood of Fire. How do we conjure Earth?"

Doran considers this for a moment. Then he picks up a stray rock and crouches into the dirt. "Let's right her a note," he suggests.

I crouch down beside him. Everything in my entire body hurts and I feel filthy. My hair is matted with sweat and ash, my knee and palms are scratched and bloodied, and my face is streaked with dirt. I've never wanted to go home—actual home, not back to Fire—more in my entire life.

"How do you know it's a *her*?" I ask.

He shrugs. "Haven't you ever heard of Mother Earth?" I shake my head, besides the pun of my own mother being an Earth, I have not.

He thinks for a minute and then carefully uses the stone to craft a message in the red dirt.

Dearest Earth,

We request the honor of your help. Ka and I, Doran, wish to return home.

If you could be ever so kind as to assist us.

Sincerely,

D & K

I'm dubious. "Do you really think that is going to work?"

"After the things I've experienced today, I'd say anything is possible," he replies.

And so we wait. We sit side by side staring out into the distance, at the rocky slopes of Xon 9's mountains and the vast uninhabited land before us. It doesn't make sense, I find myself thinking. Bina is right. Only 3,000 people came from Earth all those years ago, but then why hasn't the population grown and expanded?

Earth was huge, billions of people huge, and in comparison

the population of Xon 9 is barely a blip on the proverbial radar. I've always thought of Xon 9 as a small planet, limited mostly to my own colony, descendants of the original settlers from Earth. But looking out at the world from this vantage point, it seems much larger than I realized. Not to mention, what could be on the other side of these mountains? Or what about the Elemental Abyss—is that a planet too? Is Xon 9 actually some sort of planet within a planet? Have we not grown as a society because of this so-called Imminent Darkness of which Bina spoke? The possibilities make my head throb in protest.

"Look!" Doran whispers. The wind has picked up and the end of my ponytail stings my cheeks as it whips around. Specks of dirt kick up and float away. My t-shirt makes a snapping sound as it flaps wildly against my skin. A soft hum has escalated to a howling roar. We watch as the message in the dirt is quickly smeared away by the wind, flecks of dirt being picked up angrily and obscuring the colony lights, blotting out the sky.

As we stand together unsure about what exactly is happening, I feel the wind begin to push and pull gently, first at my arms and then at my legs, like a mother prodding along her child. It begins to swirl. I watch fascinated as the wind begins to form a cyclone around us, wrapping us tightly in its center.

I never feel my feet leave the ground. In fact, I'm not sure they ever did, but I don't know how else to describe the sensation. It's as if we're being carried away, snuggled inside protective arms. Doran's eyes are wide in surprise and a smile plays at the corners of his lips. I've never felt anything like it before, cocooned within the wind.

It doesn't last long before the wind dies down ebbing into a gentle breeze. As it does the dirt around us begins to settle and for the first time since the wind kicked up in the mountains I can see again.

Only we're no longer in the mountains. The lights of Xon 9 shimmer in the distance; we're just outside the colony Perimeter. Maybe it's because I'm so tired, or maybe it's because I'm starting to lose a little bit of my mind, but I begin to laugh. And before long, Doran joins me in deep bellyful laughter. We join hands, swinging each other around, laughing like children. Then we turn toward the mountains, our backs to the colony, and call out: "Thank you!" as we wave good-bye to the retreating wind.

. . .

In order for the cloaking cuff to work on both of us, it makes sense to hold hands. So Doran grasps my hand as we near the colony and I press the button. Before re-entering inside the Perimeter, we discussed our plan. I wanted to find Bina and Doran needed to go home, even though I got the sense that he didn't necessarily want to. Neither of us wanted to go back to Fire. At least not yet.

We walk silently toward the Underground turning down the now familiar alleyway. Most of the vendors are closed, so it must be pretty late. Or really early depending on how you look at it.

I press the button to uncloak us now that we're in the Underground. Here, no one cares about our presence. We're just one of many people who wander into the Black Bazaar.

I pause.

Something's not right. I count the trailers from the entrance and re-count it a second time. One of the trailers is quite damaged. The metal grate is bent and dented like someone banged on it with the intent to cause damage. The door hangs by a hinge and the glass light above the door is broken shards of glass.

The trailer belongs to Bina.

Drawn as if by some unstoppable force, glass crunching beneath my boots, I approach the trailer running my fingers over the damaged metal. The first time I saw Bina, she leaned right out this window and called to me. That seems like forever ago, but I now know how integral a role Bina truly played in my life.

"Bina," Doran whispers. I forget that Doran grew up in the Underground. He probably knew Bina, could have been her neighbor or her friend.

"It happened earlier tonight." A voice says from behind us. Tears sting my eyes as I turn and see Zora standing beside Doran. I'm startled by a sudden realization; pieces of a puzzle falling into place. Zora's wild curly hair and long, lithe stature is a perfect match to Doran's. Although her skin is lighter than his, their eyes have the same Fire behind them. Why hadn't I seen it before?

"You know each other?" I ask, momentarily forgetting the crime that lay before me, looking from Zora to Doran and back again.

"You know each other?" Doran asks looking from Zora to me and back again.

"You know each other?" Zora asks looking from Doran to me and back again.

"We're in Fire together," Doran explains at the same time that Zora says, "He's my kid brother," which is also at the same time that I say, "She gave me my tattoo."

We chuckle awkwardly at the realization before quickly turning somber at whatever events had taken place earlier this night.

"Come with me. It's not safe to be out like this," Zora slings an arm over Doran's shoulder and I follow them past the tattoo vendor and down the cobblestone street. Near the end of the street, almost to the bar where I'd last seen Sloan—well, seen him in actual reality—we turn to a small trailer, somewhat pushed back from the rest. There's a stand of handmade trinkets beneath an awning.

Zora leads us in and shuts the door behind me. "Where's mom?" Doran asks immediately.

"*Shhh*, you knucklehead. She's asleep!" Zora plops down onto a worn-out yellow couch. Doran disappears into the kitchen. I stand, unsure what to do with myself, my feet seeming to sink into the pea green plush carpet. "Here, sit." Zora orders sliding some magazines to the floor to make room for me on the couch.

"What happened?"

"I don't know exactly, but earlier tonight some people came. They're around sometimes, in the Underground, people in thick hooded cloaks." *Sloan,* I think immediately. Like the night I followed him and the other Water to the University Complex before Pronouncement. I push the thought quickly aside. I don't think Sloan could be so cruel. "They came and took Bina. But not before they damaged her home." Zora scowls and when she does I can see even more the family resemblance to Doran.

Doran returns from the kitchen and hands me a glass of water before easing himself into a torn leather armchair, stuffing spilling out onto the thick carpet. "So, where'd they take her?"

Zora shrugs. "No idea." She turns to me, not accusingly, but curiously. "You went and saw Bina yesterday. Did she seem worried or concerned about anything?"

"Yesterday?" So it's the same night that we left. I could have sworn that we were gone for half a day or more. But it's only been a little while. Doran and I exchange confused glances. I shake my head. "No. I mean we talked, but she didn't seem worried or anxious." Or did she? I try to recall her body language when she brought up the Imminent Darkness, but I'm too tired to remember.

"Who are the hooded figures?" Doran asks, his voice sleepy.

"Don't know that either," Zora frowns. "People talk of course. Some say they're some sort of secret society, others say that they're a kind of citizen created law enforcement. No one knows for sure."

"And no one tried to stop them?" I ask. "From taking Bina away?" Doran begins to snore softly from the armchair. With Tristen lurking around Fire and then our adventure tonight, I can't imagine

Doran's slept very soundly lately.

Zora shakes her head. "The one thing we do know, is not to get in their way. They have no qualms about using force, as evidenced by what they did to Bina's house." Her face softens. "Hey, you look beat, Girl. Maybe you should get some shut-eye too."

As soon as she says it a huge yawn escapes before I can stop it. She tosses me a large crocheted blanket before she disappears down the hallway. This is as close to home as I've felt since I left my own and before I can help it my eyes are sliding closed for the third time in this seemingly never-ending night. But this time there are no sea creatures, nor fantastical enchantments. Exhaustion washes over me and I sleep soundly, dreamlessly.

. . .

The next morning I decide that I need to find Sloan. Doran stays behind. Going back to the University Complex isn't an option right now. Not as much time has passed as I previously believed which could mean there's a chance that our absence has gone unnoticed. Once again, I need answers, and the only person they seem to be able to come from is Sloan. Rhian and Li are going to have to cover for me just a little bit longer.

Before leaving Zora hugged me tightly. "I haven't seen him smile in so long, and when he pronounced Fire, I feared I'd never see him smile again. Or see him at all for that matter. After our father…nevermind. I don't know what you did, just thank you."

Now as I walk down the cobblestone street, I have a sinking suspicion that Doran will not be returning with me to the University Complex. What will happen to him then? He's already been injected and began the Transitional Phase. Yet, he already comes from the Underground, the broken pieces of the perfectly structured visage of Xon 9. Would it matter if he stayed?

I walk past the bar which is now closed, like most of the other vendors. This early in the morning pretty much nothing in the Black Bazaar is open for business. I keep walking down to the steps at the end of the alleyway, until I reach the spot where I angrily shoved the letter back at Sloan. It's still in my messenger bag, tucked carefully inside its envelope, nestled beside the Fire stone. I've no idea how to destroy the stone; and now that Bina's gone I can no longer receive her help. All I have now is the small burlap bag of seemingly random items she gave me when I saw her for the last time.

I pause as I notice Sloan sitting on the rocky ledge as if he's been waiting for me. He doesn't turn, but stares out into the distance. Zora said the hooded figures came and took Bina, but I just can't imagine that Sloan could be capable of something so cruel. So far he's tried to protect me and guide me, at times even saving me from almost certain demise. Why then, would he belong to a group that kidnaps people and possibly harms them?

Before announcing my presence, I take in the essence that is Sloan. The brown hair curling in the wind, the tall slightly lithe, slightly muscular build. He's leaning back on his hands with his legs dangling over the side of the ledge. The side of his face that is toward me has the delicate traces of scales, the greenish silver reflecting in the early morning light.

"I know you're there, Ka." He doesn't turn around to look at me. His words also don't really surprise me. Of course he knows I'm standing here. He always seems to know exactly where I am and how to find me.

I silently make my way to the ledge and sit down next to him. "You should be at the University Complex," he chastises.

"And you should be helping me retrieve the stones from the Elemental Abyss," I reply. He turns then, a small smile hinting at the corner of his lips, but says nothing. "Why did they take Bina?" I ask after a long pause.

He sighs. "They know that she helped you."

I'm shocked. Am I somehow responsible for Bina's disappearance? "But how? How do they know?"

"I told you, trust no one."

"That's ridiculous," I respond angrily. "The only person who saw me go to Bina's is Zora."

He shakes his head. "Not Zora. Someone else." I think back to the night of my tattoo. There were two other men in the tattoo shop. Maybe it was one of them.

"What will they do to her?" I ask thinking that if the hooded figures are anything like Tristen, Bina probably won't last very long. She may be fierce, but she is older and more fragile.

He shrugs. "Hard to say."

"Will they kill her?" I ask not really wanting to know the answer.

His green eyes are piercing. "She's not much help to them dead. So I'd venture to say no."

There's no way that Sloan is part of the society of the hooded figures. Something isn't adding up. "I saw you," I blurt out. "One night, before Pronouncement, you were wearing one of the hooded cloaks. You were coming out of the Underground with another person. I followed you back to the University Complex."

This time he actually smiles. "I know."

Of course he does. I may not have had a cloaking device, but I thought that I'd done a pretty good job of concealing myself. But I don't ask him how he knew I was following him. Instead, I ask: "Are you one of them?"

His eyes sparkle and he actually chuckles. "Of course not."

"You're not?" I know deep down that his words are true, but in my head it still doesn't add up. *Your head or your heart, Kata?*

He tilts his head curiously. "You really think that little of me?"

I feel my cheeks flush as I shake my head. "Zora said that they enforce the law."

"Depends on which law you're following," he scoffs.

I pick up a stone and drag it back and forth in the loose dirt beside me. After another long silence I ask, "Who are they?"

He sighs, leaning back onto his forearm. "They're the Imminent Darkness."

"That's the Imminent Darkness?" I say dubiously. "A bunch of hooded figures?"

He laughs. "Well, not exactly. They're the physical representation of the Imminent Darkness. The thing is no one knows just what the Imminent Darkness is; that's what I've been trying to find out. I'm not part of the Imminent Darkness, well, not really." He looks up at me and smiles. "It seemed the best way to be able to protect you."

I frown. "So you're a good guy pretending to be a bad guy?"

He laughs again. "Something like that."

I feel relieved that I'm right, that Sloan isn't capable of kidnapping Bina. "Is Tristen part of the Imminent Darkness?"

"I don't know every member. But I can't say that it would surprise me."

"She's cruel. She uses physical reprimand and tortures people." The words are tumbling out now. "There's this horrible room in the lowest levels of the Fire building. There are chains in the floor and she...she burned Fire into Everly's skin because of my Mindscape. And she did something to Doran." I turn away and look at the ground. "I don't want to go back. I never want to go back." I glance back toward Sloan. "But Rhian's there and Li. I can't leave them there alone."

Sloan studies me silently. I can see his discerning eyes taking in my face, which I realize with mild horror is still probably streaked with dirt. My pants are still torn and my hair a matted mess. "Then go and get them."

"What about the Transitional Phase? Aren't we supposed to stay at the Complex throughout the Transitional Phase?"

He smiles. "I'd say you've already broken that rule—and more than once." He turns back to the view. "Soon, it's not even going to matter. The Transitional Phase will be the least of anyone's worries."

"What do you mean?"

But he shakes his head, turning cryptic once more. "I've already said too much. Remember I'm supposed to be protecting you."

I want to tell him that I've found the first stone, that it's safe inside my bag, and that I could show it to him right now. But he told me last time that he couldn't help me. I had to retrieve and destroy the stones on my own, well, at least without his help. I wonder if infiltrating the Imminent Darkness is the reason for his refusal to help me, or if it's because of something else, something that I'm missing. I mentally file the thought away to consider later.

"You're right. I should go back. Rhian's probably worried about me." I get up slowly, feeling the ache of the night's adventures deep inside my bones. Five stones; five separate trips into the Elemental Abyss. Will they all be as frightening as last night's trip?

"Yes, you should." He stands up too and faces me. Sloan says that he can't help me, only protect me from afar. The physical ache of my body reminds me of how he helped me break the enchantment; I can almost feel the burn in my lungs as I recall the enchanted dream. Only was it really a dream? It felt so real; it didn't

seem like it was a dream. Besides, are enchanted dreams the same as
normal ones?

"Thank you."

"For what?" He looks younger when he smiles. He's standing
only about a foot away from me and I realize he really is only a few
years older than me. Funny, how for so long he seemed mysterious
and aloof. Well, he's still mysterious, but I feel like I am finally
beginning to crack the shell. The pieces are starting to fall slowly
away and little fragments of his personality are beginning to shine
through.

"You were there in the enchantment. You told me how to
break it. You saved my life," I breathe. We're so close that I can feel
the heat between us, the weird mix of comfort, apprehension, and
desire that lingers between us. How had I never noticed it before? Or
had I chosen not to notice?

"Did I?" he asks, his eyes betray his lie. Somehow he knows.
Maybe he really was there and it wasn't just a dream. But how is there
any way to know, to truly know for sure? He reaches out slowly and
gently moves my ponytail out of the way. His hand is soft on my
neck, his fingers are cool on the warmth of my skin. He carefully
moves me toward him, turning me ever so slightly as he peers at the
back of my neck. The tattoo, my Elemental Star. "I like it."
Reluctantly, he lets his hand fall limply back to his side. We stand
awkwardly for a moment unsure of what to do next. "I'll walk you to
the end of the alleyway."

We move together in silence, walking side by side. Something has shifted and changed between us. He guides me down the cobblestone street and up the steps to the entrance of the alleyway. His hand is light on the small of my back; it doesn't feel strange, in fact it feels quite natural. It ends much too quickly.

"You're not coming?" I ask pausing at the sidewalk.

He shakes his head. "I can't. I have some business to attend to down here." I recall the blonde woman and feel a tiny surge of jealousy which I hurriedly squash back down. This—whatever this is—it's still nothing. It could all just be me, a story I'm telling myself in my head because it's what I want to believe.

"Alright then. I'll see you around."

"You always do," he smiles and I can see the worry behind it. "Be careful, Ka." And he's right. I do always see him. Every time that I've needed him, to hear his voice, or see his face, he's somehow found his way to me. Even if it is only in a dream.

I begrudgingly head down the sidewalk back toward the University Complex to find Rhian and Li, silently hoping that they're okay and that Tristen hasn't yet noticed my absence.

Except—

You always do.

I knew it. He *was* there. It wasn't a dream, at least not in the true sense of the word. I pause wondering if he's still standing there, at the end of the alleyway watching me.

But when I finally turn around, he's already gone.

CHAPTER 21

I press the cloaking button a couple of blocks before nearing the University Complex. My heart pounds in my chest and my stomach feels weird, like it's pushing up on my diaphragm. I guess sometimes your body can sense something is wrong before your mind.

I round the building looking for the side door that was open the last time. But this time I'm not as lucky. It's locked. I squelch the panicky feeling that's slowly clawing its way up my stomach. I continue around to the back of the building. Behind the building are a couple of smelly dumpsters and another door nestled behind some shrubs. "Maintenance" is clearly labeled in peeling white letters. I approach the door tentatively and try the handle. Unlocked. I quickly enter and pull the door silently closed behind me. I find myself inside another stairwell that only leads one way, but this time it's up instead of down. I breathe a sigh of relief and quietly make my way

up the concrete steps to the third floor. At the top of the stairs I
pause listening for the sound of voices on the other side of the door,
but I hear nothing.

I ease the door open as little as possible and slip into the
hallway. I enter into the common area. A fire burns in the ultra-
modern fireplace. No one is around. I walk down the hallway toward
our sleeping quarters.

I notice the door is ajar. At first I think—hope?—it's because
Rhian left it open for my return. But as I nudge the door further
open I quickly realize that I'm wrong.

The room is a mess. The beds are disheveled; clothes are
strewn about; books are tossed to the floor, some with pages torn out
and scattered about. The window is wide open and the chilled
morning breeze causes pages to flutter about the room.

Rhian's bed is empty.

My stomach sinks. What happened here? Did the hooded
figures kidnap Rhian too, like they did Bina? Is no one who talks to
me safe anymore? *No*, I chide myself. That's not true because then
Zora and Li would have gone missing too.

Li.

Not being as cautious, but still under the protection of the
cloaking cuff, I run down the hallway to Li's room. His door is wide
open and a similar scene greets me. It looks as if someone was
looking for something. Books, clothes, and bedding have been tossed
to the floor. The door to the bureau hangs open revealing empty
shelves. My stomach sinks and I can feel panic starting to settle in.

I sit on the edge of the bed. Not only are Rhian and Li gone, but I haven't seen or heard a single person. And it's the middle of the morning. Where has everyone gone?

That's when I notice the little silver tube on the floor, rolled beneath the desk. A message tube. They're a way to leave a message. It plays once and then immediately deletes itself with no record of it ever having been recorded. The packaging is long and slim, perfect for slipping into a pocket or into another small space. Its light is flashing green. There's a message.

I get up off the bed and push the door shut, turning the lock although I doubt that would stop anyone from entering from the looks of whatever happened in my short absence. I get down onto my knees and reach beneath the desk, my fingertips just graze the tube, but it's enough to pull it toward me.

I pop the cap and a green light emits from the top and then spreads open like those really old-fashioned fans I've seen in Old Earth history books. You know the kind women used to coyly cover their faces. A pixelated image of Li's face comes into focus.

My heart sinks at the fear that is apparent in his eyes. The message is short and to the point. "Ka, if you've found this, they've taken me. I don't know where, but I think it's somewhere in the Fire building. They're just waking people and snatching them right up. If you try to resist they spray this stuff in your face that knocks you out cold. They say it's to speed up the Transitional Phase. But something's not right." There's a loud crash and the transmission turns to static before Li's voice comes in over the garbled image.

"Find me." The time of the transmission is four hours ago.

Once the message plays it automatically deletes itself. The light turns red. No message. I stuff the tube into my pants pocket. Li didn't know where they were being taken, but I suppose I could take a guess.

I don't know enough about the Transitional Phase to understand if they were to actually speed it up what would happen. I wish Doran was with me; I could use his brain now more than ever and it was comforting to not have to face all those difficult things alone. But that's exactly what I am right now. Alone.

I head down the hallway to the elevator. The sleek black doors glide open and I step inside tapping the button for the lower level. If I were smart I'd leave, get as far away from the Fire building and away from the University Complex as possible. Go, find Sloan, and tell him something strange is happening. But I can't leave Li alone. He's counting on me to find him.

The doors open and I exit into the stone hallway. The torches cast eerie shadows across the floor and walls, even though it's morning this place feels like the middle of the night; it distorts all sense of time. The elevator doors slide silently closed behind me. I make my way through the tunnels, automatically drawn toward the room where Doran and Everly had been kept, figuring if you were going to take a bunch of people without their cooperation that would be the place Tristen would put them.

Despite the things I've seen I'm not prepared for what greets me. Two hooded figures stand at the front of the room. Their backs are toward me. In front of them stand five rows of eight Fires each. Young Fires, all between the ages of eighteen—the newly pronounced—and twenty. The golden filigree on the sides of their faces sparkle in the torch light. They're all wearing black bodysuits and black boots. They stare straight ahead at the two hooded figures.

In the second row I see Li and I try to catch his eye, but then I remember I'm cloaked anyways so it doesn't matter. He stands at attention, his brown eyes vacant and unseeing, his shoulders back, jaw set. Like a soldier.

"You are Fire, Passion, Life, and Energy. You feel these things running through your veins." A voice speaks and I'm surprised to find that it isn't Tristen, but a male. Eoin. "But now, after last night, you now feel something else. You feel a darkness, a desire that coalesces with your Fire."

All the voices respond at once: "YES, SIR!"

"You feel the power that courses through you. You are no longer a simple Elemental, you are much, much more than that." In the row behind Li I can see Rhian, her curly brown ponytail, the same absent look in her eyes and a strong set to her jaw. There's Jielle, Bryn, and Pierce. Pierce—who I once thought looked like the perfect soldier. The irony isn't lost on me.

"You are our best and brightest soldiers. They say Metals make the best soldiers, but they have yet to see the soldiers of the Imminent Darkness."

"YES, SIR!"

I can hear Eoin chuckle, pleased with the response. He turns toward the other hooded figure. "My dear?"

"Thank you, my Love. Children of Fire you have a great task before you. It will not be easy, but your sacrifice on behalf of the Imminent Darkness will not go unnoticed."

Tristen.

"YES, MA'AM!" the voices echo off the stone walls.

"Sleep, my children. You will need much rest before the battle begins. Tonight, we show the Council why Fire should be feared."

"YES, MA'AM!" This time the unanimous response is so loud I feel the reverberation in the ground beneath my feet.

Eoin and Tristen turn and I instinctively press into the wall. I hold my breath as they pass, fearing the pounding of my heart will give me away when Tristen pauses in the entrance to turn and admire her army once more. A sadistic smile plays at her lips as she loops her arm in Eoin's and together they disappear down the hallway. I stay pressed to the wall; there's now nothing between me and the Imminent Darkness's army of Fire.

I feel a shiver run down my spine. The Imminent Darkness has created an army. Are they trying to overthrow the Elemental Leadership Council? The paramilitary of Xon 9 is well-prepared and quite possibly the strongest in the galaxy—fiercer than any military that ever walked the Old Earth planet. How could a bunch of new Fires possibly compete with that?

Then again, maybe they're no longer simply Fires. I try to think like Doran, noticing the unnoticed, paying attention to the details. Li said they were going to speed up the Transitional Phase, but what if they didn't just speed up the Change, what if they somehow created an imbalance—*on purpose?* An unbalanced Fire is something to fear: they're unpredictable, controlling, forceful, and full of restless negative energy, needing to use and consume their own desires that are burning inside them, a passion that will never burn away as they themselves burn from the inside out. Indeed, Unbalanced Fires would be the perfect solider—unrelenting in their pursuit. So why then does the Council use Metals?

Because a balanced Metal is reliable, determined, and courageous.

I would take courageous over relentless any day.

I can't do this alone.

I need to find someone—Ahna, Doran, or Sloan. Even though he says he can't help me, he couldn't possibly have been prepared for this. I back out of the entryway and even though I'm invisible, I'm not intangible. I back right into someone, falling over them and hitting the floor hard with an—*UHF!*

The figure sprawled on the floor is smallish in size and wears a hood that blocks his face. "Who's there?" hisses a distinctively familiar—and female—voice. Everly. But is Everly part of the Imminent Darkness? She stands up and leans forward, almost coming nose to nose with me now that I too am standing. "I know you're there. I can feel you," she whispers.

Everly wouldn't hurt me. I press the cloaking button and hope that I'm not mistaken. When she sees me her brown eyes grow wide. "Ka!" She looks up and down the hallway before pulling me a few paces in the direction opposite of Eoin and Tristen. She opens a narrow doorway and shoves me in.

"Hey—!"

But she follows me in, pulling the door closed behind her. There's a click and a light comes on above our heads. Guess the torches are only for show. We're standing in a sort of supply closet. There's a bunch of cardboard boxes stacked one on top of the other and an old straw broom in the corner, cobwebs hang from the ceiling.

"You shouldn't be here!" she exclaims in a hushed whisper.

"Are you part of the Imminent Darkness?" I accuse.

"What?" She looks surprised. "Of course not."

"But you're wearing the hooded cloak," I point out.

"Oh, well, yes. I may have, um, borrowed one. But it's not mine," she explains to me as if it matters where she got it.

"If you aren't one of them, then why did you borrow a cloak?"

"So that I could find you before Tristen and Eoin do!"

"They noticed I was missing?" I suppose I'd figured as much, but hope has a funny way of altering your perspective.

"Oh, most definitely. And thank goodness I found you. I need to get you out of here as soon as possible." She looks worried.

"Before they expedite the Transitional Phase?" I ask.

She shakes her head and absent-mindedly runs her hands across the front of the cloak, as if she's smoothing out the wrinkles.

"Oh, no. Before they kill you."

She says it so matter-of-factly that I'm caught off guard.

"I'm sorry, what did you say?"

She gives me a sympathetic look. "I'm afraid that after I altered your data for your Mindscape it made Tristen a bit suspicious. She used her role in the Imminent Darkness to have them follow you. They know that you saw the Metal Woman and they took her for questioning."

I shake my head. "She wouldn't have said anything."

"She didn't have to. You know how we went into your Mindscape?" I nod. How could I forget? "It's similar to that, except it's called a Mind Cleanse."

"They cleansed her mind?" My heart sinks. Even the terminology sounds horrifying.

Everly nods solemnly. "I'm afraid so. It's a very quick way to get all the information you need from someone. Unfortunately, once the mind is cleansed…well, it's best not to think about it. They know all about you—who you are. And they're nervous. As far as they know you're not real, only a legend. But the great lengths people have gone to protect you has made them suspicious."

Suddenly the closet feels much too small, as if it's closing in on me, growing smaller and smaller. I feel like I can't breathe, as if I'm drowning. Only this isn't a dream or an enchantment. It's real.

Everly continues. "So you see they plan on killing you now before you can retrieve all the stones from the Elemental Abyss. They figure if it *is* true—and you are really the Impossible Girl—it's best to eliminate the threat before you can actually become one."

"So they plan on killing me." The words feel too big for my mouth, strange and foreign on my lips.

"Yes."

"How?"

She shakes her head. "I don't know. I just knew that I had to try and find you. To warn you before it's too late." She takes my hand in between hers. "You mean so much to so many people, Ka, to people you don't even know. You are something different—a future that no one knew was possible. You may be impossible, but what you represent to those who know the legend is everything in the world that *is* possible."

I know now that everything Sloan has told me is 100% true. I think that I knew it all along, but somehow hearing it right now in this moment has made me realize even more how important it is that I retrieve all of the stones, not so much for myself, but for everyone. It isn't so much the stones themselves, but the embodiment of all that they possess: a new future.

"But what about my friends?" I ask thinking of Li and Rhian, standing at attention in the torturous room, waiting for the next command from Tristen or Eoin.

Again, she shakes her head. "They're beyond your help now. You need to get out. And get out now. Go far, far away from here. Away from the Imminent Darkness and their army of Fire."

"No." She arches an eyebrow in surprise at my words. "No, they aren't beyond my help. As long as they're still alive, then they aren't beyond my help."

Everly smiles as if this is exactly what she expected me to say all along. "What are you suggesting we do?"

"Instead of an escape mission, we turn this into a rescue mission."

. . .

The rows of Fire soldiers are just wide enough to walk through. I walk up and down the rows, my brain working about a mile a minute as I try to figure out how I can save my friends. I pause peering into Rhian's face. Her brown eyes are unseeing, her posture erect—ready to pounce at the command.

Everly paces nervously in front of the soldiers, back and forth. "I'm so sorry I don't know how to reverse what's been done. I'm afraid it's beyond my expertise."

I continue to walk, stopping when I reach Li. He's a couple inches taller than me. The jaunty look that I'm used to is gone, replaced with something more sinister. *Find me*. I've found you, but I don't know how to save you.

His posture is the same as everyone else's, an expectant, nimble posture. But something is…different.

The eyes.

Brown eyes look back at me and at first I think they are vacant like the rest, but then I see something just beyond the surface. A spark, a reminder, a memory. He sees me.

"I'll save you," I whisper.

Ever so slightly he shakes his head. "No." Barely audible.

"Yes."

"You can't. You're too late." The words come out in a tumbled rush.

"I'm not. You're talking to me right now. You're aware that I'm here. You know who I am." Everly has stopped pacing, standing in front of the soldiers, watching me in the second row. There's a pleading tone in my voice, although I'm not sure why until Li's next words resonate with what my brain has already figured out.

"I know. And that's why the information has already been sent." His mouth twitches at the corner and his eyes change from a spark to—regret?

"I don't understand."

"I'm not in control, Kata. I'm tied into some sort of collective consciousness. Whatever I think," his voice catches. "I tried to fight the Change, but—but I wasn't strong enough." I can see the conflicting emotions in his eyes as they unexpectedly brim with tears. "Please don't hate me," he implores.

"I could never hate you," I whisper.

"Then run."

I take a couple of steps backward, accidentally bumping into another soldier, someone I don't know. I watch as Li tries to resist, seeing the muscles in his neck tense with the effort. He slowly raises his arms, a vein in his forehead bulges as he tries to resist what he's about to do.

I feel glued to the floor, my legs feel like they are filled with sand and even though he told me to run, I find that I can't move.

His programmed physiology overrides his heart's intent. *Heart or head?* He brings his hands slowly up as if he's cupping something even though they appear empty. Slowly—maybe because he's still trying to resist the mechanized response—I see an orange flame flicker inside his palms. "Please," he begs, "Kata, please run." The flame grows and then he pulls an arm back and launches it at me: a fireball sizzling down the aisle.

I feel firm hands grab me and yank me out of the way. Everly. The fireball lands inches from where I was standing, singeing the floor, leaving a black mark before it burns itself up and disappears. "Didn't he say run?" Everly asks as we huddle in a heap on the floor.

"But I have to save them. They're my friends." Without an audible command, the soldiers seem to waken, raising their arms slowly and I think I know what comes next. Collective consciousness. They don't need a command if they can see inside each other's heads. They break formation, whirling apart, no longer stiff and militant, but almost frighteningly graceful, moving like some sort of grotesque ballet.

Another fireball launches in our direction. Everly and I scatter apart as it lands, singes the stone floor and evaporates. What has Tristen done to them? She hasn't just created relentless soldiers, but soldiers capable of chaos and destruction. "What do we do?" Everly asks.

"I don't know!" The soldiers begin to approach, launching fireballs at us as we jump and dive out of the way. "We need some sort of shield or something to protect ourselves!" I call out.

"Here!" Everly's voice calls from behind me and I run toward her. She's standing behind a large flat metal table off to the side that I hadn't noticed before. A weird table that has leather straps flapping at its sides and which is on some sort of mechanism so that it can tilt forward and back. Fireballs hit the walls and pelt the floor as I slide in next to her. We push the heavy table up and at an angle. At least it will buy us some time.

The metal sizzles as a fireball hits its surface. "While I admire your bravery, Ka. I'm not sure this is going to work."

"You're right. We need to retreat," I agree. The door is only a few feet to our left. If we're fast we could make it. Everly follows my eyes.

"Together," she says encouragingly.

"Together," I agree. She grabs my hand and we run back into the open and toward the doorway, only it's not there anymore. Someone has slid the riveted iron door that was pushed open across the entryway.

Tristen.

We're trapped inside.

CHAPTER 22

Everly pounds on the door futilely. I grab her by the wrist, dodging the onslaught of fireballs as we hover back behind the table. "We need a plan," I say.

"We're trapped in a room with Unbalanced Fires who can conjure up their own fireballs," she says, her words tinged with panic. "I'd say we're beyond the point of a plan."

Another fireball lands inches from where I'm kneeling, burning black into the stone floor before disappearing again.

"There must be something. The fire tetrahedron in Fire Physics. You need fuel, oxygen, and…"

She nods. All Fires have taken the same classes at one point or another. "Heat and the chemical reaction."

"But the chemical reaction is happening somewhere inside their bodies. Our only chances would be to either deprive them of oxygen or to somehow alter the chemical reaction."

"The oxygen," Everly's face lights up. "Part of the combustion process is the body's own natural oils which act as the fuel, combined with their body temperature and the oxygen in our own cells."

I remember learning about this in the first week of classes. "Maybe we can use fire to fight Fire." I reach up above us, pulling one of the torches out of its stone holder and handing it to Everly. She takes it carefully. "It's a long shot."

"Better than no shot," she replies. I grab a torch from the wall and together we round the front of the table, holding the torches defensively out in front of us.

I close my eyes and take a deep breath before launching toward the nearest soldier, which happens to be Jielle. The downside to their fire creating properties is they need time to conjure up a fireball; whereas, I already have my fire so that I'm already prepared when she finally launches it at me. I take the torch like a bat and swing with all my might at the fireball.

I make contact and when I do there's a bang and a poof of smoke. Not only is the fireball gone, but so too is the flame at the end of my torch. Jielle tries to conjure up another fireball, but nothing happens. The explosion must have taken away some of the oxygen, so it isn't just their own oxygen, they need the oxygen around them as well. That must be why it takes a moment to conjure the fireball; otherwise they would just think it and it would appear in their hands almost instantaneously.

One down only about forty more to go. "It works!" I call out. "But we'll need more torches. The explosion disarms them." I'm not paying attention as I run to the wall and reach for another torch. Near my right a fireball hits the wall, turns black, then disappears. They need more practice on their aim.

I pull down the torch and see Bryn right in front of me, frizzy red hair aflame on top of her head, eyes empty. She's conjuring up a fireball and I pick up my bat ready to swing, only, another fireball comes from my left: Jielle. It must only *temporarily* disarm them. It's not a big enough explosion. I swing and make contact with Jielle's fireball, but this leaves me unarmed for the one from Bryn.

I dive to my right, rolling ungracefully, and landing hard on my ribs. Jielle and Bryn are descending on me. I'm tangled up in the strap of my messenger bag as I try to get back to my feet.

That's when I notice the hole in the canvas of my bag. A hole burned straight through—a fireball must have clipped it. Several feet away shining like a beacon in the middle of the floor is the obsidian stone.

"Everly! The stone!" I cry.

She turns to me then looks at the floor, seeing the obsidian stone. Holding her torch up high as protection, she hurries toward it, picks it up, and tosses it toward me. I catch it, but then watch in horror as Pierce launches a fireball from behind her.

"Everly!"

Her eyes are wide in shock, her mouth forming a small *o* of surprise. Her whole body bursts into a blindingly bright white light and then she's gone. Just gone.

All that's left is a black imprint on the middle of the floor where she had been standing.

. . .

The stone is cold in my palm, like ice. *Remove the source of heat.* I'm being closed in on now by Jielle, Bryn, and Pierce, slowly backed into a corner where I'm sure to suffer the same fate as Everly.

There's no Doran, no Sloan. No Li. No Everly.

I'm alone now.

Tears sting my eyes. This is not how I want it to end, crying like a baby. I want to go down with a fight, but I can't seem to help it.

A single tear pushes its way out, slides down my cheek and falls into my open palm which still holds the stone.

The tear sizzles.

In front of me three fireballs are being conjured at the same time.

Each stone is a fragment of my personality. I too am Fire.

They pull back their arms simultaneously. I have no torch to temporarily disarm them.

I am alone and I am angry. The worst thing you could do about now is back an angry, grief-stricken person into a corner.

Because they have nothing to lose.

The fireballs launch and as they soar toward me I throw the

obsidian stone at them with all of my might—if I have to sacrifice part of who I am to save myself then so be it. Fire is ugly. I don't want to be Fire.

The stone and fireballs reach each other in the middle of the air, red fire meeting white-hot fire like two indestructible forces colliding with one another. A wall of fire forms, with the soldiers on one side and me on the other. Waves of fire whoosh around me and the floor shakes beneath my feet. There are some howls of anguish on the other side of the fiery wall and I fear that I've killed my friends. That Li, like Everly, will be nothing but a black smudge of what once was.

Sweat dampens my brow from the intensity of the flames before me. Suddenly, the black stone falls out of the air, hitting the floor at my feet, appearing undamaged.

And the fire is gone.

Silence.

Bodies lay on the floor, like carnage from an Old Earth war. I'm afraid to move. Bryn is closest to me, her red hair splayed around her head like a fiery halo, eyes closed. Her chest rises and falls slowly.

They're alive.

The explosion of the stone must have deprived their fire of the additional oxygen that it needed. I crawl tentatively toward Bryn, reaching out carefully and lightly touching her chin, turning her face so that I can see the golden filigree lining her cheek. But it's not there anymore, instead a long black streak curls down her cheek like some sort of tribal tattoo.

Frightened, I pull my hand away.

I slowly make my way past Pierce and Jielle, whose chests rise and fall gently, the same tattoo running down the side of their faces. I hesitantly pick up the Fire stone, holding it tightly in my fist, afraid to let it out of my sight, before slipping it securely in my pants pocket where I can feel the weight of it pressed against my skin.

It's cold to the touch, like ice, giving no indication of the fiery battle it just waged against the Imminent Darkness's army of Fire.

I make my way through the bodies, telling myself that they're sleeping, that they're better off than the state in which they were in before the explosion. Fire still licks at the walls which have black marks singed into them like kisses from a sadistic vixen.

I reach Rhian and it's easy to tell myself that she's sleeping because the stiff set of her jaw is gone, her face is soft and relaxed. The black marks curl around her cheek and down her neck. I touch it softly, pulling my hand back because the marks are hot like the fire, as if it's been burned into their skin, much like Everly's markings after Tristen was done with her.

Near the door lies Li. I can't leave him behind. I need to take him with me. I crouch down beside him and he looks so peaceful, relieved to be free of whatever torturous concoction was flowing through his veins. But I don't know if it's actually gone, not really. And I don't know if I've hurt him in anyway.

I tentatively touch his cheek and he surprises me by wrapping his fingers around my wrist. They're hot, but not enough to burn. He slowly opens his eyes and the familiar jaunty brown peers back at me.

"You didn't run." At least the explosion didn't wipe out their memories. Then again, maybe they'll wish it had.

"No, I didn't." I say. "I'm not in the habit of running out on my friends." He smiles at this. "Does it hurt much?" I ask.

He shakes his head. "No. It's just I feel like I've been burned up from the inside out. The feelings, the burning sensation that was flowing through me. It's gone now. I feel, well, I almost feel hollow inside."

I place my hands on his back as he tries to move to a seated position. "We need to get out of here." I glance at the iron door blocking the way out. "But we're trapped inside here."

Li grins as he slowly tries to make his way to a standing position. I help him to his feet. "Oh, Kata, surely you know better than that? When you're with me, you're never trapped." He grins as he reaches down into the top of his right boot and pulls something out. A laser key. We're no longer locked in from the inside if there's a key to get us out. Li holds up the key. His grin widens. "What can I say? I know a guy."

. . .

The cloaking cuff is still on my wrist and I press the button then join hands with Li. We leave the door slid open behind us, hoping that when the others wake they can find their way out. There's no sign of anyone in the tunnels. Tristen and Eoin probably thought that Everly and I would be incinerated by their army of Fire once they sealed us in.

Li limps beside me as I drag him in the direction of the teleportation portals. When we reach it the room is empty, but the machines flash as if they've recently been used. The cowards. They ran away.

Assured that no one is around, I uncloak us and help Li onto the silver platform. I place my hand on his cheek, directly over the markings which will forever serve as a reminder of the day's events. Who knows what unseen repercussions will unfold as a result of what I've done?

"I'm sor—" I begin.

"No, Kata. You're sorry too much. What's meant to be has happened. Sorry serves no purpose." He places his hand over mine, then gently removes it from his cheek, and kisses my knuckles before letting go.

He closes his eyes and a serene look passes over his face. I know he's thinking of home, the safety and security that only a familiar place and those we love can provide. The white light encompasses him and I shield my eyes against the blinding flash as he disappears.

I climb into one of the teleportation portals and adjust my messenger bag. I pat my pocket to reassure myself of the stone's presence.

Each stone must be retrieved and destroyed.

The explosion didn't destroy the Fire stone.

I have a burlap bag with a feather, a crystal, matches, and a vial of a mysterious clear liquid. The gifts Bina gave me. Will any of those things destroy the Fire stone?

I close my eyes and imagine safety and security.

A warm feeling of never-ending love and protection; a powerful bond that seems to have no beginning and no end. I smile as the thoughts rush over me.

When I open my eyes I've arrived.

I'm in a darkened room with no natural light. A man with shaggy brown hair leans over a bed. The now familiar blonde woman sits on the other side of the bed, grasping the hand of the bed's occupant.

It took me a while to figure it out, but I understand now. My jealousy had clouded my vision, but once the jealousy dissipated it was so clear that I'm surprised I hadn't realized it sooner.

I make my way to the bed in which Bina lies. Her eyes are closed and they flutter rapidly as if she is dreaming. She mumbles incoherently. *What have they done to her?*

Sloan turns to me his green eyes bright with worry over his mother and whatever it is that the Imminent Darkness may have done to her before he could get to her. But when his eyes fall on me they soften slightly and he smiles.

"I was wondering when you'd figure it out."

Chapter 23

"Why didn't you tell me?"

We're standing in what I've come to call "our" spot, staring out into the pink night at the colony lights beyond.

I feel much better. After tending to Bina, Sloan's sister, Michaela, let me use their shower. It felt good, no, it felt *purifying* in the literal sense of the word, to wash away the sweat, soot, and loss that I experienced earlier. Everly's surprised face seems to play on an endless loop that I can't get out of my head.

Now Sloan and I sit shoulder-to-shoulder, legs dangling over the terracotta edge of the cliff.

"And what would you have thought?" he replies,

"I can't believe that I didn't make the connection sooner. Of course you grew up a Metal. You're brave, righteous, chivalrous…all of those things that make Metals such good soldiers."

"Why then, if we are all these wonderful things, are we shunned to the Underground?" I know he isn't asking me because he genuinely wants an answer, but because he is being rhetorical.

"An Unbalanced Metal is a dangerous thing." I pause thinking of Tristen and of her army of Fire. "More dangerous than an Unbalanced Fire?"

He turns to me, eyes serious. "Very. An Unbalanced Fire may be relentless, reckless even. But an Unbalanced Metal is destructive. You know how you said you could still reach Li despite what had been done to him?" I had told Sloan everything that had happened when I'd returned to the University Complex. I nod. "He showed you mercy. He tried to get you to run—for which I'm very thankful by the way—but an Unbalanced Metal would not have shown you the same sympathy. That's why Unbalanced Metals stay in the Underground. Not because they put us here, but because we've put ourselves here."

I've never known that. I always thought the Underground, the Black Bazaar, was the underside of our society. A place for all the misfits who don't fit in anywhere else. And maybe it's true, that besides as a soldier, a Metal cannot truly fit in anywhere else. All the Metals I've met and gotten to know: Bina, Zora, Doran, and even Sloan although he didn't pronounce himself as Metal, are all incredibly courageous, resolute, and have great inner-strength, but they also don't seem to belong anywhere. They don't fit any of the pre-constructed molds of our society.

'Why didn't you pronounce yourself as Metal?" I ask

curiously. I can see it in him, if not for the scales curving down the side of his face.

"My mother brought me up with a great sense of duty and honor. She told me, via her gift, at a very young age that I would grow up with a hefty responsibility. That there would be a girl I would need to protect." He glances at me sideways and my heartbeat quickens. "In order to protect her I couldn't be a soldier. I'd have to be in an accessible place where it would be easy to find her once she needed me. I always liked school and my studies, so Water seemed like a natural second choice."

"So you always knew that you'd have to protect me?" I ask.

"Well, I didn't know it was you the whole time necessarily. Bina didn't tell me until I was put at the school that I should keep my eye out for someone who fit your description. Little did I know I'd have my work cut out for me," he grins.

"I'm sorry if I was a terrible student. I was always just okay at school. School was Ahna's thing, not mine."

"That's not what I mean. When I first met you, you were insecure, completely unaware of who you are and the greatness that you're meant to achieve." The look he gives me is admiring and I feel my cheeks flush. "You've changed a lot, since you realized it, I mean. The first time I noticed that you seemed different is when you got angry with me for not helping you." He smiles sheepishly.

I remember how I reacted, throwing his letter back in his face, like a petulant child. But I didn't care what he thought. Is that when I began to feel different? Could it be that just knowing I was going to retrieve pieces of my personality somehow began to return them to me? Kind of like how your stomach gets queasy right before something bad happens or gets really excited and jumpy right before something good happens, before you're even cognizant of it happening?

"Will Bina be okay?" I wonder out loud.

"I think so. I would have liked to take her further away, but Michaela will do a good job of protecting her and taking care of her. They tried to conduct a MindCleanse on her, but MindCleanses don't work well on Metals who have sight. It kind of backfires."

"How?"

"Instead of going into my mother's Mindscape and cleansing all her thoughts and dreams, it takes the person accompanying her into their own Mindscape. I think that's why they returned her. They figured she was of no use to them. But the experience drained all of her energy. She should be better in another day or two." He moves his hand and accidentally puts his on top of mine. "Sor-"

"No," I say wrapping my fingers tightly around his. "Never sorry. Sorry serves no purpose." I echo Li's words, one of the last people I'd expect to impart wisdom.

"Who told you that?" he grins.

I shrug thinking of both Everly and Li. "Just a friend."

He considers this. "I think your friend may be right. Sorry is either an implication of wrong-doing or it's an excuse. It really does serve no purpose."

I laugh. "Okay, Teacher 4." He smiles and wraps his fingers

around mine. "So you always knew?" I ask changing the subject, coming back full circle to our previous discussion.

"Know I'd have to protect someone very important? Yes," he says slowly. "Know that I'd slowly begin to fall for her? Not so much," he chuckles. "Honestly that part kind of took me by surprise."

My heart skips a beat. "You're falling for me?" I ask teasingly.

"You mean you haven't noticed?" A flush creeps up his neck and I realize that he's nervous. It's strange to have the tables turned for once.

"I'm kidding. I think I noticed a while ago, I just hadn't connected all the dots quite yet."

"Here, let me help you connect them," he smirks. He leans in toward me and I know what's about to happen next, but before my head can get in the way my body takes over.

It's not like when Li kisses me, all fiery passion, flirtation and adventure.

Sloan's kiss is slow, purposeful, and full of promise.

A promise that was made very long ago to a girl he didn't even yet know.

. . .

"I thought you said you wouldn't help me? Actually I think the words were more specifically that you *couldn't* help me." I point out.

We're back in Michaela's apartment and I'm pacing back and forth in the living room while Sloan sits on the small sofa.

"I think things have changed a bit don't you? Some things you were meant to figure out on your own; if I was involved too soon then you couldn't draw your own conclusions, you wouldn't have made the same decisions that led you to this right now."

I pause and flop down on the couch beside him. He picks up my hand, turning it over in his own. "Okay, then, now that it's been established that you can *and* will help me, I retrieved the stone—by no means of help from you," I add, even though I understand what he means I'm still a little bitter about the whole thing.

"Technically, I did help you." And I know he's referring to telling me how to break the enchantment. How he did that, not to mention the other dream visits, is a conversation for another day. "I'll help you on the next one, I promise," he looks at me solemnly, "I swear on my favorite Universal History textbook."

I laugh and give him a playful shove in the shoulder. "In all seriousness, retrieving each stone is only half of the problem. The other half is destroying them. Your mother gave me some things, but I have to admit, I'm not sure how any of them will help."

I reach into my messenger bag and pull out the small burlap sack Bina had given me the last time I'd seen her cognizant. I pull out each of the contents and lay it on the sofa cushion between us: the speckled feather, the crystal, the pack of matches, and the small vile of clear liquid.

Sloan inspects each item studying them. Even though Bina is

his mother, I know that even if she were awake and well, she wouldn't reveal to me how to use the items. If she had wanted me to know she would have told me before. Apparently, the apple doesn't fall far from the tree, and Bina wants me to figure it out on my own.

He shakes his head. "There are only four."

I stare at him confused. "What do you mean?"

"I mean there are only four things here," he points to each of them before elaborating. "She only gave you four items, but there are five stones."

"I hadn't even noticed," I explain. Now, I'm really confused. Had Bina meant to give me five items, but in the haste of the evening only given me four of them? "Maybe she meant to give me five," I offer.

But Sloan shakes his head again. "Bina doesn't make mistakes."

"Everyone makes mistakes," I insist.

"Not my mother. Every word, every action, is concise and with purpose. She is a Metal through and through," he explains.

"Well, out of the ones I do have, which do you think could be the one to destroy the Fire stone?" I ask.

"You have the stone with you now?" I nod. It's still in the front pocket of my pants snug against my hip bone. I pull it out. The black stone is cool and smooth in my hand. Sloan holds his palm open and I carefully place it in his hand.

Truth be told, the stone frightens me. It has a power that I don't understand; it knocked out an entire army of Unbalanced Fires.

That in itself is frightening, but what truly frightens me is that this stone is a fragmented part of my personality. And if that's the case, then what does that mean I'll be capable of once it's returned to me?

Sloan slowly turns it over in his hands, inspecting it. "What was it like? The Land of Fire?"

"Terrifying. It was all fire and brimstone, literally. There were rivers of lava and the sky was black. There was a giant volcano and the stone was on a pedestal inside the base of the volcano. When it was removed from the pedestal the volcano almost seemed to erupt in protest. I didn't think we'd get out of there alive."

"We?" Sloan lifts his eyes. I just assumed he'd known that Doran had accompanied me on the trip.

"Doran and me. Tristen was…being Tristen…and he was there when I left and instead of teleporting himself home he teleported to the mountains with me. If he weren't with me, I'm not sure how far I would have gotten on my own," I concede.

"That was very brave of him," Sloan nods handing the stone back to me. I rub my thumb across it absent-mindedly.

"Born a Metal, pronounced himself as Fire. He's not so different from you," I shrug.

"Well, I'm thankful that you had help and didn't have to go alone." He leans forward inspecting each of the items on the couch between us. "Explain to me again how you stopped Tristen's army?"

"A fireball had burned a hole into my bag and the stone had slipped out. Everly, she's the one who had originally accompanied me on my Mindscape, grabbed it and tossed it to me. Because of that she couldn't get out of the way fast enough and was hit by a fireball which just completely…evaporated her." A lump forms in my throat at the memory.

Sloan reaches out and gently places his hand on my leg. "That must have been very hard for you to watch."

I nod choking back tears. "She was so kind. All she wanted to do was help me and she had this crazy faith in me that I was going to change things."

"It's not so crazy," Sloan says softly. There's a long pause; he's giving me processing time before carefully continuing, "And what happened after you caught the stone?"

I sniffle. "I'm not sure exactly. Bryn, Pierce, and Jielle were descending on me, they threw their fireballs and I threw the obsidian stone at them. There was a huge…explosion. Their fire was orange-red, but the fire from the stone, it was different."

"Different how?"

"It was white. It created a sort of wall around me and I could hear them crying out on the other side. And when it was gone, they were all just lying there. Except their Fire markings were gone, all that was left were these black tattoo-like markings," I explain. I shiver at the memory of the bodies that at first I thought were dead.

"I think that means it's gone," Sloan says softly.

"What's gone?"

"The Fire. The stone somehow took away all the Fire that was inside them, along with whatever Tristen had probably done to them. They went from having too much, to having none at all. You said they had a black tattoo where their markings had been?"

I nod.

"Fire is very different than the other Elements because its capacity for pain and control can be visual."

I think of Everly and Doran. "Like burns?"

He nods. "Like burns. It's, well, it's almost like the Fire inside them was burned up."

"It scares me," I confess. "The stone does."

Sloan's face softens. "Oh, Ka. It doesn't mean that this is your personality, that you are violent or destructive, none of those things. It was just doing its job, what it was told to do all those years ago. It was simply protecting you."

I hadn't thought of it like that before. My mother had said the words as she threw each of the stones into the Elemental Abyss: *protection, piety, promise.* This new perspective lessens my fear of having the stone destroyed and the fragment of my personality restored. I thought all Fire was ugly; maybe it is simply misunderstood, just as each Element has its own good and bad qualities, no Element is all one nor the other.

"How do we destroy it?" I ask.

Sloan picks up the matches. "I'm not sure, but based on your description it sounds like the stone caused its own explosion which was large enough to deplete enough of the oxygen in the room to remove it from the fire tetrahedron."

"You know about the fire tetrahedron?" I ask surprised. I thought that was something only Fires learned once pronounced.

He smiles. "I know a lot of things." He continues, "So once the oxygen was removed their Fire would no longer function." He twirls the pack of matches between his fingers.

"What are you suggesting?" I ask even though I think I already know the answer.

"Perhaps we should use fire to destroy the Fire stone," he grins mischievously, "Fight fire with fire."

CHAPTER 24

The wind whips across the rocky landscape blowing about debris and bits of red rock. We walked out past the colony perimeter, where I'd last been with Doran after we harnessed the power of Earth's wind to travel home. It seemed the safest place to experiment with the unexpected.

Sloan admitted he has no idea what will happen. Will it be an explosion? Will the stone simply disintegrate? It's hard to say for sure. He's crouched on the ground with the stone in front of him. I pull my jacket tighter around me to protect myself from the blustery day. He directs me to stand closer to block the wind, but not too close for fear I could be injured if the stone does indeed explode.

He takes a match from the pack and strikes it. The wind blows it out. He takes out a second match and strikes it again, this time it ignites and he hovers it above the stone waiting for a reaction.

Just before the match burns to his fingertips he drops it onto the obsidian surface. Nothing. His face scrunches up in puzzlement.

"Maybe you should try. After all, it is a fragmented part of *your* personality, not mine." He stands up and hands me the pack of matches. I crouch beside him, strike a match, and when it ignites I hold it close to the obsidian stone which gleams in its light. Nothing happens. I drag the fire along the obsidian stone's surface.

Still nothing happens.

"I don't think this is right. It worked instantaneously last time." I turn the pack of matches over in my hand. "It must be one of the other objects."

"Or the one you're missing," Sloan points out.

The pack of matches is old. The edges are slightly frayed. On the front is a faded picture of a mermaid, more specifically a siren. I flip the pack over: The Old Tavern and the Sea. I'd never heard of it before, but it's given me an idea.

"Water."

"Yeah, what about it?"

"Water can put out Fire. Fire consumes, it is always hungry, but water satiates. Maybe it's simple chemistry." I pick up the stone feeling its coolness in my fingers. It's hard to believe something so unostentatious could be so powerful.

"So what are you suggesting? That we submerge it in some water in the kitchen sink?"

"That seems too simple." I think about it for a moment. "What if we travel back to the enchanted lake?"

Sloan shakes his head. "No, I feel like that would somehow be too obvious. Also, what if it didn't work, how would we retrieve it? Swim to the bottom of the enchanted lake? You'd be consumed by your own dreams as soon as you hit the surface."

"Well, there has to be some water somewhere, doesn't there? It can't just be the sink or bathtub, it has to be significant."

"It's your personality. I didn't realize you were so high-maintenance." I scowl at him. "Actually, there is a place. Only Waters know about it."

"Where is it?" I ask shoving the stone into my front pocket then pulling him to his feet.

He hesitates, "It's in the Water Building at the University Complex."

I really was hoping to not go back there anytime soon. Sloan says rumors were already starting that the University Complex may be shut down indefinitely due to the 'unexpected manipulation of students attending.' I can only imagine the confusion and hurt that my fellow Fires must have felt upon waking from their slumber, drained of all their Fire.

And then I think of the last time I saw Sloan entering into the Water Building, with the other hooded figure, before I knew that he had joined the Imminent Darkness in order to protect me. That night they were talking about me: the eighteenth moon on the hundredth solar alignment and Sloan knew. I wonder how deep into the Darkness he's had to go in order to keep me safe.

"Then let's go. There's only one way to find out if it will

work. And maybe that's why Bina only gave me four objects; she couldn't exactly fit a lake or pool into that little burlap sack." I smile to hide my nervousness. My anxiety is not about Sloan, I realize now that I trust him—have trusted him without realizing it—fully from the beginning. It is about running into someone—or something— dangerous: Tristen, the Imminent Darkness, the list seems to keep on growing.

Sloan takes my hand and pulls me back toward the colony. The wind continues to whip around us, pushing us forward as if to say *Yes, yes! Hurry!*

The Earth has not been wrong.

Yet.

. . .

It's mid-afternoon when we approach the Water Building. Unlike the last time where I kept to the shadows in order to stay hidden, we walk out in the open. However it doesn't really matter because no one is around. We walk around to the back of the building where I'd seen Sloan enter the building with the other Water man. I wonder who that other man could be. Is he someone important? It seems that members of the Imminent Darkness have some degree of prestige in our colony. Tristen and Eoin run the entire New Elemental Fire program; Sloan is a teacher. Who else walks amongst its ranks?

I recognize the gnarled tree from before and at this angle I can see that, if you look very closely, the door that I'd seen Sloan and the other man disappear into, is actually built inside the trunk of the tree. Last time they had knocked somewhat ceremoniously and then the door had opened. But this time Sloan reaches down the collar of his shirt and pulls out a key hanging from a leather cord that I'd never noticed him wearing. The key is quite small, a tarnished brass with a small loop at one end and only a couple of teeth at the other. It is probably only the size of a paperclip.

He carefully slips the key into a very small keyhole on the right side of the wooden door. I have to admit this isn't exactly how I pictured entering the Water Building. I'm not sure what I was expecting—some sort of secret waterfall entrance or something? Then again the entrance into the Fire Building is just a regular building door, no hint of the labyrinth of tunnels and rooms that lie beneath. Maybe the Water Building has similar secrets hidden within its walls.

The lock tumbles and Sloan pulls the door open. This time no light spills out from inside. Instead what greets us is an inky black darkness. I reach into my messenger back and find the flashlight that I stashed in there on one of my now many adventures sneaking out of Fire. I hand it to Sloan and he flicks the switch illuminating the darkness.

Inside is a wooden stairwell that leads down into more darkness. Sloan steps inside then takes a step down before pulling me in behind him. There isn't enough room for two of us to fit on a single step side-by-side; they're that narrow. I pull the door closed behind me. Shutting out the red light of the afternoon; the beam of the flashlight now our sole guide.

The steps aren't only narrow, they're extremely steep. Sloan's fingers are wrapped around mine as he leads me down the steps; even though he uses the flashlight, his tread is confident. This is a path he's traveled many times.

The walls of the stairwell aren't earthen, they are wooden planks, similar to what I'd expect in the Wood Building. Is it possible that the buildings are somehow connected underground? That's when I hear the now familiar rush of water. We reach the bottom of the stairs and as we do the wood plank walls give way to stone.

The stone walls are dripping with moisture and as we get closer, the rush of water grows louder and steadier. The floor is also stone, slippery because it is covered in moisture.

"Be careful," Sloan instructs. He turns off the flashlight because once we reach the bottom of the steps it is no longer needed.

What stands before me is a beautiful, cerulean pool of water. It's illuminated by a narrow hole near the top of the far wall where pink light streams in turning part of the water the most beautiful lavender color. A waterfall gracefully slides down the stone walls to the right. It's not quite as magnificent in size as the waterfall at the Elemental Abyss, but it's magnificent in its own right. It looks magical, mystical, as if we've entered another land far, far away.

"The waterfall pulls the water from the pool and recycles it," Sloan explains.

"It's beautiful," I breathe. And it is. The colors coalescing with the light spilling in from the outside and the peaceful rush of the water.

There are stone steps that lead into the pool and some benches that are also carved into the walls of the small cavern.

"There are classes held here. It's one of the few places on Xon 9 where a Water can learn to be a Water."

"It's strange, isn't it?" I ask. "That one of our Elements is Water, yet there's no naturally occurring water anywhere on the surface of Xon 9. Why then, did they choose it as one of the Elements?"

Sloan directs me toward a bench and we sit facing the majestic pool. "Well, perhaps they understood the value of water. We could not have survived on a planet with absolutely no water, so even inhabiting one where we had to drill for it suggests the vitality of it. Maybe it's a way to still honor what we know to be sacred. Water sustains life." His voice drops conspiratorially. "But it can also take life away."

I think about how I had to drown in order to wake up from the enchantment. It was terrifying. Something I'd never want to experience ever again. Even though it wasn't real; it felt real. That's the truly frightening part.

He continues, "Water is unpredictable, Ka." I wonder if he's somehow referring to his own personality, or maybe to mine, after all I have yet to retrieve the Water stone. "It needs to always be treated with the utmost respect."

We sit in silence for a moment taking in the surrounding

beauty. "I never get tired of this place," he admits.

"I can understand why," I offer. The stone is heavy in my pocket, a reminder that we didn't come here simply to enjoy the scenery. I reach inside and pull it out, placing it in the palm of my left hand which hovers in the air between us like an omen of the monumental task that lays before us.

"Do we just throw it in and see what happens?" I ask.

Sloan shakes his head. "I doubt it will work. But it's worth a try." He curls my fingers around the stone, enclosing it in my palm. "Here, you do it. I don't think it will work if I do it."

I shrug my messenger bag over my head leaving it on the bench behind me and approach the edge of the pool, careful not to slip on the slick stones. My back is to Sloan so I take a second to close my eyes and whisper over the cool stone. *Please work. Please let me have this missing piece of myself returned. Let me have passion, energy, and life.* I take a deep breath, open my eyes and toss the stone. It arcs through the air before slicing neatly through the surface of the cerulean water with a small *plop!*

I feel Sloan come up behind me, putting his hand gently on the small of my back as we wait to see what will happen next. Seconds turn to minutes and nothing happens. "Maybe we were wrong," I sigh. "Maybe it is one of the things in the bag Bina gave me, like the crystal or something." I say the words, but I don't sound much convinced myself.

"Well, if we are wrong, someone needs to get the stone from the bottom of the pool." Sloan looks at me, a smile hinting at the corner of his lips. "Do you know how to swim?" he asks.

I shake my head. "Never in my life." But that's a lie. "I mean, never in my waking life," I correct.

Sloan kicks off his shoes, shrugs out of his jacket, and pulls his t-shirt over his head. I can see the excitement practically radiating off him. Deep down he may be a Metal, but Water brings out a different side of him, a sort of child-like joy.

He gives me an impish grin then runs agilely across the stones and dives into the blue water, barely making a splash. His brown head breaks the surface. "Come on. It's instinctive, trust me. And I'm right here if you need me."

My heart pounds as I slip off my jacket and untie my boots. With sweaty palms I pull my t-shirt over my head, so that I just have on a thin, black tank top. I know that I can't dive gracefully like Sloan, slicing through the water like a knife. I could take the steps leading into the pool. But where's the fun in that?

Again, I close my eyes and take a deep breath. My feet lead me across the stones and I jump rather ungracefully into the water. I can hear Sloan's laughter, melodious and carefree, as I break the surface a few feet to his right.

He disappears beneath the surface again and re-emerges next to me, the obsidian stone in his fist. The water is deeper than it looks; I have to tread water because I can't touch the bottom. The light is filtering through the hole and falls across Sloan's face, making his green eyes and silver scales sparkle. He hands the stone to me, but when I reach for it, he pulls me in close so that we're chest to chest, and lowers his face toward mine.

I've been here before, or somewhere similar. The dream with the cavern, where we swam until we broke the surface in the little underwater cave. It felt like this. Like no one else needed to exist and that it was just us and that was all that mattered. In all my dreams I already knew how to swim, even though in actuality this is the first time I've ever been in a pool of water not in the shower or bathtub. Is it some sort of trace left of the Water that had been taken from me as a child?

The stone is pressed in between our two palms, our fingers intertwined as we kiss in the lavender colored water, enjoying our own sort of enchantment. And for just a moment my frustration at not being able to destroy the stone slips away, just like the stone itself, tumbling down deeper and deeper, to the bottom of the pool.

And then something strange happens. A heat begins to trickle up my legs, starting at my toes and winding its way up. I'm about to ask Sloan if he feels it too, but he pulls away slightly eyes wide, and I know that he felt it. The heat continues to trickle up until it travels down my arm and into my hand where the stone burns hot, but neither of us can pull away. It's as if our hands are molded to the stone.

The stone begins to change from darkest obsidian to deep, blood red, then to a brighter red, which eventually turns pink until the stone is glowing the same white hot as it feels. And then there's a blinding burst of light, white hot flames erupt out of the stone and I can finally break free. Blue white flames surround me, seemingly burning across the surface of the water, forming a ring around me much like in the Ritual of Fire.

"Sloan!" I shout. "Sloan, I don't know what's happening!" I can't see anything, don't know if he's still there on the other side of the wall of fire. The incident the other night comes rushing back, the agonized screams ring in my ears at the memory.

I can feel panic in the pit of my stomach starting to bubble up. "Sloan, answer me!" Something isn't right. It's very wrong. I feel the familiar burn of Fire percolating beneath my skin's surface, only it's not like the Change.

This is different.

Stronger, more painful. I feel as if I'm burning up from the inside out. Is this how Li and the others felt? Is this what caused the black tattoos that will forever remind them of that day?

Heat flows through me burning through every inch of my body, as if my blood has been replaced with liquid fire. I hear excruciating screams, at first thinking they're Sloan's before realizing that they are my own.

The ring of fire rises higher and higher around me, an impenetrable wall.

I feel myself being pulled. Down and down, further and further. Burning up from the inside while I sink to the pool's watery bottom.

CHAPTER 25

His hands find me and pull me up, leading me back to the beautiful pink light just above the surface.

Dreaming, it must be another dream.

His arms are strong as he pulls my body toward the stone steps and heaves me across them. I can't see what he sees, but I can take a guess. A lifeless body with wet, knotted hair, lips tinged with blue.

I feel his mouth on mine as his breath comes into me, short bursts, of life-giving air. There's a pattern, a rhythm. One..two..three. Pause. One…two…three.

He sounds so far away, but I can hear him, on each pause, whispering. "Please, Ka. Oh, please no! Come on, Kata, breathe. Just breathe dammit." More air. This pattern goes on for three more cycles. Until—

My eyes flutter open. I cough and sputter, leaning forward as water comes up and out. I throw it up all over the stone steps. "Oh, thank you," Sloan says and he pulls me up into his arms like a small child, pressing his cheek to mine, his warm in comparison. He rocks me back and forth gently and I realize that he's crying.

"It's okay," I reassure him, which is funny, because it should be the other way around.

"I thought, I was sure, Kata, I thought you were dead," he whispers.

"But I'm not," I whisper gently.

"The fire, it practically reached the ceiling, and your screams," he shakes his head and swallows forcibly, trying to regain some composure. "That's something I'll never be able to get out of my head."

I shake my own head. I no longer feel the burn of Fire, nor do I feel hollow like I was emptied of something. Truth be told, I feel exactly the same. Was all the fanfare for nothing? "What happened?"

He helps me to the bench and wraps his jacket around me before pulling his t-shirt back over his own head. He sits next to me, putting an arm securely across my shoulders and pulling me into him. If I felt before that Sloan was keeping a watchful eye over me, I think now it will be at an entirely new level.

"You were screaming as if you were being burned up from the inside. Once the force was broken and you pulled away, the stone turned to ash in my palm, then it dissipated into the water, swirling itself into the ring of fire. That's when it turned white and the flames shot even higher; as if the stone was reversing into its full power. You just kept screaming. I heard you call my name. I realized the fire was only on the surface, I could just dive underneath it and pull you out from the ring. But as I went under, you began to sink and as you sank the fire weakened and grew smaller and smaller until it extinguished itself. I caught you in my arms, but not before you'd swallowed a substantial amount of water."

"You saved my life," I say gratefully.

The worried look evaporates as he seems to finally acknowledge that I really am okay. He smiles sheepishly. "It wouldn't be the first time. And it most likely won't be the last."

. . .

Bina's awake when we return. Michaela is sitting next to her trying to coax her mother into drinking something from a chipped mug.

"Well, look what the cat dragged in," a toothless grin spreads across her face.

The first time I met Bina I had judged her quite unfairly. I thought Unbalanced Metals were something to be feared, the dangerous ostracized members of society, kept in the Underground so as not to harm the other, more functional members of society. How unfair I had been! Truly, it's some of those so-called functional members of society that should actually be feared. Who knows what things led Bina down this path? What untold stories hide in the lines of her life weary face?

"Good to see you awake, Mom." Sloan leans in and gives her a kiss before disappearing down a hallway and returning with two towels, one of which he hands to me.

I run it through my still damp hair. Michaela hands the mug to her mother who reluctantly takes it. "Let me get you some fresh clothes," she offers. "You look about my size." She leaves the room on a mission to find me something dry to wear.

Bina peers into the mug. "Yer sister thinks this concoction will help me to heal," she says to Sloan. She scowls down at the mug then looks up at me. "Don't tell her I told yeh, but it tastes like spit." She sets the mug onto the nightstand. "Now, that Michaela's busy, sit, the both of yeh."

Sloan perches on the bed beside his mother and I lower myself into a plush armchair with a gray, knit quilt draped over the back.

"From the looks of it I see that ye've found and destroyed the Fire stone. Is that correct?" She's asking both of us, but she looks at me. I nod. "Good. That one is probably the most dangerous."

Sloan's eyes narrow. "It almost killed her." There's an anger, no, not anger, a ferocity to his words. Anger is Fire; Ferocity is Metal. Sloan may have pronounced himself as Water and it may give him a sense of joy and calm, but Metal still runs through his veins, sure as Fire runs through mine.

"But it didn't," Bina reminds him. "The Protection Charm is not easy to undo and it can only be undone by the one in which it protects."

"I couldn't have done it without help from my friends though. Ahna helped me figure out where the Elemental Abyss is located, Rhian and Li helped me to escape Fire unnoticed—or at least unnoticed at first, Doran helped me to retrieve the stone, and if it weren't for him I never would have made it past the enchanted waterfall." I look toward Sloan. "And if Sloan hadn't helped me, I wouldn't have been able to destroy the stone on my own."

Bina considers this. "Ye are greatly protected, Ka, not only by the stones, but by those who love yeh." She glances at her son for a moment. What else has she seen about us, about our future together? She turns back toward me. "Ye have much more work ahead of yeh. Retrieving and destroying the other stones will each be as arduous a process as the first one. It is good that ye have people willing to help yeh."

"Something I don't understand, Bina, if I may ask?" She nods. "Is why I don't feel any different? When the stone was being destroyed I felt as if I were burning up from the inside, as if all the Fire was being used up inside me. But I thought the stone was supposed to return that part of my personality."

"And it did, Child. Yer Fire has been restored, I can see it in the glint of yer eyes and the set of yer jaw. There's a confidence about ye that was lacking our first meeting. Perhaps ye don't feel much different because ye were already starting to find yer Fire on yer own before destroying the stone. The Fire released from the stone simply merged with what already had come to exist inside yeh."

I hadn't thought of that, but the words seem true. I've felt the change in myself and Sloan has said that he's seen it too.

Something else has been plaguing me, something that I still don't understand. "What does the Imminent Darkness want, Bina? Why would they build an army of Fire? Why would they want to control their friends and loved ones? Why would they want to destroy their own colony?"

Bina chuckles. "That's a lot of why's. Maybe those are questions best left to Sloan."

He nods. "The Imminent Darkness thrives on the motto *divide et impera.* The colony has been led to believe that we must divide and categorize ourselves because it is what's best to help us overcome, or conquer, our problems. If we choose an Elemental that best represents who we are, or who we think we are at our very core, then there will be less burden of unwanted personality traits for us to carry. But really it's a quite clever ploy on behalf of the Imminent Darkness to lead the colonists into believing it is a way to lessen the burden and help society to function. If we divide our burdens then we can conquer anything. The true meaning behind the phrase is not 'divide and conquer', but rather 'divide in order to conquer.' If the Imminent Darkness can perpetuate the belief that we must choose who we are, that it is a base desire within each of us to place ourselves within a category, then it is easier for them to exert control. If we all realized that within us all of the Elements flowed freely, regardless of what we pronounced, well, then that would be the downfall of the Imminent Darkness and their plan."

"And what's their ultimate plan?" I ask, afraid for what the answer could be. It's already clear that the Imminent Darkness's secrets are not close at hand.

"No one person knows the entire plan. Pieces of the plan are given to certain key members. Unfortunately, I fly too low on the radar to be entrusted with such knowledge. I only know about the things my mother has seen in which I have a direct role. I cannot interfere in the freewill of others," Sloan replies.

I'm forbidden to explain it to you. There are certain things you have to do on your own.

He truly couldn't help me. It must have been frustrating to be unable to intervene.

"That's why I told you I couldn't help you. There are some things which if I interfere, I can alter the natural, intended course. That's when things can become truly dangerous. My role in the Imminent Darkness is one of those things. I have to be involved enough that they accept my loyalty, but uninvolved enough to protect the ones I love."

And I know now that he is no longer just talking about his mother and sister, but of me too.

"Their entire agenda isn't yet known," Bina continues. "I've tried to see it, but I can't. Too many people are involved, which as Sloan said, was probably done on purpose to further perpetuate the secrecy. What I can see is that it is not good and that we are all in grave danger if the Imminent Darkness becomes powerful enough to overthrow the Council of Leaders. Even the pliability and steadfastness of Wood will not be able to withstand the storm that is to come." Her face turns grim and we sit in silence.

Michaela returns and hands me a stack of clean clothes. I thank her and get up to make my way to the bathroom to change. As I rise Bina's fingers enclose around my forearm. "Sometimes the Darkness must rise before people are willing to acknowledge the light."

. . .

As I walk home, it feels weird to be alone now, after all that time spent surrounded by other people. Sloan stayed behind to tend to Bina, and give Michaela a break. I left with the promise that he would pay a visit in the morning. The red sun of Xon 9 is dipping behind the terracotta-colored mountains in the distance, making the sky a blaze of pink and white. The two white moons flank either side of the sun. A warm breeze tickles the back of my neck as if to remind me of the tattoo that is there.

The Elemental Star: five points. One each of Fire, Water, Earth, Wood, and Metal.

I think of Sloan's words about how the Imminent Darkness wants us to choose and categorize ourselves. How Sloan chose Water even though Metal clearly runs through his veins. Or how Zora chose Metal even though I can see Fire clearly just beneath the surface. And Doran, just the opposite of his sister, choosing Fire even though the bravery of Metal resonates deep within his core.

I make my way toward the familiar house that I grew up in, endless afternoons playing in the yard with Li and Ahna as my mother watched on from the living room window. My mother is an Earth; she kept the truth of who I am a secret from me. What other secrets may she be keeping? Who is my mother really, deep down at her core?

A light glows inside the house. Will my parents be surprised to see me or are they expecting me? So much has changed since I last left these walls.

I'm the same, yet different.

All those years spent thinking that I'm ordinary, unable to decide for myself who I am, when in actuality, I am quite extraordinary.

Not extraordinary.

Impossibly extraordinary.

Something my mother once said floats back to me. *You can choose, but it doesn't mean that everyone does.*

I walk up to the door and try the knob.

Once the choice is made; it cannot be undone.

It's unlocked and I push the door open.

Will you choose the easy path, the path of least resistance that will give you instant gratification, or will you choose the path that challenges you, possibly the very path that you fear and keeps you awake at night with indecision, but that will make you a better person for having chosen it?

Warm golden light spills out across the front stoop.

Ultimately the choice is yours and yours alone.

I step inside the house.

I choose Fire. And I choose Water.

I choose Wood and I choose Earth.

I choose Metal.

Choose wisely.

I close the door behind me. For this moment, I am forgetting about what's been and what's to come. I am not ordinary or extraordinary; I am not possible or impossible.

Right now, I am simply Ka.

I choose them all.

ABOUT THE AUTHOR

Jennifer L. Kelly is a middle childhood educator. She resides in Cleveland, Ohio. When she isn't writing, she can be found fangirling over *Doctor Who*, doing yoga, spending time with her dog, or reading.

This is her second series for young adults. Her first novel, *The Prophecy: The Lucia Chronicles Book 1,* was published in January 2014.

Visit her website **Skim.Scheme.Scribble: www.jenniferlkelly.com**

Or say *HI!* :

✉ info@jenniferlkelly.com

🐦 JenniferLKelly3

👍 AuthorJenniferLKelly

📷 AuthorJenniferLKelly

ACKNOWLEDGEMENTS

I'd like to thank my Dad for his knowledge of the fire tetrahedron and for always being my alpha reader! You always push me to achieve both my best and my dreams. (My best dreams?) I would also like to thank my friend, Shannon, for reading! Not only were you an awesome student teacher, but you are an even more awesome friend. Thanks to my mom for her input on cover design for this series. We may never agree, but we agreed on this! Joshua at JoshuaJadon.com also deserves much kudos for taking my pencil drawing of Ka's Elemental Star and turning it into something amazing and real. And lastly, but *never* least, I'd like to thank all my readers for making it possible for me to do what I love doing most in the world. Thank you!☺

Turn the page for the beginning of ...

THE EARTH KEY

The Elementals Book 2

PROLOGUE

You'd think 800 years is a long time, right? Think of all the advances that we as a society could make in 800 freaking years. Seriously. Flying cars—no, better yet, spaceships. Crazy sleek silver spaceships that could fly around the planet. Fossil fuels, gone out with the gas guzzlers. Houses would be like glass bubbles—maybe sustainable domes with their own vegetation and solar panels to eliminate the use for the now non-existent fossil fuels. When you wanted to hang out with your friends you'd take your spaceship and drive—navigate?—to their little glass dome home. Of course, the house itself wouldn't be glass, that would be too intrusive. The house itself would be made of recycled materials because we'd used up everything else long ago. Society's menial labor tasks would be conducted by robots. Robots that could walk and talk—maybe even look just like a human being with, you know, blonde hair and blue eyes or whatever. They'd do the jobs that no one really wants to do, like build the recycled homes or construct the spaceships that replaced the cars. Computers would be obsolete. Who would need them if everyone had a robot? Maybe even the frickin library would just be a robot. You walk up and ask it a question and it would just automatically answer. Even better, you'd have a chip embedded beneath the skin of your arm and the robot would just scan it and directly load the information into your conscious. *Bam!* Anything you ever wanted to know, downloaded instantaneously. What would happen with that kind of power?

Access to anything you ever wanted to know. Ever.

800 years is a long time.

Then why are we still living in stone houses and drilling for water?

Some say it's because the Imminent Darkness is keeping us from progressing. But no one seems to know why.

800 years ago the sun died and 3,000 people left Earth to populate a new planet: Xon 9, with its two moons, never-setting sun, pink sky, and balmy temperatures that never change. There was one catch: rogue elements that would affect our human physiology sometime after puberty. Once we reach our last school year, we have to pronounce an Element, a life-long affiliation. Fire is passion and impulsiveness like the uncontrollable flicker of a flame. Wood is steadfast and wise like the sturdiest of trees. Metal is brave and strong like an iron bridge. Water is intuitive and calm like a bubbling brook. Earth is reliable and nurturing like the ground beneath your feet.

I chose Fire.

Big mistake.

Turns out the Imminent Darkness had infiltrated some of the Elements and after Tristen created her Army of Fire, well, let's just say University is out indefinitely. (Everly, this one's for you. *Gulp.* Turns to bartender, "You know I still hate the taste of that stuff, thanks to you.")

I'd always thought I was ordinary and indecisive, but I was wrong. In fact, I am quite extraordinary. I found out I'm part of some kind of legend. Weird, right? Well, yeah, so the legend goes there's a girl (an *impossible* girl) who embodies all of Xon 9's Elements: Fire, Water, Wood, Metal, and Earth. But in order to protect her, Five Elemental Stones were thrown into the Elemental Abyss. So now, she has to retrieve these Stones from the Abyss, and with each retrieval a part of her now fractured personality will be returned. And once it's all returned? Watch out, Imminent Darkness, because you're going down.

Who, you might be wondering, would throw some strange magic rocks into an abyss? Well, it's strange what lengths we'll go to in order to protect the ones we love. You know, like traveling across the planet, trekking deep into a cavern, surviving an enchanted waterfall, and then leaping over a fiery chasm just to throw a few rocks into some portals that lead to other worlds. No big. Like I said, who would do that!?

Yeah, that would be my mom.

Novea Waylon.

CHAPTER 1

After our drink at the bar vendor, we head through the little alleyway to our ledge. I love the ledge. It looks out over the colony. Little lights sparkle in the distance. The warm breeze rustles my hair and kisses the back of my neck, caressing my now-healed Elemental Star tattoo. If only I'd known then how appropriate a tattoo representing all the Elements would truly be for me. It was impulsive, just like the Fire coursing through my veins, and I was drawn to the flash on the wall like a moth to a flame. Once a tattoo is bought, it's taken off the wall never to be used again. It's mine now, just like I have my Fire back. Now, I just need to restore what else is rightfully mine.

I tenderly push the thought aside. Not much time has passed since my return from the Land of Fire and my boyfriend Sloan has practically had to stake me to the ground to convince me not to go rushing back to the Elemental Abyss for the next stone. Sloan is a few years older than me and used to be my teacher, which is weird in its own right, but then it got even weirder because I found out he had taken that position in order to watch over me and keep me safe. His mother, Bina, is an Unbalanced Metal with the gift of the Sight. She saw that the Impossible Girl was coming, but even she thought it was only a legend. However, as I got older she began to see me in detail and informed Sloan that I'd need a protector. He was up for the challenge apparently, not realizing, as he puts it, that he'd fall for the one he was protecting. Typical, right? We used to have a sort of love-hate relationship, but right now it's been more love than anything.

My leg is pressed against Sloan's as he takes a long drink of water, restoring his body's equilibrium. He turns toward me and the silvery-green scales on the right side of his face catch the pink light of Xon 9's sun. "You know, you really make Bernard crazy." He's referring to the bartender.

'Well, that one time, he totally tricked me! It wasn't very nice!" Once I secretly followed Sloan into the Underground, to the outskirts of the Black Bazaar. And when I ordered a water at the bar, having never drank before, the bartender—Bernard—had tricked me. Let's just say my choking debacle not-so-discreetly attracted Sloan and his sister, Michaela's, attention.

Sloan chuckles at the memory. "I should be getting you home." He tucks a strand of brown hair behind my ear, green eyes teasing, expecting the protest before it even leaves my lips.

"I can get home by myself just fine!"

Normally, you'd expect an argument here. But not from Sloan. Even when I'm angry, he's calm as a pool of water.

"You know my responsibility. And I don't take it lightly. Especially now that we're…well, now that you're no longer just a student." He stumbles over the words, flushing slightly. "I made a promise."

"Speaking of which. I think it's time." He raises an eyebrow at me. "Time to retrieve the next stone. I'm fully recuperated." I pat my chest as if to prove my solidity.

"You don't have enough information. Just let me see what else I can find out. You don't know what the Imminent Darkness is capable of, and let me tell you, after your stint with the army of Fire, Tristen was less than happy." In order to protect me, Sloan has gone so far as to infiltrate the lower ranks of the Imminent Darkness. Risky indeed, but unfortunately, it also means he misses out on some vital information. If he moves up in the ranks and is noticed, then he could put my life in jeopardy, the exact opposite of what we want. I look over his shoulder toward the alleyway. I am safer in the Underground. Bina told me so. What goes on in the Underground stays in the Underground. It's why the Black Bazaar is full of things you'd never see anywhere else: like fortune-tellers, tattoo shops, and bars. That doesn't mean they're invincible though. Nobody is.

"Waiting is just so frustrating!" I sigh. "You don't know what it's like. It's like I'm a broken dish and I can't put it back together because I don't have all the pieces."

His eyes sparkle. "You just compared yourself to a household item." I glare at him, but he just takes my hand and pulls me to my feet. "Time to get you home."

Before we head back, we stare out at the world below. It looks safe. However, I know that it's anything but. Secrets are hidden beneath the surface. Secrets that could change our society. Each other. Everything. His lips graze my cheek and I peer up at him.

"I promise you, we'll retrieve the next stone. Together. But it's too soon. They're waiting for something else to happen. And when it does we'll have an even more difficult time getting to the Elemental Abyss."

I sigh, resigned. Often this is how the discussion ends. "Promise?"

"Always." And I know he's good for it because he's yet to break one. He wraps me in his arms, pressing my ear against his chest and I can hear the soft beat of his heart as he rests his chin on the top of my head. "And, Ka, you're anything but broken. I've never met someone more whole."

I don't reply. I know what he's saying. That I don't need the stones to be complete. But he doesn't understand. No one does. It's like I didn't realize I was even empty until my Fire was returned to me. And somehow the return of my Fire has emphasized the other four voids that much more. I don't just want the next stone, I *need* it.

. . .

I lie awake in bed staring at the ceiling. I should be in University, adjusting to life with my fellow Elementals. But I'm not. I shut down that operation. Well, not me alone. I had Everly's help and Doran's. Everly is one of the first Fires I had met after initiation. She accompanied me into my Mindscape. A Mindscape is this super trippy thing where you're basically in your own consciousness, interacting with your own thoughts and dreams. Everly could only act as a witness, recording all that she observed. Only she had to lie about my Mindscape. Apparently, she saw things about myself that I didn't even know about yet, like the whole Impossible Girl thing.

One of the memories we traveled to was when I was just a kid. My mother had met with a Metal Woman, whom I now know to be Bina, Sloan's mother. She was concerned because I'd shown tendencies for all the Elements. She feared that I was the legend come to life. Bina gave my mother five stones, one representing each of the Elements and instructed her to travel to the Elemental Abyss and throw each stone in reciting the mantra: Protection. Piety. Promise. With each toss of the stone, a piece of my personality was taken away...or rather I suppose put away for safe-keeping. Because now in order to defeat the Imminent Darkness I have to retrieve each of the stones.

I know my mom was only trying to help me. But how could she watch me be so lost all those years? I was always a plain kind of kid. I didn't excel at any one particular thing, not like my best friend Ahna who is a stellar student. No guys were ever interested in me, except Li, Ahna's twin brother, but that hardly counts because he's interested in everybody. For the last eighteen years I was just, I don't know, *there*. Not above average, nor below average. Just average. And that all changed when Everly told me she knew who I really was. She went to great lengths to protect me, even dying in battle, sacrificing her life to return the Fire stone to me. Then POOF! She was hit by a fireball from Tristen's army of Fire, and incinerated. As if she never even existed. Just a black smudge of soot on the stone floor.

My stomach recoils at the memory. I've tried to talk to Sloan about it. He tries to understand and I know that to some extent he does. After all his mother had a MindCleanse because of me. Luckily, it backfired because of her Sight and instead cleansed the mind of the person administering it. But not before Bina had a significant amount of her life energy drained. So, I know that he has just as much to lose as I do. But Everly died for me. Okay, maybe that's a little self-centered. She didn't die for me exactly, she died for what I represented to her.

Sloan put it best. At the University Complex is a great iron archway with the words: *divide et impera* scrolled across it in beautiful, metal calligraphy. I never thought much about it, but Sloan was my Universal History Teacher, so he's all into that sort of stuff. I just assumed it meant that if we divide ourselves we can conquer anything, not like Xon 9 is in danger of being attacked or anything, but I guess more like we could control the rogue Elements if we divided ourselves up, and chose our Elemental affiliation. But Sloan insists that's wrong. He says the motto is a reminder to the Imminent Darkness that they divide us in order to conquer us. That in order for them to exert control, they must create separation. Sure, we all get along more or less, any Element can marry another for example, but some matches are better than others. My mother is an Earth and my father a Wood. A good, solid match. But Sloan and me...well, Water and Fire both complement one another, where I am passionate he is calm, but both are quite unpredictable. And an Unbalanced Elemental is a completely different thing. Unbalanced Elementals can be extremely dangerous. That's why I always thought Unbalanced Metals lived in the Underground. Because the rest of the colony put them there, but in actuality it is self-imposed. Metal is invasive and the most likely to become Unbalanced. Metals make up our entire military. (It's just good sense to be prepared, even though we've never been attacked or anything like that. If I've learned anything, it's that there's always a first time for everything.) Metals are brave and strong. But an Unbalanced Metal can be aggressive and deceitful, thus the nature of the Black Bazar. Only recently did I learn that many people show qualities of more than one Element, yet they're forced to choose only one, and wear that label for the rest of their lives.

None of it makes any sense. Why would anyone not want our society to thrive? What would the Imminent Darkness gain from dividing us up into these little categories? I feel a headache forming behind my eyelids, pulsing inside my skull. I haven't slept much since I came back home. My nights are filled with dreams. Sometimes they're sweet, like Sloan and me swimming in a vast sea, the likes of which I've never seen except in my dreams. But usually they're nightmares. Everly's death replays over and over on endless loop. Or it's me drowning in order for the real me to survive the enchanted waterfall at the Abyss. Or Li telling me to run before the collective conscious registered that he recognized me, the veins bulging in his forehead as he tried to resist the fireball already conjuring in his hand.

The black tattoo that was once golden filigree on the side of my roommate Rhian's face as she lay barely breathing after the explosion.

I finger the back of my neck where my Elemental tattoo is usually hidden by my long, brown hair. It's healed now. Smooth to the touch, except one of the star's points. As I was getting ready for my date with Sloan earlier tonight I noticed that it seemed...different. I leaned over my dresser, inspecting it closer in the mirror. At first I thought my eyes were playing tricks on me. The point of the star representing Fire, realistic flames carefully drawn by my friend Zora, seemed to shimmer golden in the pink light from my bedroom window. Just like the beautiful filigree that adorns the faces of the Fires. Just like I thought it would inevitably adorn my own face.

Li and the others had been injected with something to rapidly expedite the Change, virtually eliminating the Transitional Phase all new Elementals go through. It could have killed them. It almost did. I move my hand to the right side of my face. Smooth. I can practically feel the Fire coursing through my veins, not burning like it did at first, but more like an aliveness, a sort of energy buzzing from the top of my head to the bottom of my toes. I turn onto my side. The curtains on my window blow in the warm breeze and the deep pink of the sun casts a perfect square onto the bedroom floor. I close my eyes and wait for sleep to come.

. . .

The first thing I notice is the smokiness in the air that burns my eyes. I squeeze them shut then open them to slits. The sky is black. Something hits the top of my head and I reach up and touch my hair. Something soft. I hold my fingers close to my face to better inspect them. Ash. I know where I am. I am in the Land of Fire. It's where I went to retrieve the first stone. Last time my friend Doran, Zora's brother, went with me. And I am thankful he did, because he was spared Li and Rhian's fate as Fire soldiers. This time I am alone.

I'm wearing boots and I can feel the hot ground permeating their soles. In the distance I can see the volcano which housed the Fire stone, on a pedestal. Its removal caused the eruption. I'm not sure why I'm here this time. If it's raining ash then the volcano already erupted. I shield my eyes and try to scan the horizon, but the smoke is too thick. I look down at my feet and now I understand why the soles of my boots feel like they're on fire. They practically are. Lava in the various stages of cooling is all around me. It's definitely after the stone's retrieval. But I don't know how long. I didn't pay enough attention in Science class I guess.

I decide to walk toward the volcano. I am wearing a jacket and I pull my hood up and over to try and shield my eyes, periodically lifting my gaze to make sure I am headed in the right direction. At first I think I am imagining it. Through the haziness I see a smoky shadow that appears to be coming toward me. I'm aware that I'm dreaming and safe in my bed at home, but like all my dreams this one feels very real. The figure is getting closer and through the smoke I see that it is taking the shape of a small figure wearing a hooded cloak. My heart pounds in my chest. Is it a member of the Imminent Darkness?

Soon the figure is close enough where I see gray eyes peering at me from beneath the hood and then a nearly toothless smile. Bina. "Ye visited this Land once, Girl, why do ye keep coming back?"

Her words catch me off guard. "How do you know I keep coming back?" I haven't told Bina about my nightmares. Or Sloan for that matter.

She ignores my question. "Ye need to move on. The answers you seek are no longer here. Ye got what ye came for." As if in response the volcano in the distance lets out a rumble.

"Well, then where do I find them?" I ask exasperatedly. The raining ash seems to come down in thicker swirls. And even though Bina only stands a foot away it gives her a strange ethereal affect.

"'Tis right in front of yer face! Ye will find the answers at the beginning not at the end."

"That doesn't even make sense!" I protest. But she just smiles and begins to fade away, although I'm not sure if she's truly fading away, or if it's just the effect of the ash and haze.

Her voice languidly floats to me through the smoke. "The beginning has the answers ye seek."

THE EARTH KEY

The Elementals Book 2

12.06.16

www.ingramcontent.com/pod-product-compliance
Lightning Source LLC
Chambersburg PA
CBHW022135170626
46807CB00005B/1947